THE OILMEN

D1738821

Books by Scott A. Dondershine

Project MK Ultra
Double Conundrum

The Oilmen

By Scott A. Dondershine

Published by Stonewall Stories, LLC

Dedication

In memory of my father and his eternal optimism.

Acknowledgements

I could not have written this book without the assistance of a few special people in my life. My wife Diane, children Alex and Zachary, and brother Steven, provided me with a mixture of space, editing advice, encouragement, and love that helped me along the journey. I also want to acknowledge the help of a variety of people who provided me with technical and writing assistance: professional editors Nina Catanese (plot development) and Beth Skony (copy-editing), Michael Adelberg, David Blake, Tim Colwell, and Kim Lisa Sobotta (plot development and editing), and Gil Armendariz (technical assistance).

Chapter 1

Fred Turner fiddled with his Texas A&M Aggie ring as he positioned his chiseled face into the retinal scanner. A brown Stetson hat stood tall on the large man's head, toothpick sticking out of his mouth. He had arrived in Lisbon, Portugal, earlier in the day, courtesy of his company's private jet.

Although he had done it many times before, the procedure never changed even as the venue rotated. *Will my contacts make a difference? Of course not!* The door opened.

He entered through the kitchen of the Portuguese restaurant. Meetings were always in the morning, no matter the location, before the afternoon help arrived to start dinner. Turner had glanced at the menu, discovering that it included grilled octopus, garlic shrimp, salted cod, and other local delicacies. *Ugh!* He preferred simple delicacies like a thick steak or medium-rare burger.

Turner took the stairs down into the basement and opened the door. A tall white man wearing a navy suit frisked him, confiscating all electronics, including his watch. Security was paramount. Once the guard cleared Turner, an inner door opened, allowing him to enter the meeting room.

The other five members rounding out the Oilmen nodded at his arrival. They sat silently, waiting for the Benefactor to call in.

The Benefactor called ten minutes late, voice filtered, sounding deep and monotone. Although the Benefactor could watch the Oilmen, they could not see the syndicate's leader.

1

Turner wasn't sure if anybody at the table had even met or could identify the person. He didn't even know the gender of the Benefactor, whether a *he*, *she*, or one of the "new age" categories. Turner only knew not to ask. Period.

The only clue as to the person's identity was that the five other representatives were from North America, South America, Asia, Africa, and Europe. Nobody represented the Middle East, which, although not technically a continent, had obvious importance to the Oilmen's mantra.

"Good day, gentlemen. I see everybody made it. I have a busy schedule, so let's get on with it," the Benefactor said through an obscured voice.

"Let's start with our representative from Asia. Tell me about any developments in your sector."

Turner and the representatives from South America and Europe turned to watch their Chinese counterpart, impeccably dressed in a dark blue pinstripe suit. The short man with chubby cheeks and glasses looked up from his notes before responding in perfect English, honed by years of Western schooling.

"Thank you for letting me speak," he evenly replied. "The use of fossil fuels continues unabated, even increasing in certain areas."

"Such as?"

"Southeast Asia, in particular, as the developing nations position for affordable energy to support their rapid growth."

"Care to quantify that?" The other representatives stole glances at their own notes, knowing that one of them would be next.

"An eighty percent surge in overall demand, doubling the use of fossil fuels since 2000."

"Impressive, but is that the entire picture?" the metallic voice inquired.

The Asian representative drew a deep breath and replied, "I see no reason why it wouldn't. Yes, there are threats, but high start-up costs for renewables remain a limiting factor."

"Limiting factor, eh? Is that what you think? That's for me to decide! I have told you imbeciles before! Honest opinions here. Don't water it down for me. Now, start again."

The man paused before replying, this time giving a more balanced account. "Many Asian countries, like China, are going to have to switch to cleaner fuel. The air in large cities like Delhi, Peshawar, Karachi, Beijing, and Narayangonj has become polluted with PM2.5."

"PM2.5?" asked the Benefactor.

"Tiny particles that can penetrate deep into the lungs. People are dying in increasing numbers from heart disease, lung cancer, respiratory infections, and other serious health problems."

"But the citizens of most countries in your region have little power to change the situation. Isn't that right?"

The representative took a drink from his water glass before responding. "That is true, historically, at least. However, it's becoming more difficult for even the wealthy to avoid exposure. They used to be able to hide indoors or in country villas, but as the air gets worse, it has become more difficult to filter out the pollutants before permeating their center-city buildings and exurban residences. Even plutocrats care when their children develop asthma due to rancid air."

"I see…thank you for your honesty," the Benefactor replied.

Next came the updates from Europe, Africa, and South America, each given with Turner squirming in his seat, twisting his ring.

"We'll talk about our worldwide coordinated response after lunch is served. But first, let's hear from the American," the Benefactor said with a pause. "Mr. Turner, what is the situation like in North America? You don't seem to have the same level of problems. Can the threat of renewables be suppressed there?"

Turner cleared his throat. "Our situation is hard to predict. The threat of renewable energy had thankfully subsided during the Trump years, but now seems to be rearing its ugly head again. We need to change the politics — and fast, which we're trying to do, of course." He stopped, letting the Benefactor guide the discussion.

"Go on, Mr. Turner."

"We discussed before, our plan involves solidifying our influence. One of the more powerful lobbyists is, or *used to be,* it now seems, Benji Hammer."

"Hammer?" the obscured voice revealed a hint of surprise.

"Yes. Hero of the fossil fuel industry. Credited with killing the federal cap-and-trade movement."

"Federal?"

"Yes. Mr. Hammer's efforts lead to litigation and payoffs that killed any U.S. national efforts, limiting the movement to a handful of states. And he's been instrumental in other helpful efforts over the years."

"That seems good, no? What's happened?"

"According to my contact, he's about to represent one of the OPEC countries. I don't know which one."

"I'm not following you. What's the problem?"

"His new client apparently wants to diversify into renewable energies."

"That would be horrible! If one member state did that, others might follow, and then…"

"The whole system would collapse."

"Yes…the consequences could be devastating!"

"Have you discovered which country?" the Benefactor asked.

"No."

"Hmm. Why did Hammer switch sides?"

The Texan shrugged. "The client gave him a better offer."

"That's a troubling development," the Benefactor said. "I think we'll have to alter the agenda, continuing the discussion while you eat…."

Chapter 2

Dr. Lawrence Meridian sat in his white Washington Gas van, waiting in a new development of colonials, each one with exactly four shapely shrubs and one six-foot tree, located just off the Greenway in Loudoun County, Virginia. Perspiration from the summer humidity, white hard hat, and black beard, even at 5:30 PM, drenched his chest and torso, adding dark navy spots to his light-blue field uniform. His left elbow rested on the inside of the door, left hand stroking the thick crinkly hair he had glued to his face earlier.

A few birds became visible through his windshield, momentarily diverting his focus from the task at hand. He had no idea of the type of bird, and detested people that knew such things. Real men, he reminded himself, didn't have time for such pedestrian activities. The hatred had been one of many reasons why he had chosen a solitary lifestyle.

The sitting and waiting bothered him. Meridian was a doer, not a waiter. Not that he didn't understand the importance of planning; he strove to be a consummate planner, at least when time permitted. And, if all went well, he would get to perform something special.

Meridian watched as David Grigorio drove his black Mercedes convertible into the driveway of his two-story brick colonial house, opening his garage door late, but in the nick of time. Meridian could hear

Linkin Park blasting from the open roof of David's car, even after it pulled into the garage.

Another nerd overcompensating, he thought. *If David only knew he was being watched.*

"Subject just arrived," Meridian reported to his boss. He was to be a catalyst of sorts. Striking the match that would start it all — literally and figuratively.

He had been watching David over the past two weeks, cataloguing his movements: The time David left for work at Earthcare's D.C. headquarters, the Farragut Square lunch places David frequented (too snobby to eat a bagged lunch), how long he stayed at work. Meridian even rented a hotel room at the posh Mayflower Hotel from which he watched the lights turn on and off in David's corner office. Sometimes Meridian treated himself to the hotel's famous jumbo prawns, all expenses paid by his current employer.

"Good, and the pressure point?"

Meridian bit his lip, not wanting to sound over-confident. "In place."

"Are you ready then?"

"Yes."

"Then proceed carefully." The line clicked off as the syndicate's American asset, Fred Turner, ended the call.

Meridian smiled. The hyper, intense man lived for these moments. He had worked hard to have the opportunities. In his early twenties, Meridian had tried to enroll at the University of Virginia School of Medicine, hoping to become a surgeon and fulfilling a childhood dream.

He had been eight years old when an attacker shot his mother in the chest during a mugging on the streets of Richmond. The paramedics transferred mother and son to the VCU Medical Center. The young boy stole glances at the operating table as the door opened and closed several times. Hours later, the doctors breathed easier. The patient would live.

He knew his destiny after watching the doctors save Mom. Only, the usual path wouldn't work for him. High school had been a slog. History class? *Pointless.* Gym class? *Waste of time.* The only subjects that interested him were math and science.

He also found it difficult to make friends. Men found his uncompromising personality difficult. Girls were too much work. Drinking beer made him gassy and left him with a headache.

The only activity was weightlifting, which he dutifully performed on machine that his parents purchased for his use. Best of all, he could do it alone.

Graduating high school signaled the beginning of his independence; he could live the way he wanted.

Unfortunately, college proved even more of a grind than high school. After his first semester of boring subjects which produced uneven grades, he knew he wouldn't be able to attend medical school through the traditional route.

And so, he prepared a fake transcript showing he had graduated from college with honors and a fabricated MCAT test result with an elite score, even though he hadn't even finished college. The ruse worked, gaining admission to the Med school at the University of Maryland. But one day of medical school classes made him realize the fallacy of his plan. He quickly left College Park, narrowly suppressing the urge to go postal, in search of a new career.

Having no formal education suitable for the white-collar world, and no appetite to work his way up the blue-collar ladder, he was trapped in the working class with no options. Maybe he could practice medicine after all, he realized after watching two reruns of *Grey's Anatomy.*

He continued to believe it the next morning, cementing the plan as neither folly nor fallacy. Years later, he had earned sufficient bona fides leading to his current position.

Meridian continued to watch the house, waiting for the sun to set. At one point, two people crossed the sidewalk in front of the house, each walking a dog. He sneered at the polite manner in which they passed each other, careful not to step on any of the surrounding blades of grass. "Fucking suburbanites," he whispered.

Gone from their faces were the senseless masks that people had worn during the dark days of the pandemic. Fauci's communist policies had backfired, delaying the point of herd immunity and COVID's natural progression.

Meridian didn't mind. Sure, COVID killed more than a million Americans, but that number was deceptive. Most were elderly who would be dead in a decade anyway.

His beard and hard hat caused his skin and scalp to itch. Meridian needed adjustments and had some time to spare before Act II. Against his better judgment, he put his hat on the passenger seat before driving to a nearby strip mall. Meridian glanced at the traffic light turning green as he turned into the mall.

Once there, he removed his beard and wiped his face and head with wipes. The naturally pale man, with platinum hair and blue eyes resembling an albino, ate a mixture of nuts and dried fruit and guzzled water, imagining David and his fiancée eating their dinner. *Hopefully, meatloaf or pasta with ice cream for dessert, fattening them up*, he thought to himself, smiling.

Meridian's legs and back began to cramp and strain. An active person, he couldn't temper his sudden desire to stretch his legs and rotate his torso and neck. After returning to the van, he reapplied his disguise and watched the sunset. He anxiously waited for the coming darkness.

Good things happened in the night.

After dusk fell, he reapplied his helmet and drove to David's house. *Good*, he said to himself upon arriving. It looked like inside lights were on in several rooms, although he couldn't see anybody through the window treatments.

Meridian calmly exited, retrieved his tool bag, walked to the door, and rang the doorbell. He hesitated when he looked at the white mask with the words "Washington Gas" on the right corner but decided to wear it.

David answered after the third ring. "Yes?" he asked impatiently, red spaghetti sauce dotted on his light blue shirt.

Meridian studied his mark. Up close, he looked worse than from a distance. David's disheveled sandy brown hair, unruly mad scientist eyebrows, and round belly bubbling out from the bottom of his stained shirt provided Meridian with even more inspiration.

"Gas leak, sir. Someone reported a smell."

"Cindy," David snarled towards the kitchen. "Did you report a gas leak?"

"Gas, you say?"

"Yes, gas. Did YOU report a leak?"

"No, why?"

David ignored the question being yelled at him. "We didn't report one, sir. You must have the wrong house."

Meridian handed David a business card with an elongated shoulder shrug. "All I know," Meridian replied, "is what I was told by my dispatcher. *Somebody* reported a gas leak. Anybody else in the house?"

"Just my fiancée. Didn't you hear her just shout that she hasn't smelled anything?"

Ignoring David's condescending tone, Meridian said evenly, "That's good. Probably a neighbor or deliveryman. Must have smelled it on the outside. Most likely near the meter. Happens all the time. Joints rust, gas starts leaking. Easy to fix. I'll quickly check inside. Confirm nothing's there. Then look outside."

David glanced at the card, thinking about how annoying the man's short bursts of speech were, not wanting to delay it any further. He opened the door and led Meridian to the entrance of the basement. There, he gestured for Meridian to go down the stairs.

A short, skinny woman with a pointy nose approached David before he descended, introducing herself as Cindy.

"Evening, Ma'am," Meridian said to the woman, who replied with a simple hello.

David and his fiancée paused at the top of the stairs; neither seemed to want to go down and listen any more to the worker.

"Where's the furnace? I'll start there. Probably where the gas line first enters the house, I imagine."

David told Meridian where to look, and then he and Cindy walked away.

"Thanks. I'll let you know if I find something. Please leave the door open. I can call you down if needed," Meridian said before proceeding down the steps.

The furnace room sat to the left of the stairs in an unfinished area. He looked around at the rest of the sparsely decorated basement first. Simple beige carpet, brown walls, and no furniture. *Couple of kids pop out and then the man cave goes up,* he figured before entering the furnace room.

Meridian retrieved a gas meter from his bag and looked around the room. A furnace with patch tape around the ducts and dents in the metal lay next to a hot water heater located on the wall to the left of the door. Shelving containing picture albums, computer equipment, two sleeping bags, clothes, and paint cans were stuffed into two metal storage units. The units formed a ninety-degree angle to the right of the furnace, with a gap at the apex of the angle where two white folding tables and six black metal chairs were wedged.

Meridian removed a small canister from his tool bag and nestled it in one of the sleeping bags on a shelf near the furnace. He twisted the top of the canister and then put the gas meter on a folding table that he set up near the furnace.

He looked at the meter and, satisfied with the reading, walked out of the room and up the stairs. There, he shouted in a raised voice, "Sir! Madame! Can you come down here, please? I located the source."

The couple walked down the stairs, following Meridian into the room, brows furrowed. It was obvious to Meridian that they wanted him to leave the house as soon as possible. He knew they were to be married soon and assumed they wanted to have at it, like bunny rabbits. *What a shame*, he smirked.

"I'll show you what I found. Look at my meter, by the furnace," he said, pointing to his meter.

David bent over to look at the meter that Meridian had placed. Cindy peered over his shoulder.

David began to say something when Cindy let out a loud yelp!

Both turned around. Cindy clawed at a hypodermic needle sticking out of her buttocks.

Meridian, after removing his COVID mask, pointed his homemade syringe injector gun alternatively at both. He had thought of the idea after finding a commercial syringe injector, used to treat farm animals, online. While the ones available for sale didn't have the capability to launch a needle, Meridian had been able to design a wooden spring-loaded gun.

He waved the weapon at them, finger twitching, threatening more. "Do not scream. Everything will be fine. Do as I say, and this will be over soon."

Cindy slurred something in an unintelligible scream that began strong before fading fast. She collapsed in David's arms while Meridian continued.

"You need to remain calm. Put her in the chair. Do not make me shoot you. It's only midazolam. She'll be fine."

"What do you want with us?! Is this about money?"

"I don't have time for questions."

Before David could respond, Meridian shot another needle that he had fished out from his bag, striking David in the thigh. "Don't worry," he said. "Milder dose. It will relax you. Scream, and it'll get much worse." Meridian stood tall to stretch, the movement causing the front of his uniform to lift, revealing to David a handgun jutting out from his waistband.

When David protested, Meridian clobbered him over the head with the butt of the gun, knocking him out. *People never listen, everybody wants to be a hero.*

With both targets out cold, Meridian carried Cindy and deposited her into a folding chair that he positioned close to one of the shelving units. Meridian tied her against the chair with rope and gagged her mouth with a piece of cloth before doing the same to David on a different chair.

Cindy's head flopped down in front of her. Meridian liked this part of the ritual; it showed his power over the subject.

Next, Meridian changed into a white gown before carefully laying out a white paper towel that he had neatly separated along the perforated marks on one of the folding tables. Then, he placed a scalpel, surgical scissors, a small mirror, gauze pads, and, in case of an emergency, a needle filled with morphine. Smelling salts were added to the collection, each small packet lined up with matching edges perfectly in a vertical row.

Placing each object in a straight line separated a centimeter from each other, he thought of the doctors that had saved his mom's life. Even as a little boy, he knew that they had acted methodically with God-like skills.

With Cindy secured and the instruments set, he proceeded to the next step. Holding the smelling salt under David's nose, he slapped him a few times across his cheeks. David stirred and awoke to an unimaginable scene.

The husband-to-be began to thrash and scream, albeit muffled through the gag. Meridian watched him, trying to stifle a grin that he knew would make the thrashing worse.

Satisfied that the bindings were tight, he said calmly, "You need to see. You need to understand. So, you'll make the correct decision later."

David continued to scream, the gag muffling the sound.

"Nobody's going to hear you down here. If you don't calm down, you'll never see your Cindy again. If you cooperate, you will. I'm not interested in killing her or you. Nod if you understand."

David slowed down his protests before nodding his head up and down. Meridian knew he had won.

Meridian checked Cindy's pulse, blood oxygen level, and heart rate. Satisfied that her measurements were normal, he gave her an additional shot of anesthesia.

The scalpel came next, leading David to struggle and scream again. Meridian flashed a grin and turned to David. "I learned watching YouTube. It's called *yubitsume*. Lots of fun. A new procedure for me. Calm yourself, you don't want to disturb me."

He made his first cut just above the knuckle of Cindy's left pinky finger. Blood emerged but didn't squirt as it did earlier in Meridian's career. It didn't take long for the finger to sever completely. Meridian applied an antibiotic and wrapped the remaining finger carefully with gauze. "See how careful I am?"

Only David didn't seem to care, continuing his struggle. Meridian watched in amusement. He recalled seeing Dr. Phil discuss a strategy of parents letting their babies tire out from screaming. Intervening too quickly could encourage future protests, the television doctor pointed out.

Sure enough, Dr. Phil's advice worked. David calmed a bit, apparently realizing that hurting his forearm and shins was doing nothing to help Cindy.

"Now that I've got your attention," Meridian began as he cleaned up, "the people I work for own you, at least for now. I'll be borrowing your wife. Like checking out a book at library." Meridian chortled at the last part before continuing, "Don't worry. We'll return her undamaged if you do what we want. Don't want any library fines after all! But if not, then…" Meridian paused for effect, waving the scalpel before finishing, "Understand?"

David nodded.

"Great, I'm glad we settled that. There's one more detail, however."

Meridian retrieved a sheet of paper with a blank signature line towards the bottom and thick tape covering the text below and above the line. He foisted the paper in front of David, saying with a devilish twang, "Sign where indicated. It's your receipt to redeem Cindy later."

"What's beneath the tape?"

Meridian swatted David's head hard with his open right hand. *Some people just don't learn!* "Want me to use the scalpel again?"

David relented and signed on the line.

"Good choice. No law enforcement. No telling anybody. Any slipup and you'll never see your Cindy again, at least alive. I'm handing you a thumb drive. Open it at work this coming Monday. Start with the readme file. I'll give you an additional sedative. You'll wake up. I'll be gone. Nod if you understand."

David nodded affirmatively.

Meridian smiled before jabbing a needle into David's arm.

Chapter 3

David twitched awake later that night. He had trouble focusing and felt groggy. Initially, he thought he was in a surgical recovery room. Only there were no nurses, and the room was dark.

A biting headache contributed to his general delusion before the dreadful events of earlier in the evening hit like an avalanche. He felt the crusted blood on his head and stared at the ceiling, crying out for Cindy, knowing full well that she couldn't come and be with him. She had been taken from him by that monster, the fake utility worker/demented doctor. Strange, he didn't even know his name or anything about him.

A sliver of light showed from the bottom of a door, and he realized the monster had moved him into the guest bedroom on the basement level.

David tried to get up, only to be driven back onto the bed by intense nausea. He felt an object in his front pocket, reached into his pants, and retrieved the thumb drive. Head beginning to clear, he remembered. The Washington Gas man. He knew he didn't have time to cry, couldn't call the police, FBI, or anybody else. Not if he ever wanted to see Cindy alive again.

His second attempt at sitting up worked. He slithered to the bathroom, where he relieved himself, splashed some water on his face, and walked to his now-familiar furnace room. The table and chairs were back in their former place, the basement floor looked slick, and even the shelving and furnace looked clean.

David again thought about calling the police. *How can I possibly get her back on my own?* He thought about examining the thumb drive, but paused, remembering Meridian's warning.

As he contemplated what to do, his thoughts drifted to their first date. The night began awkwardly. An introvert, he had little experience dating. A mutual friend set them up for the date, and he and Cindy had agreed to meet at a Chinese restaurant.

He had asked his mother for advice about what to wear, only Mom didn't really know what to say, having been out of the dating game herself for nearly forty years. An hour was spent fiddling with his collection of raggedy clothes only to throw his arms up in despair. Business attire - his navy suit, white shirt, and red tie - would have to do.

He had waited at the table before figuring out that he should have stayed up front, heart beating faster from the panic. When Cindy arrived a few minutes later, his arm nearly tipped over a glass of water as he stood. She had dressed casually in a purple V-neck shirt and a faded jean skirt. A hint of lavender sprung from her body as she drew closer. *I still remember the smell.*

He silently cursed to himself, looking for the exit.

Cindy could've commented on his attire, a meaningless platitude or joke, but she didn't, instead giving him an awkward hug before they both sat down. It took them an hour just to order, talk coming natural to both. Giggling each time the waiter approached, they ordered nothing, having not even looked at the cocktail menu. Dinner ended three hours later with both going to their separate Washington, D.C. apartments, each too afraid to verbalize what they both knew each wanted. It would be their last night apart, until now.

He decided to ignore the warning of Cindy's captor. Time was precious, he realized before making his way carefully to his home office upstairs. Once there, he inserted the thumb drive into his PC and waited.

The drive registered the standard Windows recognition: several quick beeps signaling success followed the familiar message: "USB Drive (E:) Select to Choose What Happens with Removable Drives."

So far, so good.

David opened File Explorer and examined the contents. The readme file and two executable program files appeared on his screen. *Why two?* he wondered when he had expected there to be one.

He clicked on the readme file. The following text appeared:

Insert this thumb drive into the Dell Precision 5820 computer that Earthcare brought for your use on June 15 of this year and became operational on June 18. Do this on Monday of this coming week. Note the time on your clock, located immediately to your left, near the picture on the shelf of you and your wife taken at the Ritz-Carlton in San Francisco when you proposed to her on July 10. Leave the thumb drive inserted for five minutes, at which time it will reformat automatically, erasing all contents. We will know if you inserted it into your HP EliteDesk, your home office computer. If you did, your screen will go blank one minute after you click on the file, and you should consider this your one warning. Do not involve the police or take any other action. We are watching you.

David chewed at his left index finger as the screen went blank. He quickly removed the thumb drive, hoping the nightmare would end.

When it didn't, he rocked his body back on his desk chair and closed his eyes. He tried to think of his options. He couldn't possibly comply, could he?

Frustrated and afraid, his thoughts wandered to the day that he had proposed to Cindy. They were in San Francisco eight days ago, staying atop the city at the Ritz-Carlton. After a romantic meal in the dining room, they had walked out to the rooftop lounge for drinks. The sun began to set as he kneeled in front of her to propose in front of the distant skyline. He saw bright spots on the windows of the buildings on Fremont Street. Still nothing compared to watching Cindy's face light up as she said yes.

The memory faded, replaced by his new reality. The blackmailers, whoever they were, had been in his office and home. They had access to his business records and were obviously well-prepared. Professionals.

David thought about what the program had to do with Earthcare. The evil doctor and the tyrants he worked for wanted him to use an Earthcare computer as opposed to his home computer. It obviously had to do with tapping into the Earthcare network.

David wondered if they, whoever they were, were ecoterrorists of some kind — and needed information that only a small number of insiders like him possessed. Nobody would suspect Earthcare's third-longest tenured employee, who joined shortly after Suzanne Harper formed the nonprofit. David had wanted to make a difference and had been attracted by the stated mission of "preserving a livable Earth for future generations."

He considered why he had been targeted instead of somebody else at the company. The classic *why me?* In addition to helping to manage the nonprofit's carbon reduction division, he served as Earthcare's CTO, managing Earthcare's computer systems and network.

David's duties as CTO gave him charge of the network that the perpetrators were apparently targeting. Wouldn't this mean that he would be in the best position to defeat whatever transpired? Was that the answer to *why me?*

He thrummed his fingers on his desk, thinking. Another possibility occurred to him, and it terrified him. Suzanne trusted him more than anybody, and his position made him the perfect fall guy. He had little choice but to oblige. The alternative, calling the police, scared him even more.

Chapter 4

On Monday, the day after Cindy's kidnapping, David drove his Mercedes into Earthcare's parking lot. Summer usually meant less traffic in Washington, D.C. as Congress's usual anemic pace slowed even further, giving the cantankerous lobbyists, lawyers, and Capitol Hill staff some needed time to heal their wounds and escape the long stretches of 95-degree days.

David usually used his solitary time to listen to podcasts, the news, or his favorite Sirius heavy metal channel. But today was different, and it wasn't because of the rare morning hailstorm pounding the roof of his car.

Nerves on fire, colitis boiling, nostrils flaring, he chewed a stick of gum in a vain attempt to forget what he had to do. What he *needed* to do.

Earthcare occupied most of the 5th floor of the ten-story brown building, a sign of the organization's growth as more people began to think about global warming. Some of the offices and cubicles, empty during the heart of the pandemic, had recently begun to be re-occupied. Others remained unused by people who had gotten used to the comforts of home, a few employees having moved out of the area, taking advantage of Earthcare's flexible work policies.

After emerging from the bathroom, David mumbled "hello" to the rent-a-guard in the lobby, keeping his head down and taking the stairs when he usually waited for the elevators. David began huffing when he reached the fourth floor, remembering Cindy and their joint New Year's resolution to buy a treadmill. They had made the resolution in each of the last three years of living together in their extended engagement, in what became a constant joke throughout the rest of the year.

David walked by the vacant L-shaped receptionist desk and worked his way through a maze of cubicles to his corner office. Reflexively, he looked at the clock and the photo of himself and Cindy as he walked in the door. His desk looked like it had just been bombed, with papers, sticky notes, pens, paper clips, and binder clips mixed together, crying out for some organizational therapy.

After setting down his brown leather briefcase on the floor, he went to the kitchen to retrieve what would be the first of four cups of coffee needed to get through the day. David returned to his office, closed his door, and fired up his computer.

He thought again about calling the police. A glance up at the photo taken at the Ritz rooftop lounge in San Francisco on the night he had proposed sealed the decision to proceed. The extortionist doctor and his organization had shown they knew intimate details about David's office and home. The doctor had established himself as a real menace by slicing off a good chunk of Cindy's left pinky finger, proving that the man was capable of far worse.

Both the doctor and the readme file he reviewed on Sunday said to insert the thumb drive today, Monday. What choice did he have if he wanted to see Cindy again alive?

David carefully removed the thumb drive from a pocket in his briefcase. After taking a deep breath, he inserted it into one of the USB ports, clicked on the first of the two executable programs that appeared, and noted the time — 8:10 a.m. Nothing happened, which for a moment brought relief but then terror. Would the miscreants think he designed a counter measure, a program that would negate the instructions?

He simultaneously pressed the ALT, CTRL, and Delete keys and then clicked on Task Manager. Two programs that David didn't recognize —

DHLPTX47 and DHLPTX48 — came into view, using a combined between 5% and 2% of the computer's CPU power. The files must have been linked; clicking on the first activated both.

The suspicious programs continued to use CPU power over the next several minutes, a telling sign that something was happening. At 8:15 a.m., five minutes after inserting the thumb drive into the computer, the computer began reformatting the thumb drive and Task Manager reported that the two programs no longer used any CPU power. *That's it? Now I get Cindy back?*

David took out the thumb drive, put it in his front pocket, and left the office. Shortly after returning home, he sent Suzanne an email explaining that he didn't feel well and would work from home. "Don't worry," he explained at the end of his email, "it's not COVID-19."

At home, David paced in the living room of his house, waiting for word that he had performed as asked and that Cindy would be returned. Day turned into night, and the next day - still nothing. He thought again about going to the police and again came to the same conclusion. He had no choice but to wait at home. Going to work was out of the question.

The wait didn't last long, but with an outcome he didn't expect either. Wednesday night he received an email with the subject line — DHLPTX48 — and a simple instruction to "Click Here" in the body of the email. He complied and a secure web portal came into view that, after satisfying a required two-step authentication, spit out the following message:

"Be patient, there's more work to do. Business as usual for now."

Chapter 5

On Saturday afternoon, the fifth day following insertion of the thumb drive into Earthcare's network, Bircher Smith, a freckly teenager with a squarish face, aimed his yellow Frisbee with its stylish red racing stripe at his girlfriend, Trudy Lamonte. They were in Golden Gate Park on a sunny afternoon.

Bircher stared at Trudy as her long black hair bounced around her slender upper body, elevated from a breeze that brought fresh salty air onto the grounds. Jet black, the kind that older people, including Bircher's mom, could only accomplish with artificial coloring. As with her hair, she also had a natural tan. *Remarkable*, he thought, no artificial dye or sunning needed on that girl.

He cocked his right arm behind his body and let it fly with the flick of his wrist. A golden Labrador in the distance licking vanilla ice cream from the leg of its owner distracted him, causing the Frisbee to veer slightly off course.

Bircher turned his focus back to his girlfriend. Carried by her pencil-thin legs, she chased the errant throw, arriving just in time. She held out her left hand, palm facing up to the sky, as if attempting to catch rain.

With her right hand, she clapped down in an awkward attempt at catching the incoming object. Her impatient timing caused the Frisbee to hit her hands as they joined together a moment too soon, causing her fingers to sting. With a thud, the Frisbee fell to the ground, causing Bircher to cackle, teasing her.

"You got to catch it with your fingers, silly, not by clapping. You look like you're applauding at one of those fancy shows your parents drag you to. Let me show you," Bircher said as he ran towards her, eager for the chance to get close. The light splash of perfume drove him wild.

She suddenly ran away, giggling, dodging to the left and then the right in a playful attempt to evade her boyfriend's embrace as he approached. Only Bircher knew her moves. As usual, he let her evade his advance with her first move to the left but delicately tackled her to the ground on the next move to the right.

Bircher wrapped his arms around Trudy and kissed her. When they finished the embrace, Trudy composed herself and sighed, "So, remind me, where are we going tonight? Some guy's house?" Her voice cracked when she said "guy," leading both to stitches.

Bircher looked into her eyes and replied, "It's not just some guy's house, honey. It's the Techno House. Remember? Jason and Laurie went there last Friday night and had a blast. Coolest party ever. We talked about this yesterday. Do you still want to go?"

"I'm sorry, Birch. I know we talked about it. I'm just nervous. Remember, my parents are tracking me. They even insisted on your cell phone number and are probably monitoring you too."

"Well…," he said patiently at first, trying unsuccessfully to stifle a rise, "that's ridiculous! I don't understand what their problem is, to be honest, Trudy. You're a year away from college. Nobody's getting sick anymore, except for old people! And we've all been fully vaxxed and boosted, several times I might add!"

"I know…I know. But remember that my mom lost her brother to the virus, and they're hyper-sensitive to new variants emerging."

Bircher considered his words carefully, not wanting to point out that Uncle Edward had diabetes and weighed about 300 pounds on a good day.

"I do understand, Trudy. I'm sorry. I got a little excited. That's all. If you don't want to go, just say the word!"

"No, let's go. We've talked about this before, and I agreed. Besides, like you said, pretty soon we'll be in college."

"Great. Remember our plan. Even if they are tracking, we have it covered. You told them we're going to the movies? Right? Right?"

"Yes, of course."

"You'll leave your phone in my car."

"Yes, I *know*, Birch. We've been through this. You promised we'll leave at 11:30 as we agreed. Right?"

"I guess so, but 11:30's ridiculous. Jason told me the place was rocking until two in the morning! Can we just see how it goes? We can be a little late," Bircher said realizing his mistake after saying the words.

"So, I need to remember the plan, but you don't? If I'm leaving my cell phone in your car, they'll understand that I silenced it during the movie, but then after that, I need to answer."

"Sure, honey. That's what we agreed to. 11:30 it is," Bircher said before adding his clincher. "Honey, I don't want to make you do something you don't want to. I know it's tough. We can see a movie *instead,* if you want. I'm fine with that. Seriously."

"No, Birch. As you said, it's my senior year. It'll be good practice for college."

Bircher smiled sheepishly, hiding his relief. "It will, but let me know if you change your mind. I'll pick you up at eight." They kissed again before departing, each going home separately.

***

The parking lot for the movie theatre was crowded. Bircher pulled the car into an empty slot to the left of a tall black light post that illuminated the area. The air mixed with the smells of smoke and gas from the traffic and people walking nearby.

Bircher's green jacket and Trudy's button-down blue denim jacket provided sufficient protection from the evening's chill. Both wore jeans but Trudy's were darker with bell bottom finishes. Trudy applied perfume and lipstick before leaving the car.

Bircher led the way towards the Techno House.

"You know where you're going, Birch?" Trudy asked once they exited the main street onto a more residential area.

"Of course, honey. We'll be there in ten," Bircher responded.

The houses in Oakland consisted of a mixture of older shotgun structures, townhouses, duplexes, and ramblers, each residing on a zero-lot line. The cars tended to be older with a few RVs. Five minutes later, they entered an area containing small commercial buildings and warehouses.

"You sure you know where you're going, Birch?" asked Trudy more stridently than the last.

Bircher ignored his girlfriend and continued walking. A few minutes later, they came upon a two-story structure, bigger than the surrounding ones, with lights summoning them closer. They stopped and looked at it from a distance.

"It doesn't look like a house, Birch," Trudy said.

"No, it doesn't, Trudy. It's way cooler though, just like Jason described it," Bircher gaped.

They could see more details the closer they approached. The exterior walls were made of painted white brick. Three small windows were evenly spaced on the side facing them. The words, "Welcome to the Techno House" were painted in blue calligraphy on a large sign mounted at a ninety-degree angle from the flat roof. Decorative string lights extending from the edge of the roof gutter to poles on the sidewalk formed a makeshift canopy along the side, leading to the door.

They watched as a group of young, well-groomed college boys, wearing preppy clothing and looking a few years older than them, walked up to the door and knocked. The door opened after an extended pause, and the college boys looked relieved.

The sound of Grateful Dead music emanated from inside. The guys walked in, and the door quickly closed, silencing the music. Bircher strangely thought of the Star Trek enterprise where small groups would teleport into a foreign land.

"See, honey!" Bircher exclaimed. "Those guys look clean-cut, harmless. They look like they're in college. Last chance. We're good?"

"Sure, Birch. It looks interesting. Let's check it out. You'll leave if I want, right?"

"Of course. Say the word and we're out of there," Bircher replied.

They knocked and the door opened, allowing the music to escape. A man with an unkept, curly brown beard and an earring, and wearing a Phish shirt, answered the door. Trudy struggled to overcome the body odor. The man was talking on the phone and simply waved them in.

Bircher began to explain that they were friends of Jason, but the man put a finger to his lips and pointed to the phone. He motioned them into the house with a simple inward wave.

Trudy looked at Bircher and whispered, "Was he expecting us? Who is that?"

Bircher shrugged his shoulders and said in a low voice, "No idea. Jason just told me about the house and said only that it shouldn't be a problem."

They held hands and walked in, nerves blazing as they entered.

The excitement that Bircher experienced outside while watching the college kids enter and then walk through the entrance himself with Trudy evaporated once they walked into the structure. To the left of the entrance area, a large room contained a group of older men and women who sat on worn-down furniture. A woman wearing a short-sleeve white T-shirt with armpit hair visible through the end of her sleeve and strumming an acoustic guitar sat in the middle of a couch and sang:

Driving that train
High on cocaine
Casey Jones you better
Watch your speed

Trudy and Bircher left the room and the armpit hair strummer and walked back towards the entrance, not finding anybody of interest. In the room immediately to the right of the entrance, Bircher peeped through the crack of a partially closed door with a sign that read, "The Gallery." Inside another group stood drinking wine and beer, peering at art on the walls. They walked past the gallery towards the back of the structure.

There, a large group gathered, sitting around a large, round table in the kitchen, taking turns bouncing quarters into a glass filled with beer. A keg in a rubber tub filled with ice sat on the white linoleum floor by the sink. A tall woman with long blond hair opened a black refrigerator to retrieve a White Claw.

Nobody looked up at Bircher and Trudy as they watched the action. Even the woman who, after retrieving her White Claw, walked past them into the gallery without acknowledging their presence.

Bircher looked at Trudy, who, with a frown, shrugged her shoulders. Jason had described the Techno House as cool, and while it may have been "cool" to Jason, so far it felt awkward to Bircher. He felt guilty for bullying his girlfriend into going to a lame party. Maybe they should have gone to the movies.

Bircher wondered whether they belonged. He had shied away from alcohol at parties, having tried beer before but hating the taste, not understanding the hype. He tried a shot of whiskey once as a sophomore, only to gag and nearly toss it back up, while Jason and others laughed at him.

The combination of cigarettes and pot created a noxious odor. The smoke was getting into his eyes, causing them to water.

He had talked Trudy into going, thinking it would be good for both of them. But now he realized he had made a terrible mistake. Everybody seemed preoccupied, and there didn't seem anything for them to do. They were the youngest people in the house by at least a decade. He wanted to leave before they both began to reek of smoke and alcohol. *What would Trudy tell her parents if they smelled her walking in the house?*

Bircher was working up the resolve to apologize to his girlfriend for ruining their night when he saw it. To the right of the circuit breaker panel by the back exit, a beam of light rose from a hole in the floor, beckoning him to explore further. He began walking towards the light without uttering a sound, as if in a trance. Once there, he began descending a skinny wooden staircase.

"Where are you going, Birch?" Trudy shouted in a voice that Bircher barely heard.

Hearing no answer, she hurried to catch up to him and descended as well.

The light seared their eyes as they reached the basement floor. Bircher thought about a miniaturized version of the sun hanging from the ceiling, incinerating everything in its path. A chill ran through him.

"Look over there, Birch," Trudy said before adding, "I wonder if we're allowed down here."

"I don't think anybody cares what we do in this place. The people playing quarters must have seen us go down. Nobody said anything," Bircher said, shrugging his shoulders.

They walked over to where Trudy had pointed. Four rows of neatly stacked bright-green potted plants sat on shelves held up by a metal frame.

The basement walls, ceiling, and foundation surrounding the plants were lined with reflective fabric, causing the artificial light to bounce back, stimulating growth.

Above it all contained the God-like source. Four separate panels of LED lights hung about a foot above one of the four shelves. Bircher had never seen lights that bright. It almost seemed impossible, but what did he know?

A grey metallic stand with a laptop sat near the plants. *Methodical*, Bircher thought to himself.

"She's a beauty! Isn't she?" asked a voice rising from behind them, jolting them back to reality.

Bircher and Trudy turned, facing the man with the earing that they had seen earlier.

"I'm Caesar, just like the chimp," he laughed before continuing in a more somber tone. "Seriously, you're not supposed to be here. Gonna have to kill you now!" he said before chuckling again.

Caesar barely acknowledged Bircher's presence with a side glance, directing his icebreaker to Trudy. She beamed, flashing him a wide smile.

The two of them talked and laughed for a few minutes while Bircher stood and watched from six inches away. His heart began to pound.

The man looked at Trudy and said, "Is this your brother? You look like siblings." Bircher curled both hands, tightening them up into balls, but he knew he didn't have the guts to pummel the old man. Trudy appeared to be having a horrible night before meeting Caesar; now, she would probably laugh it off and spend the rest of the night with the man who seemed to draw her attention. He would have to drive home alone.

Only Trudy didn't do any of that; instead, she put her arms around Bircher, pulling him into her, saying, "No, he's my boyfriend! Don't be silly!"

The man replied, "Of course! I was just kidding. What do you think of our setup? We refer to her as 'the gorilla.' She's a beauty, isn't she?"

"Yes, she is," Bircher mumbled. "Is it always this bright?"

"Hmm. No, it's not actually. I thought only one row should be lit at a time. But what do I know? I'm not the guy that runs it. We had somebody in to check out the system a few months ago. So, it must be right!" Caesar gawked before slapping Bircher hard on the back.

"And the computer?"

"Hooked to the Internet, so we're able to monitor it from anywhere. The repair guy set that up when he was here."

"Interesting," Trudy said.

"Well, gotta go! You need to leave this area as well. I'll follow you up the stairs."

When they reached the kitchen, Caesar asked, "Can I get either of you a White Claw or a beer from our keg?"

Trudy said, "That'd be great. A White Claw, please."

"Same for me," Bircher said awkwardly, following it up with, "This place looks cool. Do you live here?"

"Cool? That's funny I haven't heard that word in about ten years." Caesar chuckled, slapping Bircher on the back. "Yes, I do. Right over there," he said pointing to a small room in the back of the loft, visible from their position in the common area on the floor.

Trudy asked, "How many people live in this place?"

Caesar replied, "Twenty! Can you believe it? The owner of the place never pays any attention to it. I think only about half of us pay rent." He then added in a whisper, "The amount we pay is dirt cheap, and now you know how we pay for even that! Let me get those drinks for you."

Trudy smiled at Bircher and said, "Birch, this is exactly what I needed. Thank you for taking me here." She stood tall and embraced Bircher.

Caesar walked up and handed them their White Claws and said, "Enjoy your stay here. Explore, be merry, we're all friends here. There's an upstairs loft too!" He walked away.

Trudy pointed to a staircase to their left. "Let's see what's up there," she said.

They walked up wooden stairs that creaked as they walked. "Be careful, honey," Bircher said, pointing at worn away portions that contained chips and holes. The railing moved as Bircher touched it.

***

Trudy walked onto a piece of dark blue and red shag carpet at the landing of the staircase, relieved that she had made it there alive. The air was smoky and the lighting uneven. Still, there was something special about the place. Everybody seemed happy, calm, relaxed, unlike at some of the high school parties she had attended.

It seemed like a scene out of *American Graffiti*. Trudy half expected to be transported to nearby Haight-Ashbury in the '60s. A chill ran through her as she became excited.

A table held a stereo receiver playing a mixture of rock 'n' roll music. To the right of the table, she noticed a green couch with rips covered by duct tape. She imagined it had been found on the side of the road.

A second couch, this one blue and without any visible duct tape, formed a ninety-degree angle with the green couch. About ten people were squeezed onto both pieces of furniture, with another five sitting on bridge chairs pointed haphazardly a few feet away.

Trudy noticed the three college boys that had entered the Techno House immediately before she and Bircher had entered. They were sitting awkwardly on the chairs, wearing their preppy outfits.

She compared the college kids to the others in the loft, not only in and around the couches but standing and walking in and out of the rooms and the common areas of the loft and downstairs. It was a mixture of women and men that Trudy guessed were in their thirties and forties. People were smiling, laughing, and talking.

Two scruffy men in their forties were sitting on the green couch. They wore red, yellow, and blue tie-dyes and gestured for Trudy to sit in between their smelly bodies. As she sat down, they introduced themselves as Ned and Benji. "NedBen," chuckled the one called Benji, offering Trudy a joint. Trudy accepted giggling, and sat in between NedBen, drawing a concerned stare from Bircher. Trudy ignored her boyfriend, taking a large drag that sent her into a coughing fit.

The college kids offered Bircher a drag from a different joint. He initially refused as he was singularly focused on NedBen seemingly hitting on his girlfriend. After a while, he calmed, realizing that any talk had been harmless. Nothing inappropriate seemed to be going on between NedBen and Trudy. He then accepted and learned from Trudy's mistake, drawing the smoke evenly, taking smaller puffs. He began to relax a few minutes later.

***

It was Bircher who noticed it first. All of the lights brightened at the same time. A few minutes later, a strange smell emanated from a nearby room. He didn't want to say anything out loud, fearing he would disappoint Trudy, who seemed happier than she had been since before the pandemic. Besides, there were so many strange smells.

But as the smell became more pronounced, he began shouting her name.

***

Trudy saw the bright flame before Bircher because it came from a room behind Bircher's back but was right in her line of sight. She screamed, "Fire, fire!" just as Bircher began shouting her name about the smell.

The blaze grew larger as the wood on and around the loft quickly began to burn. The inferno seemed to rage even harder downstairs. Still, they had no choice. They had to race through the first level and out either the front or back door.

Everybody on the loft had the same thought. The staircase caught as people tried to push other people out of the way.

Bircher took hold of Trudy and tried to push her to the front, but she fell. Smoke was accumulating, and he worried they didn't have much time. He screamed for her and reached down to get her, but one of the college kids pushed past him, causing Bircher to fall near Trudy. The hippiness of a few minutes ago had disappeared in a flash.

Bircher was able to help Trudy up from the floor. They pulled their shirts up against their faces to filter out some of the smoke, but it didn't help much.

He maneuvered her to the front of the line, and she stepped onto the staircase. But the weight proved too great for the rickety structure weakened by fire. It collapsed, leaving a void where the staircase had once been. Bircher grabbed Trudy's right hand just in time.

Her body waved in midair while Bircher held her in a desperate attempt to prevent her from falling into the flames below. He couldn't increase his grip because he needed his other hand to grasp a piece of the floor, preventing him, and by extension Trudy, from falling off the loft.

She continued to hang in mid-air. Smoke and heat began to overwhelm her. She feared the worst.

"Save yourself!" she screamed at him, "Let go!"

Bircher either did not hear, or ignored, her pleas.

"Escape through a window or look for the roof!"

They locked eyes, both sobbing and terrified.

How can this happen? Bircher thought. *There must be something I can do. It can't end like this.* He cried for somebody to help.

Ned and Benji took notice of the teens. They grabbed onto Bircher, freeing him to use his other hand to grab Trudy's left hand.

He succeeded, and with the help of Ned and Benji, they hoisted Trudy back up to the loft. Trudy and Bircher quickly embraced as somebody shouted from one of the rooms that they had discovered a different way out. The smoke seemed less concentrated in the direction of the screams.

Bircher, Trudy, Ned, and Benji approached a room where people were discussing how to break down an exit. The door had been closed with a towel shoved under it to slow the accumulation of smoke. Bircher quickly opened the door, forcing it over the towel, allowing everybody to enter. A bald guy with a black stud earring pushed them aside and repositioned the towel, enclosing the now-crowded room.

Some of the inhabitants had gathered around a back door that led to another room where there was a window leading to a fire escape outside the building. Only the door was locked. Nobody had a key.

After a few minutes of watching and observing the dismay of the people that were already there, Benji barked at them to move aside. He began kicking. When that didn't work, the group picked up a heavy chair from the room in a vain attempt to use it as a battering ram.

Trudy pulled Bircher aside. "This isn't going to work. Let's look for another exit. The smoke is less here, but they're going to get trapped. That door's not going to open."

They began to open the inner door, as the others pleaded with them to quickly shut it. But by that time, it was too late.

They all heard a terrifying noise: wood breaking. A moment later, their entire world collapsed onto the first floor.

Bircher coughed while frantically digging himself out of a pile of rubble. The lack of smoke in his area provided a glimmer of hope. His right foot and ankle hurt, and his legs were bleeding, but he had miraculously landed on his feet and thought he could move.

He located Trudy nearby and crawled towards her, that area also strangely free of smoke. Ned, Benji, and the others from the loft were further away and closer to the flames. He detected no movement from their position, and they were probably dying from the fall or choked-out by the smoke.

"Trudy, we have to go!" he said forcefully, shaking her. She stirred, in much worse shape than him.

He repeated, "We have to go – now!"

Bircher helped Trudy to her feet and surveyed the first floor. It was a mess. Dead, mangled, charred bodies were everywhere. Suddenly, they heard screams from the area where Ned, Benji, and the others were located. They were alive!

Bircher thought about trying to help them, but the flames and smoke looked too intense. His lungs were burning, and he couldn't abandon Trudy.

Bircher put his arm around his girlfriend and helped her towards the open front door. A police officer, apparently there before the fire engines, screamed at them from across the room, trying to reach their position. Bircher and Trudy made progress, avoiding obstacles in their path, making it to about twenty feet from the officer.

We'll make it after all, Bircher told himself, seeing an end to the nightmare.

That is until bits of the roof began falling all around them. Trudy screamed as a chunk of wood hit her on the head, knocking her to the ground.

Bircher turned to get her. As he reached down to pull her up, a wooden beam hit him on the head. He fell, out cold, blood gushing from the side wound on his head.

***

Trudy shrieked hysterically for Bircher to get up, but he wouldn't move. She could no longer see the officer. She tried everything, slapping his face, yelling his name. No movement. She frantically searched for a pulse and realized he was dead.

She thought about lying down with him, giving up, not having the strength to go further. Then she thought of her parents.

She kissed Bircher on the lips, closed his eyes, stood, and began limping through the smoke towards the open door, moving towards the faint light in the distance. The light became stronger. She thought of the lighthouse that she and her family had seen on a trip to Maine, and she imagined she was a boat in a storm guided by the lighthouse.

The police officer worked his way towards her, begging her to move more quickly. Fire fighters and emergency responders had also arrived.

Seeing the officer boosted her confidence. She would make it out alive. The officer had reached with his hand to assist Trudy, who had reached out to grab the officer's hand. Then it happened.

A loud explosion emanated from the cellar below, the sound that lightning would make if it hit a few feet away. An overpowering force hit her from below, knocking her into the air. She landed with a thud as a mixture of brick and wood fell, crushing her chest. As she faded away, she thought of Bircher and the last instructions from her father before they left her house a couple of hours ago: stay safe and make the right choices. And, then Trudy LaMonte felt nothing.

Chapter 6

Chetan Maka parked her pickup truck emblazoned with the Oakland Fire Department's red and yellow crossed-hatchet logo, filling a void in the mishmash of fire engines, police cars, ambulances, media, and other vehicles that had assembled around the now mostly smoldering Techno House. Portable light towers mounted on several of the fire trucks lit up the scene. Bugs flew around the rays of light in random patterns amidst all the fuss. Though it was 3:00 a.m., it seemed like the middle of the day, except for the areas not illuminated.

The fire had surprisingly been brought under control in a mere four hours. A compressed debris field helped consolidate remnants of the destroyed structure, allowing the abundance of firefighters called to a catastrophic scene to extinguish the flames.

Conditions were safe enough for Chetan to enter, beginning the process of reconstructing how and why the fire had begun. She would have to step gingerly, avoiding any gaps that would cause her to fall to the basement below. Embers would hamper her work. Still, she felt it important to survey the inside before critical evidence became tainted, a lesson she had learned earlier in her career.

She stepped out of her truck and began to put on her uniform. Her helmet and face shield protected her dark brown complexion and shiny black hair that had been neatly tied into a long ponytail extending down half her back. Chetan stepped her smallish, skinny figure into her protective outer pants and coat. She double-checked the fit of her gloves, helmet, and breathing apparatus while surveying the scene.

An abyss of collapsed floors and walls filled with charring flesh lay before her. Low flames were visible in a few areas but were being extinguished. Smoke and water vapor, visible in the spotlights, rose like an ascending angel. The air reeked from burnt wood, plastic, rubber, and flesh.

Chetan approached the structure from behind. Fires didn't use the front door, so she didn't either. The walls and doors had collapsed into the pit. Before stepping into the mess, she looked at the Suits that had gathered near the assembled media. *Posing for pictures and no doubt offering details and expert opinion when they know nothing*, Chetan mused to herself.

One of the Suits stood out from the rest, standing emotionless as if waiting patiently to enter a museum. He was tall and skinny, wearing thick glasses, his black hair parted to the side. Chetan briefly caught his gaze before the man's eyes darted away.

Must be a real winner, Chetan thought.

Although her boots protected her feet and legs from nearby debris, she had to be careful about falling into a void, twisting an ankle, or worse. Firefighters nodded respectfully at her, moving out of her way.

Chetan took a deep breath; she had to remain strong. Strength had helped her rise through the ranks first at Cal Fire and now the Oakland Fire Department, no easy task for any woman, much less a Sioux Indian raised on South Dakota's Rosebud Indian Reservation.

When she first joined Cal Fire, initially in its forest management division, some of her male colleagues refused to work with her, claiming she could put their lives in jeopardy. She was not smart, strong, or agile enough to cull the forests, and was putting her platoon at risk, at least that is what some of the men said. Others called her Pocahontas or The Savage.

One particular asshole performed an exaggerated cryfest for her with hoots of: "See you on the Trail of Tears."

At first, she thought about challenging them the way she learned to defend herself growing up with two older brothers. They would wrestle, box, and play hot hands. Not as strong as her brothers, she had been forced to outwit them at first through distraction, and later superior technique.

In high school, she had been more interested in continuing with wrestling and boxing even though there were no girls' teams. Title IX apparently did not apply to the Indian sovereign nation. The coach didn't allow her to participate at first. But she would show up before practice, daring the boys to fight or wrestle. Word spread of her defeating several of the boys, and the coach eventually relented.

She knew it would be the same drill at Cal Fire. People are similar, even if the situation is different. She needed to bide her time until the right moment. Fortunately, she didn't have to wait long.

One day, shortly after Chetan's first anniversary with the forest management division, strong Diablo winds toppled several electrical poles. A swirling fire followed. Firefighters working sixteen-hour days became desperate and tired, a few had even died.

During the worst of the blaze, Chetan's six-person platoon, including three men who had mocked her the loudest, came across a cabin. Chetan started to enter, when two of her platoon mates shoved her aside, berating "Pocahontas" for entering without permission. All five of the men chortled as she let them pass.

Soon after the five men entered the cabin, with Chetan still outside, the roof collapsed. Ignoring the danger, she rescued her colleagues one by one.

Then-Governor Jerry Brown awarded her the Medal of Valor, publicly lauding her efforts. Gone were the racist taunts as she began to climb up the ladder. The Oakland Fire Department stole her away with the prestige position of Chief Investigator, reporting directly to the Fire Marshall,

Antonio Gonzalez. Continued hard work and bravery earned her respect throughout the emergency services.

Chetan glanced at Jerry, the department's medical examiner. She knew that after photographing a body, Jerry's two assistants would delicately place the corpse in a bag and mark the area with a triangular, yellow sign.

Chetan stepped carefully through the debris, taking pictures of wires and anything suspicious. She would return the next day for a more detailed look during the daylight, but wanted a record of the conditions before the site was disturbed by water, foam, and the inevitable scavengers who would set upon the site after the firefighters left.

She found the remnants of the kitchen and noted that nothing seemed unusual. Then, she located the circuit breaker box on the back wall. The breakers seemed in place, although, curiously, one looked cleaner than others.

Next, she noted the staircase leading down to the basement. Although the second floor had caved into the first floor, experience told her that the foundation and cast-iron ceiling support beams would have protected the basement. Firefighters had already hosed the area down, clearing the staircase from any rubble.

While the concrete floor looked relatively unharmed, burn marks told her that flames must have run up the inner wall near a junction box. Wires could have overheated, igniting boxes, paper, or other flammable material nearby, the result of too much electricity being forced through overloaded wiring.

Four damaged rows of light fixtures held by a metal frame were hanging over a melted mess near the junction box. Something was being grown. Chetan considered the burgeoning home pot-growing industry but couldn't tell for sure. A badly damaged computer near the apparatus could have been operating the system.

She traced the burn marks near the junction box. While almost everything seemed at least partially incinerated, she noted a pattern. The wooden portion of the ceiling had also been deeply charred. If not for the cast-iron beams, the ceiling might have collapsed. Flames likely burned up from the junction box and then up the staircase, drawn by oxygen.

Chetan revisited the circuit breaker box. She recalled that one of the breakers looked new. After examining the breakers more closely, she realized that a new thirty-amp breaker was installed where a fifteen-amp breaker should have been.

A theory germinated in her mind. Hustling downstairs back to the junction box, she determined that using a thirty-amp breaker may not have tripped, protecting against an overload of the grow lights, especially if all were illuminated at the same time. *But how and why would that have happened?*

After finishing her notes and taking pictures, Chetan walked back up the staircase. Making her way to the front of the house, she spotted a body that had not yet been removed, a few feet away from the door. Jerry's assistants were hunched over on either side of the corpse.

Chetan stared at the body, inexplicably drawn to it, before screaming, "Do not touch that body! Move away! Before I cut off your hand!" she repeated, brandishing her axe for emphasis.

The assistants looked angry as they turned around to confront the small woman yelling at them. They cooled, recognizing her as Chetan with the words "CHIEF INVESTIGATOR" on her helmet and uniform, and quickly backed away.

Chetan knelt closer. Judging by the smallish frame and skinny legs, she thought it might be a young woman, perhaps a teenager. The teeth were small and round in contrast to choppy and square, a sign that the deceased had been female.

So young, with her life ahead of her, she said to herself. Her arms flailed about like a toppled flamenco dancer. *So close to making it out. She must have thought she'd survive until something, probably an explosion from the basement, propelled her into the air like a jumping jack, causing her to land on her back.*

Her chest had been crushed by what Chetan assumed to be falling debris. Her face looked contorted by a chin expanded downward, stretching her visage. *The tortured panic she must have felt at the end,* thought Chetan. Her face bore a striking resemblance to Edvard Munch's *The Scream.*

Chetan walked out of the building, needing to get some air. The girl's face threatened to bubble up repressed memories. Dozens more had also died. She had seen a lot of tragedy investigating for Cal Fire and the Oakland Fire Department, but nothing like this fire.

She looked around, glancing at her cellphone– 4:30 a.m. While some of the spectators had left, one had not. The man with the blank expression remained, observing, holding a cell phone against his ear. Like the young woman, he didn't fit in either.

Chapter 7

Meridian stifled a yawn as he talked to Fred Turner. Turner's pompous attitude annoyed Meridian on a normal day. And at 4:30 a.m., after being up all night watching the bonfire he had started, Meridian had no patience for string-pullers.

Turner demanded to know every intricate detail. It took all of Meridian's available self-control to refrain from yelling what he *really* wanted to say: *If you want to know everything, then you should've been here yourself!* He could have gotten away with it too, since the Benefactor had merely loaned Meridian's services to Turner for the mission.

Ten minutes into the call, Turner finally asked something meaningful, "Are you sure Hammer's dead?"

"I saw his body being taken out,"

"How do you know it was him?"

"I recognized his bright tie-dye shirt as two lackeys picked up his body replacing it with an adorable yellow sign; his inseparable friend, Ned, came next."

"Hmm."

"Hmm."

"And the collateral damage we discussed?"

"Significant, very significant. Bunch of hippies nobody will miss."

"Obscuring the real target," Turner pointed out.

"Yes."

"So, the program really worked. Caused the overload."

Obviously, asshole! "Yes."

"And what about the thirty-amp breaker being where a fifteen-amp breaker should've been?"

"Nobody will figure that one out. We're talking about the Oakland Fire Department after all," Meridian said, watching the Chief Investigator poke around the scene.

"Good point."

"Good night."

Chapter 8

The closing night revealed the first shades of the approaching day's light when Chetan arrived at her apartment in West Oakland.

The apartment located in a former industrial area of Oakland, consisted of three large rectangular buildings. The buildings were aligned in a U-shape with the vertex forming the middle of a dead-end. Two years ago, the structures featured broken glass, vermin, strewn garbage, and graffiti, bearing a resemblance to a zombie land depicted by shows like *The Walking Dead*.

A developer had purchased the complex, converting the buildings into residential studios and single apartments. A mixing pot of singles, hipsters, elderly, and young couples moved in, followed by small retail shops, restaurants, and coffee houses lining the ground-floor levels. The exteriors were cleaned and repaired, with each exterior taking on the original reddish brick hue of its original appearance.

The interior of Chetan's building, like the two others, had tall ceilings, oakwood floors, and large glass panes. It looked new, with few signs of the older structure.

She began renting her unit on the second floor when the building first opened. Her boss, Antonio Gonzalez, had authorized a monthly stipend as part of the package to entice her away from Cal Fire. The stipend reimbursed her for use of a second room as a home office that she used when not in the field, as part of the agency's bid to reduce the need for more expensive office space.

Chetan crawled into bed after closing her blinds, not even bothering to slip off her smoke and sweat-drenched undergarments. She wore an eye mask to help block out the emerging sun that would soon burst through her thin window shades.

Zonta, her white fluffy cat with an adorable pink nose, snuggled up to her as she desperately tried to doze. The feline had followed Chetan home one night, looking for a handout, and the two had immediately bonded. Her name meant trustworthy in Lakota, aptly suiting her personality. Chetan could tell her anything, and Zonta never told a soul. They were best friends, a commentary on the life of a Sioux still trying nearly twenty years later to adapt to life off the reservation.

Unlike Zonta, who quickly fell asleep, tired out from her purring, sleep evaded Chetan as she struggled with her restless thoughts. At first, she thought about the young woman that lay dead by the door at the Techno House. Visions of *The Scream* overwhelmed the sheep she tried to count. *And how did the woman wind up at the Techno House in the first place?* Chetan had learned from talking to a cop who had interviewed the witnesses that, except for a handful of younger college or high-school aged visitors, the rest of the crowd consisted of older hippies, artists, and homeless. *Who did the woman go with? She didn't go alone, that's for sure.*

Chetan's tired thoughts drifted into sleep and then into a recurring nightmare of an event that shaped her life a long time ago when she was fifteen.

Dad's Ford Torino that he had purchased earlier in the summer at an estate sale lurched as it moved across the bumpy reservation road. He flashed a smile at my mom in the passenger seat. Dad had been happy that day, at least in the beginning.

The Oilmen

Our car turned onto Route 83 heading south towards Nebraska for a picnic in a grassy field off the reservation. Mom had packed food and blankets for the occasion and a Frisbee too!

I sat in the back, squeezed against the right window, on torn seats patched with black duct tape. Hotah elbowed me after I pinched his leg, egging him on, while Tashunka tried to ignore us. It usually started between me and Hotah before spreading to Tashunka, who always tried to initially play it cool, like Switzerland, Mom had said once, although we didn't really know what that meant. The three of us were crammed in like three pieces of one of those chocolate almond bars Dad sometimes brought home after work.

Mom turned around with a frown, scowling at me, knowing that I had started all the fuss. We all knew that was part of the game and that she was never really mad.

Twenty miles later, we passed the green and blue sign pronouncing, "Nebraska...the good life."

Hotah saw it first from his middle seat, yelling at my dad to slow down. A blue semi-truck sped towards our car from the other direction. Mom and I screamed while Tashunka looked terrified.

Dad swerved our car hard to the left, missing the truck but flying off the side of the road down an embankment. I turned my gaze away to shield myself from an oncoming tree, holding Hotah's arm tight. Our car jerked to the right back towards the road, and, for a second, I was sure that we would land back where we started from and would laugh it all off. That was when we hit another tree, causing everybody to fly forward, Hotah the most.

Relatively unscathed since I hit Mom's headrest and bounced back. I smelled gas and screamed for everybody to get out. But nobody responded...

***

47

Chetan's iPhone alarm awoke her at 7:00 a.m., a mere two hours after finally falling asleep. Eager to get back to the scene, she quickly showered and gulped down two cups of coffee, a banana, and a stale donut. She then fed Zonta, put out fresh water, and changed the litter in her litterbox.

The morning chill hit as she entered her car to return to the Techno House. Thinking about her recurring nightmare made her depressed. The dream ended at the same place each time. She knew it had all happened, culminating in a fiery explosion ignited by the gas. She also knew that Hotah hadn't survived, unlike the rest of her family. But she couldn't remember anything after the point of screaming for everybody to leave.

Did I fail you, Hotah? Could I have saved you, somehow?

***

Chetan pulled into the lot in front of the Techno House. Police monitored the cordon set up around the building, and a collection of people from the ABCs of government milled about on the premises. Antonio acknowledged Chetan with a scowl as she entered the site, pointing to his watch. *Fuck off,* she felt like saying, still feeling the effects of little sleep.

A lieutenant with the Oakland Police Department handed her a list of known people discovered to have been at the fire, with the dead or injured notated and an indication of where they died or had been injured. The officer told her about a shared website being established for any interview notes, leads, and background information obtained by any of the investigators. She would receive an invite by the end of the day.

Chetan spent the next six hours meticulously going over the grounds, taking detailed notes and pictures. First, she walked the site looking at the list and where each person died or became injured. Where some of the dead or injured were in the front, it seemed likely that the second floor collapsing into the first floor and excessive smoke inhalation had been the cause. The rate of calamities was much higher, and body damage much more significant, in the back of the house towards the kitchen, reinforcing the pattern of the fire spreading from below, into the kitchen, and then to the rest of the house.

Next, Chetan looked for other suspicious starting points beyond what she had found earlier about the basement. Not finding any, she double-checked her theory about the basement before leaving after her stomach began to growl.

Chapter 9

On Monday, a week after he had inserted the thumb drive into his Earthcare computer, David Grigorio paced back and forth between his living room and kitchen. He wore only an undersized pair of unfashionable white Hanes underwear he had retrieved from the bottom of his drawer. He tried to do laundry over the weekend, but he had mistakenly poured bleach into the washing machine, thinking it had been detergent. Portions of his hair stood up as if he had been electrocuted, and thick stubble threatened to turn into something more permanent.

David had done everything asked of him, but the mad doctor and his bosses had yet to reciprocate. He began dialing the police on his cell phone, but then quickly disconnected before hearing the first ring. More pacing. David called his mom, but he hung up on her too, before she answered. More pacing.

A minute later, his cell phone rang. His heart began to pound so fast he thought about saying the Lord's Prayer as he answered weakly, "Hello?"

Meridian mocked him in a cheerful singsong but with his usual short bursts, "Hello! Hola. Wife all good!"

David bit his lip and replied dryly, suppressing deeper emotions. "I did what you wanted me to do. Do I pick her up somewhere? Or can you drop her off?"

"Want to know? How many fingers left?"

"I did everything you asked. Don't make me call the cops."

"Relax. Just kidding! Haha! Be at 351 Sandy Street at 8:00 p.m. tomorrow. Come alone. She's all yours." The line went dead.

David breathed easier. The nightmare would soon be over. He would quit Earthcare. They would move away and start again. The damage created by whatever virus he helped unleash on the server wouldn't be his issue.

***

The houses on Sandy Street had aged in the decades since they were built near Telegraph Road in Alexandria. Like the other streets in the area, the houses were occupied by mid-level government workers needing an inexpensive place to live close to D.C. The houses were mostly one-level ramblers that looked like shotgun houses turned to face parallel to the street.

David's stomach, already on the verge of exploding, growled even more as he pulled into the stub-like drive leading up to 351 Sandy Street. A Long and Foster for sale sign stood proudly to the left of the driveway. No lights were visible inside, except for one light near what David imagined to be the front hallway.

He looked around before pressing the doorbell that he had to find using his iPhone flashlight. A realtor lockbox hung on the doorknob. An elderly black man puffed on a cigar on his lit front porch across the street.

Nobody answered the door as he continually rang. He let loose a few F-bombs and looked at the cigar man, who had been watching.

This can't be right. Did Meridian say a different address? What do I do now?

Cigar Man continued to puff. "Can I help you, young man?" he called out.

David walked over to him. "Ah...I was told to meet somebody here."

"Son, there hasn't been anyone in that house in quite a while. You sure you got the right address?"

"Yes, I think so. 351 Sandy Street."

"Well, that's the right address, but nobody's been there since Lucinda died."

"How long ago did that happen?"

"About a year ago. It's been on the market ever since. I haven't seen anybody tour it in the past couple of months. My brother told me that if a house isn't sold in two months, it's never going to sell."

David clenched his left fist. "Anybody service the house recently? Maybe from Washington Gas?"

"The gas company, you say?"

"Yes, sir."

"Not that I've seen. Why?"

"Never mind," David grunted before walking back to his car.

***

David raced home, speeding on the Beltway. Forty minutes later, he arrived. After parking in the garage, he slowly opened the door to the house. Everything seemed in order. He even checked the furnace room. Nothing.

He knew he had no choice but to wait. Meridian had called before and would call again. He had followed the instructions. Something must have happened at Meridian's end.

David retrieved a pint of coffee ice cream from his freezer. Eating out of the container, he began to think about *what-ifs* and *whys*. *What if Cindy had tried to escape?* He knew the answer to that. Cindy was not a runner. *What if I had called the cops after the nightmare began a week ago? What if I call tomorrow? Why is this happening? Why did the crazy doctor pick me?*

He would give it one more day, he resolved as he hit the bottom of the pint. David walked upstairs to the bedroom. He would watch television in his bed for a few hours.

That wouldn't happen either, however. As he entered the room, something hit him in the neck. *A dart*, he thought silently before collapsing. Then he couldn't move.

"Gotcha! Walked right into it. Back from Sandy Street? Haha!"

Meridian's silvery hair shined at the terrified David being hoisted onto the bed. Next, he retrieved Cindy from the guest bedroom, placing her next to her fiancé.

"Got you a present!" Meridian said to David. "Nod if you like it."

When the paralyzed David didn't move, Meridian asked, "No likey? Should I return her?"

Meridian, wearing surgical gloves, positioned both sitting next to each other with their backs against the headboard of the bed. Neither victim moved, except for their traumatized eyes darting back and forth.

Meridian read a letter to them, and when finished, he placed it on David's knee. The letter had answered the "what-ifs" and "whys" David had been asking himself earlier in the evening – and a whole lot more.

The monster doctor then placed David's limp index finger on the trigger of a gun. Two shots were fired. Meridian placed Cindy's left hand by the left side of her skull before forcing David's limp finger to fire the first shot.

The bullet tore off the remaining portion of Cindy's left pinky finger, hiding the earlier torture from the meddling cops, who would soon invade the house like maggots milling about a dead corpse. The bullet next entered the left side of Cindy's skull, spraying her brains all over the bedroom, including onto David and Meridian.

The second shot occurred with David's involuntary hand shooting himself under the chin. Many people committing suicide make the mistake of yanking the gun away at the last minute, causing severing of the nose, but not death. Meridian made sure that mistake didn't happen.

Chapter 10

Suzanne Harper lay in her bed on a Tuesday morning, staring at the ceiling as if the new day had been a Saturday or Sunday. On most weekdays, she rose early, eager to go to work at Earthcare, the environmental nonprofit that she had founded nearly a decade ago. But on this morning, Suzanne had been overwhelmed by troubling thoughts.

Something must have happened to her most trusted employee, David. Earthcare's third employee, he had been with Suzanne from the beginning. They had a special bond, unlike any other at the office. David had his quirks – messy, snarky, and nerdy – but he had been loyal, without any secrets or hidden agendas.

Last Monday, eight days ago, David left work early, claiming to be sick. Sure, he had been sick before, but never without checking in on a daily basis. The remainder of that week he had been available to work, but only at home, and any interactions were rushed and terse. *Maybe he had a breakthrough infection? Was he rotting away on a ventilator?*

David's assistant had similar concerns – yesterday remarking to Suzanne as work ended for the day, "David told me in an email that he was sick, and I haven't heard from him since. I thought he had been vaccinated. Is he all right?"

Suzanne shrugged her shoulders before replying, "If he doesn't report in tomorrow, I'll contact him."

Suzanne eventually slithered out of her bed, careful not to wake her retired husband, George. She went to the bathroom, where she consulted the mirror for answers that never arrived.

A short woman in her mid-fifties with a rounded belly stared back. Her shoulder-length blonde hair that normally shined was in need of its daily grooming, and her long olive face with a button nose needed washing.

After showering, dressing, and applying a light dose of makeup, which included reinforcing her dwindling eyebrows, she walked down the hallway towards the master bedroom, where George had just stirred awake.

Like many retired men, George had gained weight, causing his belly to flop slightly over his midline. An avid runner in his younger days, his aches and pains had slowed him down. His black coiled hair varied from being tight and short after a haircut to a tumbled mess when longer and unkept. His dark brown skin, accentuated by a neat, trimmed beard, had accumulated a few notches over the years, from accidents, acts of bravado, or fights while in the military and growing up.

His dress habits matched the changes to his frame, lately not caring as much about his attire. Simple shirts that didn't fit as well as they used to and that often became untucked from his baggy jeans were commonplace.

"How's the leg feel?" George asked, referring to Suzanne's left leg that throbbed on most mornings. Her college sweetheart of over forty years frequently had to massage her leg just below the knee to calm the nerves that otherwise set her teeth on edge. Sometimes it worked, often it didn't.

Her pain had become incessant, intolerable at times. On bad days, George liked to point out that, "You'd feel better if you took some damn pain killers! That's why they make them."

But she refused, her typical retort being something like, "Grammy lived to ninety-eight and never took that crap. She did not believe in taking pills, and neither do I." George eventually gave up trying, shifting his energy into "doing it her way."

Suzanne injured her leg when operatives working for France's intelligence services attached two limpet mines to her ship owned by Greenpeace, for whom she worked at the time. The *Rainbow Warrior* had tried to disrupt a French nuclear test being staged on Mururoa, an atoll located in the South Pacific Ocean about 1,200 kilometers to the east of Tahiti. The operation failed when the mines, detonated ten minutes apart, sank the ship while it was still in port before it even left to travel to the planned test site.

Suzanne refused to leave the ship, which initially didn't sink, seeking instead to help Connor Boucher search for his brother, Ronan. Ronan worked in the engineering room, located a floor below sea level. As the area began to flood, a panicked Connor flagged down Suzanne, who agreed to help.

A stellar swimmer, she was able to locate Ronan. The second explosion hit as she and Connor were escorting Ronan to safety. Although the Boucher brothers were not hurt, the explosion sent a large chunk of metal flying from God-knows-where, embedding itself deep into Suzanne's leg. She passed out from the pain and had to be carried off by the Boucher boys before the vessel sank.

After several surgeries to pin her fibula in place to heal and to repair damaged nerves, her condition stabilized. But she would never be the same, having failed to regain the balance, stamina, and stability needed to take pictures aboard a ship or at a march or protest. The pain had also become too much to bear. Management deemed her too great of a liability for fieldwork.

***

Suzanne ate a cheese omelet, watching two deer in her backyard pick at her rose bushes. Her Black Lab, Mercy, walked over to her table, sniffing the ground under her feet. The dog then stretched and walked to the front door, waiting for her master.

Suzanne finished her meal and looked to make sure that her nosy next-door neighbor, Mr. Winestone, wasn't walking his Pitbull. Finding the cul-de-sac empty, she ventured out with Mercy.

She and George had the good fortune of buying their modern Tudor styled house in an expensive area of Arlington during the 2008 real estate crash from a builder who had become overextended. The brick house had pitched roofs above the garage and main house, with diamond-paned windows below the vertex. After walking the dog and kissing George goodbye, she began her commute to her K Street offices.

The traffic remained light as the pandemic had caused many businesses to downsize their use of office space. Some people preferred to work at home, including many who had been vaccinated but had gotten used to working wearing only a T-shirt and pair of sweatpants. Not Suzanne or David though; Suzanne found the quiet offices relaxing, and David needed quick access to Earthcare's server room.

Suzanne waved at the sleepy guard monitoring the curvy ramp down to her office building's underground parking lot. Her pearl blue Prius easily navigated the tight ramp with walls that had black scrape marks made from larger gas guzzling SUVs, trucks, and full-size cars.

An elevator opened, depositing Suzanne on the third floor that her company occupied in full. She strutted confidently past the pale, freckly, red-haired receptionist, Molly, who she usually ignored, considering her a busybody. But today she doubled back and asked her, "Is David in?"

Molly, Earthcare's receptionist/office manager, flashed her a wide fake smile and then said, "No. Sorry, he hasn't arrived yet."

Suzanne grunted and walked to her large executive corner office. She dialed David's home and cell. No answer. She resolved to try again later.

For the rest of the day, she made donor calls and handled personnel and management issues. With over two hundred staff working in the D.C. area and satellite offices in Europe, Asia, and Africa, there was a lot to do.

David remained in her thoughts, though, after two more attempts to reach him failed.

Chapter 11

A fter finishing her work on Friday, Suzanne drove her car out of the garage, debating what to do next. David last came to work two Mondays ago, and she hadn't been able to reach him except for a few terse communications last week – and none this week. *Is David in the hospital? Jail? Should I call the police and have them do a welfare check? And where is Cindy?*

Distracted, she ignored the brick warning strip on the sidewalk and had to slam on her brakes to avoid hitting a pedestrian. The tall, millennial made an obscene gesture at Suzanne as she sincerely mouthed a "sorry" and issued a polite wave.

Once outside the city, Suzanne called George to check on dinner. Although the sun, in the throes of summer solstice, made it feel like mid-afternoon, her hungry stomach begged to differ. It was 6:30 after all, time for dinner.

And like David, George didn't answer either. *What is going on?*

A half-hour later, she eased her car onto her street in her sleepy community. It was quiet except for a few other workers arriving home.

There were no lights on inside her house. George must be out getting dinner, which she welcomed because she didn't feel like cooking.

Suzanne inserted the key, turned the knob, and disabled the alarm they had installed a year before when the Beckers were robbed. Months later with no issues, she had considered using the system's chime without arming it, but George reminded her that crime comes in cycles and could quickly return, so she relented. It wasn't a lot of work to arm the system in the morning before leaving for work and disarming it in the evening. They both had, – or, in George's case, used to have before he retired from the NSA – high profile jobs.

She called out for George and received no reply. She looked in the garage. No car. She tried to reach George again, but she got his voicemail message.

If he's running an errand or picking up dinner, he'd answer my call or at least return it right away. It's not like him. Maybe the NSA had called him back in to consult on an urgent matter. He could be in a secure facility.

Suzanne continued to call for George, but then gave up. She grabbed a handful of nuts from a jar in the kitchen, hungry, but also due to a nervous habit she had picked up from her mom.

Suzanne had put a second mouthful of nuts into her mouth when she heard a loud bang on her front door. A male voice shouted, "F-B-I! OPEN UP – NOW!"

She moved to the door and looked through the peephole at a badge thrust in her sightline.

F-B-I! OPEN UP – NOW!"

She opened the door slowly.

"Are you Suzanne Harper?" asked a tall Asian man with several pock marks on each cheek as he flashed his badge. This time, Suzanne could read it: *Agent Charles Ridley.*

A second agent, a white woman with black curly hair, stood next to Agent Ridley. She, too, held out her badge: *Agent Nicole Harmon.*

Both were wearing camo pants and a navy jacket with FBI in bright yellow letters on the back. Agent Ridley had not buttoned his jacket, exposing his bulletproof vest. Their Glock 9mm handguns were visible in their holsters.

Suzanne peered past Agents Ridley and Harmon and noticed two other officers standing on the lawn near the front door stoop. Two white cars with a navy stripe emblazoned with the word "FBI" and the logo on the side and a black, unmarked Chevy Suburban were visible in the distance.

"Yes, I'm Suzanne Harper. Is everything all right? Is this about my husband George? He hasn't come home yet. I can't reach him."

"He's with us, ma'am. At the station," replied Agent Ridley.

Suzanne tried to remain calm, but she was baffled. "Huh? What is this about? Why would he be at the station? Is he a witness to something? Did something happen?"

"Ma'am, come with us. We'll sort it all out," Agent Ridley said, calmly and sternly.

"I'm not going anywhere until you answer my questions. Why do you have my husband?"

Agent Harmon interjected quickly before Agent Ridley could speak, "Just get in the car! Now!"

Agent Ridley flashed Agent Harmon a dirty look. "Please, come with me," he said gently, easing her arm.

Suzanne shook him off and said loudly, "I'm not going anywhere without some answers first!"

"Fine, have it your way," Agent Harmon said. "We'll make this much worse for you unless you get in the car now."

"Much worse? How? Do you have a warrant for my arrest? Have I done something wrong?"

Agent Ridley calmly said in a low tone, "Your husband is there already. I suggest you come and answer a few questions." He lowered his voice even further and added, "Don't make us read you your rights, not in front of your neighbors and all. Come quietly and we'll sort this out before this goes any further."

"Oh, we're beyond that, *sir*! The damage has already occurred."

Suzanne looked around at the collection of neighbors that were watching from their own stoops. She considered her options. *This could get uglier. They can't arrest me since I didn't do anything wrong. George is probably a witness to something. That asshole neighbor, Mr. Winestone, is now watching. He's sure to make this go viral if it gets more heated. He'll get his jerky kid to do it for him...*

She thought about calling her lawyer first, but she only knew the lawyer for her business. He wouldn't be able to help her, anyway. She could call him and get a referral, but lawyering up could be perceived as a sign of weakness, that she did something wrong – when she didn't. She had nothing to be afraid of.

"Why all the firepower if you're not arresting me?"

Agent Ridley nodded, responding politely. "Getting a lot of heat these days, as you probably know, even losing a few agents to gunfire."

"OK. I'll go with you, but quietly. Deal?"

The agents nodded their heads with the bait having been swallowed.

"Deal, and again, we're *not* arresting you. We just want you to come down to the station to talk," Agent Ridley reassured her.

"How long will it take?"

"Not more than a few hours at the station. Then we'll drive you back."

I don't have to go. I mean I'm not under arrest."

"That's correct. My partner just said that. We just want to talk," Agent Harmon said impatiently.

"Can you tell me what it's about?"

"We were just told to pick you up. Your husband is already there. That's all we know," Agent Ridley said, shrugging.

Suzanne turned her back towards them and walked several steps away. She tried George again on her cell phone, but again, she couldn't reach him.

"Ma'am, he's being questioned right now. His cell phone has been confiscated for the interview. I'm sorry, but that's protocol," Agent Ridley said in a soft voice.

"Ok," she relented, fighting a budding headache, "let me get my coat."

They walked out of the house, but not before Suzanne grabbed a few power bars to shovel down on the ride. She looked quickly at Mr. Winestone. He had a big grin and looked like he was biting his lower lip, probably to keep from smiling any wider, Suzanne mused. Agent Harmon opened the car door and motioned for Suzanne to enter.

***

It took thirty minutes for Agents Ridley and Harmon to drive their detainee through the light traffic to the FBI's field office in D.C. Nobody talked, each passenger was aware of the legalities of the situation. Protocols needed to be followed.

Suzanne tried to reach George again, but he didn't answer. She watched the dancing reflection of the setting sun against the Potomac River at ground level below the highway as the car zoomed down the George Washington Parkway.

She couldn't figure out why the FBI wanted to talk, and she immediately began to think the worst. *Am I or George being framed? For what? By whom? Are we both witnesses to a crime that somebody else has committed?* She began to relax, *knowing* that they couldn't possibly have done anything wrong. They were probably only witnesses.

Their car pulled into a driveway leading into an office building. A brown aluminum gate opened, allowing them to pass into the bowels of the structure. The gate shut quickly behind them, like the spring of a rat trap.

"Right this way, ma'am," Agent Ridley said, motioning as they exited the car.

"I hope you're taking me to see my husband. His cell phone is not picking up," Suzanne said.

"We told you before, he's inside a secure area. We have to hold his phone. It's the same way in other secure buildings. I'll need to collect your phone too. You might as well hand it over now," Agent Harmon said in a serious tone.

Suzanne thought about what she had been told. Although it made sense, she didn't want to give up too soon. "Not until I see George," she said.

"You know we can't do that, ma'am. We can't change our procedure for you," Agent Ridley said.

Agent Harmon, this time in an even more demanding tone, repeated her request, "Now, hand over your phone, please, or we'll drive you back home and do this another time."

Suzanne relented, powering down the phone before handing it to Agent Harmon.

"Thank you. This way, ma'am," Agent Ridley said with a gesture.

Suzanne followed Agent Ridley into an elevator with Agent Harmon entering last, and the door opened on the third floor, where the agents escorted her into a stale room with light brown painted walls and simple, square, acoustical ceiling tiles. The only upgrade, and a slight one at that, had been to the floor with its dark brown carpet laid out in square patterns.

The familiar tools were already in attendance in the middle of the room: a black rectangular table, two silver chairs symmetrically arranged on each side of the table, a legal pad and pen proudly waiting on top of the table for their prominent role, and an ominous recorder. Suzanne sat in the chair opposite the pen and pad, facing a large rectangular window on the wall behind where she assumed her interviewer would sit. Suzanne had no illusions that she was alone, even though her escorts walked out of the room, letting the door close with a loud thud.

A few minutes later, the door opened and a small, rotund, bald man wearing a brown suit entered. The man could have been a ringer for Danny DeVito.

"Good evening, Mrs. Harper. I'm Agent Proctano. Can I get you some water?" he asked with a forced smile. His voice even sounded like DeVito.

Suzanne would have laughed had the situation not been so serious. Instead, she muttered, "Yes, please," before stopping herself from thanking him.

Agent Proctano gestured towards the window that he wanted a drink. A moment later, Agent Ridley entered with two glasses and a clear plastic pitcher filled with water and ice.

The agent poured two glasses, and a piece of ice fell into one of the glasses, causing a *thunk*. A splash of water fell onto the table. Proctano wiped the water away with his shirt sleeve. *Perfect DeVito* thought Suzanne.

He handed the second glass to Suzanne. She gulped it down, washing away the remnants of the power bars that the famished woman had devoured in the car, and poured herself a refill, not knowing when she would get another opportunity.

"Now, before we begin, do you have any questions?"

"Just about my husband, George. Is he still here?"

"Yep, but he's finished and waiting for you. We'll drive both of you home after you're done. Is that *acceptable* to you?"

Suzanne became suspicious at the hollow gesture, remembering that she didn't see George's Tesla at the house.

"I'd like to see him before we begin."

Had he been lying about the car? Forgot? Didn't remember? *He probably didn't know*, she settled on. *Bureaucratic sloppiness.*

The agent shifted his weight in his seat. "We're running out of time. There are reasons why we can't do that."

"Like what?"

"Figure it out. Now, let's begin. I'll try to move it along as fast as possible. OK?"

Suzanne stared blankly without committing. *Figure it out?* She again thought about calling her lawyer, but she decided to get it over with, making the same decision calculus as before. Neither she nor George had done anything wrong. The FBI probably thought they were witnesses to a crime, although she didn't know to what.

The agent armed himself with the pen, readied the pad, and continued, hearing no response from Suzanne.

"I'm going to skip the formalities and jump right into it as it's already late. I'm turning on the recorder."

Proctano then announced the date, time, and Suzanne's name for the record before asking his first substantive question.

"Can you tell me what Earthcare does? Something that I can't read on your website or in the newspaper."

Suzanne looked around the room, gathering her thoughts, glancing at the window before answering.

"Well, there's not that much more than you already know then. We're mostly concerned with addressing environmental concerns, clean water, air, global warming..."

"Yes, but what do you actually do? Your mission is very broad, don't you think? I'm interested in *how* you accomplish your goals. Let's start with your funding. Where does it come from?"

Suzanne paused before answering, thinking about her missing CTO. *Did David embezzle? Is that what this is about? Should I speculate and ask?* No, she decided, that would only raise more questions. The FBI could be inquiring about something else.

Agent Proctano began strumming his pad with his pen until she spoke.

"Well, about thirty percent of it comes from grants from foundations, like the Bill and Melinda Gates Foundation. We also receive a lot of different charitable contributions made by wealthy individuals. Some people add us to their will or living trust, while others set up a charitable trust for our benefit. We also receive money from corporations sitting on extra cash. Our last source is money generated from our programs."

"What kind of programs?"

"One example is our corporate benefit program. LL Bean, for instance, offers customers the option of donating a few dollars to a collection of charities at checkout. Since we are an approved LL Bean charity, we get ten percent of the donations they collect. All of this is disclosed in our tax returns that are publicly available through our website as required. Do we really need to go over this?"

"Yes, we do. Details and confirmations are important, Mrs. Harper. We've already done our homework on that." Agent Proctano huffed before adding, "Thank you for the tip, though. What do you do with all that money?"

"We educate the public about climate change, ways for people to lower their carbon footprint. You know, helping a family become carbon neutral. We also organize events to clean up plastic in waterways and improve the quality of rivers, streams, bays, and ponds."

"Do you feel like you're making progress?" the agent asked, staring into Suzanne's eyes while sipping his water.

"That's a good question. I'd say yes and no, to be honest. At the micro level, yes, we've made progress. You can look at a stream after we've cleaned it up and taken away the trash. But, on the *macro* level, it's more difficult to assess, and our progress stalled during the last administration."

Agent Proctano leaned forward. "Does that bother you?"

Suzanne paused before answering, thinking, *Where is this going?*

"Yes, it does, I must confess. Yes, it does."

"Have you thought about changing your methods then? Look for a better way?"

"Of course. We're always looking for a better way. Look, Agent Proctano, what is this all about? It's getting late, and my husband George is waiting for me."

He ignored the question, responding, "I apologize for that. But the sooner you answer my questions, the sooner you can join him and go home. Do you believe that it's possible to influence behavior in some way?"

Suzanne cocked her head at him. "I don't understand your question. I talked before about educating people on the issues we're concerned about. Is that what you mean?"

"No, not really. I'm talking about beyond education. Can you use technology to achieve your goals?"

"Technology? I don't understand. Look, I've had enough," Suzanne said, starting to get up. *Does this have to do with David? Is he in this building?*

"Please sit down, Mrs. Harper," Agent Proctano scoffed. "Do you know David Grigorio?"

Suzanne looked at her questioner. "Yes, he's one of our employees. Been with me since just about the beginning. He's currently our CTO. Information that is *also* available on our website."

"What can you tell me about what he does?"

"Is this about him? Did he do something wrong? I can assure you that he's an honest person." Suzanne thought about telling the agent that he was missing, but she wanted to hold onto that piece of information, at least for now.

"Mrs. Harper, please just answer the question."

"I think it's obvious from his title. He handles all of our technological needs, running the association's computer and technology operations," Suzanne responded before adding loudly, "Why are you asking me that? This is getting tiring!"

Proctano ignored her and asked evenly, "In that role, does he ever have to write any software programs?"

"Program? Software? Is that what this is about?" Suzanne cocked her head to the right.

"Just answer my question, please. Is he any good at that?"

"I don't know, you'd have to ask him."

"Are you aware of him ever writing a program?"

"No. Well, maybe, I guess. I think he told me once about playing around with HTML, Python, Java."

"Anything else?"

"Not that I'm aware of."

Proctano took a sip of water. "What would he write a program for?"

"How the *hell* am I supposed to know? *He's* the computer nerd, not me. Probably something to do with the website or some other purpose. That's his area. I wouldn't know anything about that."

"Did he ever write a program for other purposes? I mean, for external use?"

"Outside? You mean as opposed to our internal operations?"

"Yes."

"No, not that I'm aware of."

"You sure? Not for anything?"

"I don't understand what you're asking here. Is there an issue with this? Has somebody made a complaint?" Suzanne asked, fidgeting in her seat.

Agent Proctano's eyes bore into Suzanne, ignoring her question. "Have you ever heard of a program that can cause something to happen? Does that sound familiar?"

"Isn't that what all programs do?"

"Well, good point. But I'm talking about causing something *bad* to happen."

"What? Like an accident, embezzlement, or theft, you mean? That's ridiculous. I don't know what you're talking about. That doesn't even seem possible."

"No? Not possible? Are you sure? It's been done before. The most famous example being Stuxnet, which was a virus that allegedly caused Iran's centrifuges to spin out of control, destroying about twenty percent of their inventory."

"Caused by the U.S. and Israel, if I remember right. *That* was all over the news. You think David did something like that? Are you crazy?" Suzanne could not grasp the agent's reasoning.

"Crazy? Have you ever heard of the Techno House fire? It's been in the news."

"You mean that fire in San Francisco?" Suzanne glanced at the white and black clock on the wall to her right.

"Actually Oakland, but yes."

"What about it? What does that have to do with me or Earthcare? Isn't the fire a local police matter?"

"Usually, it is. But this one's different," Agent Proctano replied quickly before continuing. "We believe that the fire began with something causing a sudden unsafe surge in the electrical system. We couldn't figure out what caused the surge, but now we know."

She looked at the agent in disbelief. *Is that possible?*

Suzanne rose as she finally spoke. "That doesn't make sense to me. And I *still* don't understand what this has to do with your questions, me, or my association. And you never answered my question about why the FBI is interested in this."

Agent Proctano took a sip of water before deflecting Suzanne's question.

"A few more questions and you'll understand why we're looking into this. Have you talked to David Grigorio recently?"

Suzanne stared at her questioner and then picked up her glass. After a long sip, she said evenly, "I haven't been able to reach him."

"When did you see him last?"

"He left the office last Monday. I haven't seen him since."

"Call him?"

"Yes, I did. Several times. No answer."

Proctano showed little but didn't seem to be surprised by this.

"Are you holding him?" Suzanne asked.

"No. Holding him? He's dead! You didn't know that?"

"Dead?" Suzanne stood up. "Oh my. I can't believe that. I need to leave here. I...I..." she stammered, "I need to leave. He's been with me since the beginning..."

Proctano looked at her, eyes drawn narrow before placidly saying, "I'm sorry for your loss. He was found in his house. With his wife. Both dead since, we believe, last Tuesday. Three days ago."

Suzanne sat back down, but on the edge of her seat. "Nobody's been able to reach him. I can't believe this. We're going to have to end this interview. I need to leave."

"Don't you want to know what happened to him?"

"Of course, tell me. Please. What does this have to do with me and the FBI?"

"We're investigating use of the internet to commit an interstate crime – the fire. And topping it all off is that he and his wife were both found dead in their home. Looks like a murder-suicide..."

Suzanne jumped up and shouted, "What? Oh my God. I can't believe this. I need to leave now! Not another question. So, unless you're charging me with something, I'm leaving. I need you to take me to George. Now!"

Proctano sighed before escorting her out to meet George.

Chapter 12

Suzanne tried to contain her emotions on the way out of the FBI's office as she walked towards the elevator to the P2 level where George had parked.

Alone in the elevator, George hugged his wife and whispered, "It's going to be alright. We're going home. We can talk about it there."

Suzanne disengaged. "Alright? How can it be alright? Everything will never be the same! *George*!" Suzanne chided before adding, "David and Cindy are both dead…"

"Dead? That's why the FBI wanted to question you?" He hugged her again and whispered, "Let's talk about it at home. Not here or in the car. Understand?"

Suzanne nodded, deferring to her husband's knowledge about such matters.

The elevator opened, and they walked in silence towards George's car, a black Tesla Model 3. Suzanne stared out the window in silence on the way home as George drove through the empty streets. His left hand gripped the wheel, freeing up his right hand to comfort his wife.

Mr. Winestone's bedroom light went on as George pulled into the cul-de-sac and then into their driveway. Suzanne looked at the house, flashing her middle finger towards his direction.

George grunted as they walked into the house. After they entered, he whispered into Suzanne's ear, "Let me check for bugs. Then we can talk."

It took him fifteen minutes to declare the downstairs bug free before joining his wife in their kitchen. In the meantime, Suzanne changed out of her sweat-stained work clothes, retrieved some trail mix, and poured two glasses of Chardonnay. They sat at their L-shaped white and brown marble countertops with six azure chairs. Stainless steel appliances were spaced on three of the walls. Vases filled with flowers and other decorations accented open spaces of the recently remodeled kitchen inspired by a picture Suzanne found in *Best Home Design*.

"Now, tell me what you know about David and Cindy, how you wound up at the FBI office, and exactly what happened there," George requested as he sat down and began to eat and drink.

After Suzanne replayed her experience, she asked George for his story.

"Well, unlike yours, my story is pretty simple. You remember Fred Daffney?"

"Yes, one of the people you used to work with at the NSA?"

"That's right. Although Fred wasn't just one of my co-workers. He's a guy I passed on my way up to the Deputy Director position. He thought he deserved the job, not me. Never had the guts to tell me what he thought. Somebody else did."

"What about him?"

"He called while I was home around 3:00 in the afternoon summoning me. Said they had some questions about David. Made it sound, without saying it, that it was just a background investigation. I speculated – foolishly, I now realize – that it wasn't going to be that much different from the ones I'd been involved with hundreds of times during my career in government. They'd thought through their strategy. Whatever it takes to get me there. They didn't exactly lie, just told a kernel of the truth. Smart, huh?"

"Sure, brilliant, George. Just great," she said dryly, staring ahead, taking a long sip of her wine. She didn't want to say what she was really thinking:

Please, George, get to the point faster! I love you, but sometimes you can go on and on!

"Why didn't you call me though?" Suzanne asked in a demanding tone.

"Because I wasn't allowed to. You know the rules. He told me that it would compromise the investigation. Blah, blah, blah."

Suzanne took another sip. "Let's move on. We have a lot to cover. What did they ask you?"

"*They* turned out to be just one agent. Fred saw me in but turned me over to the guy. Proctano was his name. Asked me all sorts of questions about David and Earthcare and never mentioned or even hinted that he had died! At first, it seemed routine, just fishing for background information. Nothing urgent. The questions grew more serious, though, when he began asking specific questions about what he was working on. I really didn't know what to say, so I just shrugged."

"Did he ask anything about me?"

"Not really. Just asked whether I knew anything about your relationship with him. Whether the two of you were close, that sort of thing. We talked for a couple of hours, and then he thanked me and said you were on your way in. I questioned why, and he just shrugged and said, more of the same sort of questions."

"Did you think that was unusual?"

"About half-way through, I thought the whole thing was strange, yes. I continued, though, because I figured maybe I'd learn something about what they were after. I wasn't telling Proctano anything useful anyway."

Suzanne finished her food and gestured to relocate to the living room. They settled on cushions that sagged in the middle of their past-its-prime couch. She poured George and herself a second glass of wine and rested the bottle on the table.

The two of them sat in silence, drinking their wine. George dutifully waited for Suzanne to direct the discussion.

When ready she said, "Something doesn't add up. Why the FBI? Do they *even* have jurisdiction for this type of case?"

"That's been bothering me too. In my experience, they are not known to extend beyond their boundaries. Pure local matters? That's not their sandbox. One time…"

"George, honey, please," Suzanne cut George off. "It's getting late. I need to figure out what comes next. I'm going to reach out to David's family and help with any arrangements. But I also need to protect myself. What did he do to interest the FBI in what should be a local matter?"

"Why use me to get to you? They treated you like a key puzzle piece, somebody they wanted to come to the FBI's offices where they could tape the discussion, watch you from the window. Not just a witness, but potentially a suspect," George said.

"Yes, that's what bothers me. I need to consult with somebody. Have anybody in mind?"

George stroked the neatly trimmed beard under his chin. "As a matter of fact I do. I have the perfect person. One of the smartest women I know – next to yourself, of course. You'll love her. She's even got two first names!"

Suzanne laughed herself to tears. It was so George — corny joke at the wrong moment. Not funny, but amusingly strange. She laughed so hard tears formed because it had been such an awful day.

George understood, holding her tight.

Chapter 13

Sleep came in spurts to Suzanne. At 2:00 a.m., at the point of reaching the REM sleep stage, a thunderstorm shook her awake. Mercy began to pant and hid under their bed. An hour later, with the storm passing, Suzanne, still half-asleep, started thinking about David and the interview with the FBI. By four, she fell asleep, but not for long. At dawn, a woodpecker began chipping away at a vent on the roof and a robin began to sing, protecting his turf while looking for a mate.

A frustrated Suzanne thrust her fists into the mattress and bounced out of bed. Two espressos would have to serve as her crutch. At nine, she talked to David's brother and offered him any resource he needed to help plan a memorial service or address any problems.

Next, she called Earthcare's corporate attorney, who vouched for the criminal counsel – Sheila Lauren – that George had recommended. Sheila's online reviews provided further affirmation, with the last one touting her as a "tireless hard worker who gets results." The cliché-like review proved correct as she answered her phone on a Saturday, and they made arrangements to meet later that day.

Suzanne looked at Sheila when she entered her office on the 7th floor of a modern office building tucked behind the Tysons Corner II Mall. Sheila was maybe 5'3'' in heels but nearly crushed Suzanne's hand with an aggressive shake. Her shoulder length red hair bounced against her shoulders as she strode behind her desk after gesturing for Suzanne to sit at a chair. Pictures of her husband and three girls sat behind her on a credenza against the window.

"Tell me your story. In your own words, of course. What brings you here today?" Sheila began.

For three hours, the women nitpicked all of Suzanne's actual and theoretical allegations. She learned more than she wanted to know about criminal conspiracy, murder, cybercrime, software piracy, computer fraud, and computer espionage. Half the time had been spent on procedural issues that nearly put Suzanne to sleep.

And at the end, Sheila looked her client in the eye and said, "It sounds to me as if you did the right thing, hiring me. It may be nothing, but it's better to be safe. I'll contact Agent Proctano and let you know what he says."

"Thank you, especially for meeting me on a Saturday. I feel better already," Suzanne said before walking out of the office.

***

The sleep-deprived Suzanne slept late on Monday and would have continued catching up had she not received an urgent call. George, habitually up early, even in retirement, made the mistake of answering his wife's cell phone on her behalf. He had no choice but to awaken sleeping beauty.

Suzanne cringed when she saw her husband's strained face. Either Sheila had horrible news for her, or somebody else was in trouble. *Couldn't get much worse than that,* she thought, hearing Sheila's voice as George shoved the phone into her ear.

Sheila explained that Agent Proctano had called to warn her that the FBI was about to search their offices. Anticipating her client's next question, Sheila added that they did not have any choice. Proctano had sent Sheila a copy of the warrant, and it looked legitimate. There appeared to be sufficient probable cause, based simply on a typewritten confession that David had left on the bed before killing himself and Cindy.

"Like what?" Suzanne shouted into the phone, interrupting Sheila while a terrified George looked on.

"I'd rather discuss that in my office. How soon can you be here?"

"Forty-five minutes. I need to get dressed."

"OK, I'll see you then. Don't worry about calling your office. It's better that you don't. I'm sending my associate, William, who's already arranged to be there with your corporate attorney. They'll arrive before the FBI in about an hour from now. Anybody else there at this time of day?"

"Just our receptionist, Molly."

"Does she know your corporate attorney, Jake Stein is his name, I believe?"

"Yes, and yes."

"Great, then William and Jake will take care of it. See you in forty-five minutes. We have a lot to discuss, and I'd rather do it in person."

"Sounds like a lot of fun. See you then."

"Wait," Suzanne said before hanging up, "can George participate?"

"Honestly, Suzanne, no. It's better that he doesn't. I don't want to jeopardize the attorney-client privilege."

"Yes, but he's my husband!" Suzanne looked at George.

"I understand, but it's a risk. The law's not entirely clear on this point with spouses, and we don't know where this is heading..."

"*If* it's headed…"

"Of course. *If* charges are brought."

George, who had been listening, whispered, "Honey, she's right. I think the best I can do for you is to conduct my own independent investigation using my NSA resources."

"He's right, Suzanne. Our substantive discussions should be in private. The two of you can talk to each other, since you generally have spousal immunity protecting your discussions in criminal matters. But George shouldn't be in on our discussions. See you soon?"

"Yes, see you soon."

***

Suzanne arrived at Sheila's office on time — a rare feat for her. She settled in the same seat she had sat in two days earlier.

Suzanne leaned forward. "How did they get a warrant this quick? Is that unusual? Is it legal?"

"Let's take this step by step, okay? Methodically. I want to talk to you about the warrant, my discussion with Agent Proctano, and next steps."

Suzanne nodded.

"On the issue of the warrant, it's not unusual for the FBI to issue warrants as soon as possible. A judge would've had to sign off, of course, but it wouldn't have taken that much evidence to convince a judge."

"Evidence? Like what? Proctano didn't seem to know that much when he questioned me."

"I think he knows more than you think, Suzanne. I was going to talk about this after the search warrant, but let's jump to that and get back to the warrant later. First, you want something to drink? This may take a while."

"Cup of coffee, black, please."

Sheila requested two cups of coffee from her secretary.

"As I was saying, they have more evidence than you might think. Calling you in on Friday wasn't just for background." Sheila looked down at her notes before adding, "You said that the meeting with Proctano ended after he told you about David's death. Did he tell you about the suicide note?"

Suzanne's clasped her hands together. "No, he didn't. To be honest, I had difficulty concentrating after he told me about David and Cindy. Why, what did he say to you about it?"

"I'm going to tell you, but I want you to promise me that you're going to remain calm."

Suzanne replied quietly, "Yes, of course. What did he tell you?"

"Apparently, a type-written note was found near their bodies in the bedroom."

"Okay, spit it out, please."

"According to Proctano, David not only confessed to writing the program that started the Techno House fire, but he said that you conspired with him to do it."

"What? That's crazy! Why would I do that?"

"I asked Proctano. One of the victims that died was Benji Hammer – an influential..."

Suzanne launched herself out of her chair upon hearing the name.

"Benji Hammer? This is getting weirder by the minute!"

"Yes, it is. The two of you have butted heads over the years. Earthcare's and Hammer's interests are diametrically opposed to each other, right?"

"Of course," Suzanne said, beginning to pace around the room. "He's an asshole, but I didn't want him dead, for God's sake! I'm *not* a *murderer*. Hammer just works for the bad guys. Amongst other victories, he's blocked important cap-and-trade legislation that would have compelled his clients – major oil producers and distributors – to either pay millions for their crimes against humanity or change the way they do business. As I said before, I didn't want him killed, not in the physical sense, at least."

"I understand, Suzanne. We'll get to the bottom of this, I assure you. But you should also know that your work at Greenpeace and stint on the *Rainbow Warrior* provides additional fodder for Proctano to exploit."

"Fodder?"

"Greenpeace has a history of committing crimes. Hijacking and ramming into ships, destroying property. All in the name of activism, but crimes, nevertheless. Your participation provides Proctano a pattern he can exploit," Sheila said, watching Suzanne, who was still pacing. She paused before asking, "Can you sit down?"

Suzanne complied with her attorney's request and returned to her chair before saying loudly, "That's a bunch of bullshit, Sheila, and he should know it. I didn't do anything wrong *then*, and I haven't done anything wrong *now*."

"Yes, I understand. Please, don't shoot the messenger."

"Did he say anything about the program that David supposedly built to start a fire at some warehouse in San Francisco or Oakland, wherever the hell it was? Proctano likened it to Stuxnet, the virus that damaged Iran's nuclear ambitions. Can you believe that crap?"

"I imagine that the suicide note and their theory about the program gave them the probable cause they needed," Sheila replied.

Suzanne looked at Sheila, waiting for her to continue.

Sheila's receptionist interrupted the silence to announce that William was on the line. She turned back to her client a few minutes later.

"That was William. It's over. They left with your computer and David's computer, but nothing else."

"My computer? I don't understand, why would they take that? Can you get it back? How am I supposed to work?"

"I'm afraid not. The warrant specifically allows for the seizure of both computers."

"I can understand David's computer, but why mine?"

"That's a good question, but there's one explanation for that, which you're not going to like."

Sheila explained her theory, and Suzanne responded with a simple, "Shit. That's not good."

Chapter 14

Suzanne drove to work after her meeting with Sheila, first thinking about David and then about her stint on the *Rainbow Warrior* ship. Sheila's mention of the day back in July 1985 when French operatives blew up the vessel had resurrected bad memories.

Her permanent injuries forced Greenpeace to assign her to its version of Siberia – office work at its Washington, D.C. headquarters. Her first HQ job had been in the promotions department, helping to assemble Greenpeace's marketing collateral – not as exciting as the adventures she had enjoyed aboard the *Rainbow Warrior,* but at least she could continue her personal mission to save the planet.

Unfortunately, laying out pictures taken by somebody else who had all the fun made her feel worse. She took classes from Georgetown at night pursuing an MBA in business management. After graduating, Greenpeace assigned her the duties of a mid-level accounting manager. Suzanne rose through the ranks, but her career path topped out at assistant controller.

Reaching her ceiling turned out to be a welcome development; counting beans did not satisfy her activist passion anyway. She yearned to advance. If she could not work in the field anymore, at least she could develop and execute advocacy strategies.   It would never happen; all positions above her were mostly filled by men, and only those with a significant amount of experience working in public accounting or consulting.

The years dragged on with the same disappointments. After a while, she quit. Then came several short stints working for NGOs, but those jobs also failed to satisfy her passion for many of the same reasons.

At around the same time, George had reached the apex of his military career. Although George did get to work as a field officer for the Marine Corps Intelligence Department, he hadn't been able to advance past lieutenant colonel. This, despite being commended for being adept at his craft.

His friend, Brigadier General Gil Meyer, confided that the issue was his wife, deemed an *obstacle* because of her field work in Greenpeace. Now, with Suzanne years removed from that position, his career path would no longer be blocked.

And so, the two titans struck a marital bargain. They agreed to devote some of their savings for Suzanne to use as seed money to fund Earthcare. The nonprofit's stated purpose would be fostering opportunities for renewable energy and reducing global warming, with the mission of "Preserving a livable Earth for future generations."

George would springboard off his wife's career change to apply for one of the more senior jobs at the three letter agencies. A person with his background in military intelligence would be in high demand.

They moved into a house in North Arlington, Virginia. The location made it easier for both to access downtown D.C. Suzanne would establish Earthcare near many of other the D.C. NGOs; George would be closer to the intelligence community.

The plan worked. Suzanne grew Earthcare into a thriving nonprofit, drawing donations and funding from multi-national companies looking to park their guilt money. George began a successful career at the NSA, rising through the ranks, eventually becoming a deputy director in the clandestine operations branch.

Now her success, and George's too, might all be for naught. Something had happened, causing her to be a target, maybe even framed. Unless she could figure out the truth...

Chapter 15

Chetan stood at her mahogany standup desk, staring at her laptop computer screen. Her wrist cramped, and her legs began aching. She pressed on, continuing after glancing at Zonta resting comfortably on her donut-shaped bed.

While she had developed a theory that an overload at the junction box in the basement caused the fire, she didn't understand how and why. Did somebody intentionally switch a fifteen-amp with a thirty-amp breaker so that the circuit breaker wouldn't prevent a fire in the event of an overload? And what would have caused the overload to begin with?

Chetan researched the twenty people who lived at the Techno House and all of the known guests of the party, some of whom would later burn in the catastrophic inferno. Details were important. Why was each person there? What is each person's backstory? Any obvious motives? Mental problems? Insurance money?

Exhausted, she looked again at pictures of the dead. How to tell their story since they can't tell it themselves. She picked up the picture of Trudy last since it haunted her the most.

Her notes indicated that she had been a mere teenager attending the party with her boyfriend. Her mother sobbed hysterically showing Chetan a photograph of the girl, who was to begin college at UCLA in the fall. She had attended the party with her freckly boyfriend. Two teenagers in the prime of their lives, soon to begin the next phase of their lives.

Chetan picked up the picture and thought about the poor girl lying dead on the watered ground close to the front door. It still produced chills for her, bringing back memories of Hotah and that horrible car crash that she had experienced a long time ago.

***

Chetan stood and walked towards the kitchen. Zonta bounced up from her bed and rubbed against Chetan's leg after she arrived at the refrigerator. She retrieved a plate of cold pizza and placed it into the oven. She turned on the light and gestured for Zonta to take a look. The cat jumped on the counter next to the oven and licked her lips at the smell and sight.

Her iPhone rang, interrupting her food search.

A crisp male voice said, "I'm looking for Chetan Maka. You Ms. Maka?"

"Yep," Chetan replied, although she didn't like being called Ms. Maka. It made her sound old and lonely.

The man introduced himself as Agent Proctano and explained that he had some questions about the Techno House fire.

"Techno House fire? The FBI's interested in that?" Chetan asked skeptically. She had heard of other turf battles – some she had even been involved with herself – but rarely with the feds.

"Interested is an understatement. We have evidence proving that a cybercrime started the fire. The FBI has jurisdiction over cybercrimes."

Sure, Chetan thought to herself. She quickly Googled Proctano while on the phone and learned that he worked out of the agency's Washington D.C. field office.

"You solved this? *From Washington?*"

Chetan's initial skepticism subsided as she learned about the suspected murder-suicide of David Grigorio and his fiancée, Cindy Chalmers. Next, Proctano described the suicide note before telling her about Earthcare and Suzanne Harper.

"The note actually said *that?* David confessed to writing some sort of…
killer program? You sure?"

"Yes, I'm sure. Think I'm an idiot, chasing my tail?"

"Nope. Just making sure I heard right."

Proctano sighed and then explained how it might have worked.

"I understand. Like the Stuxnet virus, right?"

"Yes, ma'am. That's exactly how I'm describing it to others."

"Do you think it's possible that David designed it on his own?"

"We have their computers. We don't just make this stuff up, Ms. Maka."

"Chetan. Call me Chetan. Ms. Maka makes me sound wrinkled."

"Yes, well, Chetan, the digital footprints are still there."

"Please explain."

"It's not enough to erase a program, you also must reuse the storage
space it occupied. Forensics was able to recover enough to show that it was
there, on both of their computers, actually."

"Why both?"

"Meaning?"

"Wouldn't they try to minimize the, as you call it, footprint by having
it just on one?"

"I see what you mean," Proctano snarled. "Look, criminals are not the
brightest bulbs, and they never think they're going to get caught. They
obviously were both involved. We think David designed it – he's the one
with the technical background after all – but his boss, Suzanne,
orchestrated the effort."

"You'll need to explain more if you want us to cede control to you."

"Cede control? Sure, Chetan. Cede control. First off, Suzanne Harper is
a bit of a rebel, you know. Former activist with that criminal band,
Greenpeace."

Chetan had heard of Greenpeace and knew they were activists, but
criminals?

"The environmental group?" she asked.

"Yes, that group. History of trespassing onto ships, hijacking their activities. Activists charged with piracy, trespassing, and other crimes."

"That's a long way from what's happened here, though," Chetan pointed out.

"True, but the motive is the same old environmental crap. And a crime's still a crime in the end. Petty crimes become gateway drugs to the more destructive variety – murder – this time with Benji Hammer being the apparent target."

"Why Hammer?"

"In lefty circles, Hammer is public enemy #1. The guy who blocked laws to make oil companies pay after spills, blocking renewable energy funding, and other offenses real and perceived."

"Why do you think that she wanted to take him out?"

"Give me a second, you'll understand once I read you an email exchange between Suzanne and David," Proctano replied.

Chetan could hear the man rustle through some papers.

"Here it is…"

"Suzanne begins the exchange writing, *'That asshole is single-handedly killing us!'*

David then replies, *'You saw that the fuel-efficiency bill's been killed?'*

Here's Suzanne's reply: *'Yes. Add that to Hammer's greatest hits. Killing the federal cap-and-trade proposal, protecting the coal industry against regulation, expanding drilling offshore and in Alaska. The list goes on and on. He needs to be taken out. I've had enough. I hate that man.'*"

"So, you're saying she conspired with David?"

"Yes, and forensics tells us that it had been launched from Suzanne's computer."

"Anything else?" Chetan asked.

"David's suicide note. He confessed – specifically mentioning Suzanne's involvement – to starting the fire in order to kill Benji Hammer."

Chetan thought about Proctano's evidence before pressing further.

"But, if David and Suzanne succeeded in killing Benji Hammer as you suggested, why would David *then* kill himself and his fiancé?"

"Ah. Good question, but the evidence for that crime is also irrefutable," Proctano replied. "We have his signature on a receipt for the purchase of a gun, earlier on the day he decided to kill himself after he offed his poor fiancée. Fingerprints too, all over the gun."

"Guilt?"

"Exactly. He must have gotten scared, realizing what he did. Happens a lot. Criminals are a fickle bunch. Succeed and then ramifications hit you like a freight train. Not to mention that I'm sure he never would have expected the collateral damage, all of those innocent people killed."

"Plausible, I guess," Chetan considered before shifting the discussion. "Do you have any evidence of the program being received at the Techno House? It may have been launched, but can you prove that it actually started the fire? I quickly Googled the Stuxnet virus while you were talking. It says here that the virus may have worked by affecting the equipment that ran the centrifuges. What do you think happened in this case?"

"We think that somebody – probably David, although we can't interview him, of course – set something up on the premises to trigger a fire when instructed by the program. That's how the program works, apparently, according to our computer experts."

Chetan thought again about her theory about the seemingly new thirty-amp breaker being installed in the slot normally reserved for a fifteen-amp breaker. Agent Proctano's theory about a program triggering the fire seemed plausible. The burn marks seemed to originate from the junction box, where flammable material could have been placed in the basement.

After explaining what she found, she asked, "Do your experts know what the program would've targeted?"

"They have an idea, yes. Some type of light source, but that's what I wanted to ask you since you were there. You see anything that makes sense?"

"Well, yes, actually. Turns out they were growing something, pot I imagine, in the basement. I traced the source of the fire to the local junction box covering the grow system."

"Could the apparatus have caused an overload?"

"My working theory is the lights. It's supposed to rotate power to four rows of lights, one at a time, to avoid flooding the system. If the program you're talking about caused all four rows to turn on at the same time, then that could've caused an overload."

"Wouldn't the circuit breaker have shut it down?"

"That's what's *supposed* to happen. Only it looks like somebody may have installed a thirty-amp circuit where there once had been a fifteen-amp circuit. Could've been by design or a mistake."

"Or it could've been done intentionally."

"But by whom?"

"I think I may have an answer to that. David Grigorio proposed to his fiancée at the Ritz in San Fran two weeks before the fire."

Chetan thought about what she had learned before responding.

"You're thinking he went to the Techno House to switch the breakers during his trip there?"

"Something like that. Lots of people going in and out of that place. Maybe he pretended to be a worker of sorts," Proctano suggested.

"I suppose it's possible," Chetan conceded.

"Well, you've been very helpful, Ms. Maka – sorry, Chetan. All signs point towards this direction."

"What now, then?"

"I need to talk to my superiors here, and then we'll let you know. Thanks for taking my call," Proctano said before hanging up.

Chetan thought about what she had learned. It seemed to fit, but maybe a little too perfectly. All loose ends seemingly tied up...

Chapter 16

The discussion Chetan had with Agent Proctano left her unsettled. He had seemed a bit too full of himself, even though she had to admit that the evidence pointed towards Suzanne and David as having caused the fire. A quick Google search confirmed that programs can infiltrate and manipulate technology. Countless examples of malware, trojan horses, and viruses proved the point.

Still, she wondered. The explanation about wanting to eliminate Benji Hammer was plausible, but a stretch. Sure, the man had orchestrated the devastating effort to kill cap-and-trade policies. But Hammer was really no different than a thousand other effective lobbyists.

As for Suzanne, her work for Greenpeace and on the *Rainbow Warrior* indicated that she once was reckless, even dangerous, but that was a long time ago. Since then, she had started Earthcare and had served her environmental cause perfectly legally.

Chetan thought about her own experiences. At first, her parents would have applauded Hammer's work. Tax revenues and grants from oil and gas producers built schools and housing for Rosebud citizens, including her high school.

But then people began getting sick from contaminated groundwater. Chetan knew three people who had childhood leukemia, one of whom had died.

Turning back to present matters, she thought about why David would have succeeded with the program only to then kill his fiancée and commit suicide. He didn't seem unstable, based upon her scan of the Internet, including the public access portions of LinkedIn and Facebook.

Did killing Benji Hammer and numerous other partygoers at the Techno House make him crazy enough to buy a gun and then kill his fiancée and himself? Was he crazed with guilt, suddenly afraid of getting caught, then left to rot on death row?

Proctano seemed to have amassed indisputable evidence of David purchasing the gun he used later the same day. There was even fingerprint evidence. Proctano also had proof of Suzanne's computer being used to trigger the fateful program and an expressed desire to eliminate her foe. Chetan certainly didn't have any evidence exonerating either David or Suzanne.

Antonio Gonzalez, Chetan's Fire Chief boss, answered his cellphone on the third ring. She envisioned him limping to answer the phone. A few years ago, he had the embarrassing bad luck of slipping on a spill at a supermarket. The resulting constant back and hip pain caused him to sit in his leather reclining chair for long stretches, listening to Brahms and Chopin, sipping brandy, rather than interacting with busy, able-bodied humans.

Chetan had been the exception, both forming a bond of not fitting in with mainstream society. She appreciated his gruff personality and scanty praise and never looked down on him for his supermarket fall. He considered her work indispensable to the Oakland Fire Department and his own success and found ways to let her know without what they both considered too-easily-dispensed praise in the modern workplace.

Chetan heard Antonio's two best friends, his dogs Cowboy and Blue, barking in the background. Cowboy, the German shepherd, was the elder statesman of the Antonio household, overweight and slow, and Blue was the marble-colored young sheltie lass that ran circles around everybody. Antonio developed the bond of a single parent-child with both pooches.

"Shhh! I'm on the phone," he said in a vain attempt to calm them down.

Doesn't he realize they don't speak English? Chetan half-heartedly asked herself, knowing that she often did the same with Zonta. She then replayed the discussion she had with Agent Proctano, telling her boss that it all felt too neat and that maybe she should continue to investigate, at the very least to confirm Agent Proctano's theory. What could be the harm?

"I'm sorry, Chetan. I'm making the call. We have enough on our plate as is, and if the FBI's prosecuting, let them have at it. It *is* the FBI, after all."

"With only an unsigned confession? Why would he kill his fiancée and himself after succeeding? Does that make sense to you?"

"These cases don't always make sense. But it sounds as if they have motive, the digital footprints left on his and Suzanne's computers, and confirmation from PG&E that an unexplained power surge had caused the fire."

"Still, it's a bit too tidy."

"Hah! Tidy? These cases are never one hundred percent. Believe me, it's stronger than most of the other cases I've seen."

"Yeah, I guess so."

"Look, it's not your problem anymore. Let the FBI have it, and move on," Antonio said as dog yelps arose in the background. "I have to go."

Chetan also understood what Antonino *wasn't* saying. He had mentioned the feds multiple times in his reasoning. Going against the FBI could strain the relationship between the feds and the fire department, potentially jeopardizing their good will the next time Oakland needed federal resources on an investigation with interstate implications.

Chetan wasn't happy, but she didn't have enough to press further. "Time to move on," she muttered to herself.

Tonight, would be for unwinding, treating herself to well-deserved night out. She texted her closest human friend, Celina Romera. The two arranged to meet at their favorite bar.

***

The crisp nighttime air felt refreshing as Chetan walked across the street to Trios, a bar that tonight featured an open mic night. Celina, who lived in the same building as Trios, was already there, sitting at the bar by herself, playing *Words with Friends* on her iPhone while sipping a mojito.

Celina had dyed her hair, changing it from black into a sandy color, but she had not dyed her eyebrows. Her dark complexion, black eyebrows, and light hair had given her an exotic look that, combined with her shapely body, lured men as she bored into her phone. Celina was not interested in them, swearing off men after recently having broken up with her longtime boyfriend.

Chetan approached, wearing white pants and silky red button-down top. Her high heels made her an inch taller. Like her friend, Chetan also attracted a lot of looks. She too wasn't interested, preferring instead to simply relax with her friend, listen to the amateur performers, and laugh at the scene.

Especially tonight. Several performers took the stage one at a time, in a succession of mediocrity that drew little more than curious glances as the crowd drank, laughed, and chatted amongst themselves.

The fourth act was different though. A tall man in his forties, with a bushy black afro and long sideburns, mounted the stage and sat on a wooden stool that he had pushed closer to the mic stand.

The familiar lyrics captured Chetan's attention:

"There's a lady who's sure
All that glitters is gold
And she's buying a stairway to Heaven
When she gets there she knows

If the stores are all closed
With a word she can get what she came for
Oh oh oh oh and she's buying a stairway to Heaven
There's a sign on the wall
But she wants to be sure
'Cause you know sometimes words have two meanings
In a tree by the brook
There's a songbird who sings
Sometimes all of our thoughts are misgiving"

Most of the crowd stopped what they were doing and paid attention, hearing the Jamaican singer hit the notes with a hint of reggae. For Chetan, the song invoked a different reaction-overpowering grief.

She and her brother Hotah used to sing the song together, belting out the lyrics in near perfect harmony. At the end, they would laugh together, and sometimes she would tear up slightly. She loved both of her brothers, although she didn't enjoy the same bond with Tashunka.

Chetan quashed an urge to run out of the bar. *How would she explain herself to Celina?* She initially stayed quiet, but then began singing, softly at first, and then louder to the point where she developed a rhythm and harmony that matched the performer.

It ended abruptly. The singer took his break, leaving Chetan to transpose the image of Hotah onto the stage as if he had been singing. Only he was not. He just sat on the same stool with the look of *The Scream* stenciled on his face.

Chapter 17

Chetan awoke, staring at her ceiling, thinking about the night at Trios. It had been fun to enjoy the night out with her friend, Celina. But listening to the inspiring cover of *Stairway to Heaven* had twisted her mind into a pretzel. She had tried to suppress the memories of the fire that had burned Hotah to death, only to have them pop up at the most awkward moments.

The ring of Chetan's cellphone interrupted her thoughts. Nurse Amy Renu called with sad news about Chetan's mom, Kangee. Chetan instantly felt guilty for not being able to see her as much as she would have liked. It had only been a few times throughout the pandemic. Kangee had severe dementia: short-term memory obliterated; long-term memory rarely worked. She lived in a nursing home, located near the Rosebud Indian Reservation.

With distress in her voice, Nurse Ranu explained that Kangee had caught COVID. During the height of the pandemic, a more virulent strain had wiped out one third of the nursing home residents. Still, even the weaker strains could be deadly to the elderly, even when vaccinated. They had no choice but to transfer her mom to the local hospital.

Nurse Renu told Chetan that her mom might not make it another week. She offered to arrange a FaceTime meeting so that Chetan could say goodbye.

However, Chetan refused to say goodbye that way. Getting there in time would pose the next obstacle. By car, it would take a full day.

Unfortunately, the other options were not much better. There were few flights to the Rosebud Sioux Tribal Airport even from South Dakota's biggest city, Sioux Falls — a problem made worse by labor shortages and pent-up demand sapping resources to more profitable locations. And there were no flights or bus lines from Oakland to Sioux Falls, without a transfer or two.

Still, she remained determined. Saying goodbye was vital to the closure that would be needed later. Failure would haunt her for the rest of her life.

Chetan loaded the car with camping equipment, a suitcase full of clothes and toiletries, food and drink gathered like a Mama bear for the ride. A curious Zonta kept her chin low, watching her owner prepare to leave on a journey. Her ears perked as Chetan picked her up, depositing her into the loaded car. Moments later, they began the journey.

The congestion eased after she passed Sacramento on Interstate 80. She stroked Zonta, who purred, sitting on her lap. Blasting tunes with the window open, a cool breeze gave her chills as they meandered around the Sierra Nevada mountains near Truckee.

As daylight began to recede, the travelers set up camp at a KOA campground near Salt Lake City. Pitching a tent was second nature to Chetan growing up on the reservation.

They repeated the drill the next day, this time closer to the reservation. The second night, she had difficulty sleeping, worrying about her mom. Questions ran amok. *Will Mom even recognize me? Will I be allowed to even see her? Is she even alive?*

The next day, after breaking down camp and completing the journey, she pulled up to the two-story brown brick building. A blue and yellow banner that said *HEROES WORK HERE* made Chetan melancholy and anxious.

Zonta purred words of encouragement. Chetan stroked her one last time making sure to crack the window before exiting. She put on her mask while walking towards the hospital.

Nurse Renu, who had called Chetan in Oakland, attempted a weak smile before checking Chetan's temperature and administering the COVID screening questions. After passing, she provided blue scrubs for Chetan and ushered her into the room, along the way passing through a wing cordoned off with thick clear plastic.

Mom stared at the ceiling, eyes open, pupils dilated, skin pale. Her stained teeth were visible through the two-inch gap of her crusted, chapped lips. Seeing the stoic expression on her mom's stoic face, Chetan began crying inside her mask. Lacking the ability to wipe away the tears, they dried, tickling her cheeks.

Chetan overcame her initial shock and leaned over to kiss her mom on the forehead when Nurse Renu barked, forcing to her to hold Mom's hand instead. The touch of Chetan's hand registered. Mom began saying, "Hotah… Hotah… Hotah…"

Chetan took the framed picture of the family from a shelf in the room and held it close to her shielded face, lovingly.

"Fire… Fire…" her mom weakly repeated, until Chetan's truncated memory of the crash returned, breaking through the amnesia. This time, she remembered the ending.

***

At first, the gasoline smell was present but not overwhelming. I knew I didn't have long, but I couldn't possibly leave the car without my family.

Mama had a large piece of glass sticking out of her head, making my stomach churn. But I knew she was still alive. She had to be alive!

"Mama! Mama!" I screamed. Only she wouldn't awaken.

I climbed over her body and pushed on her door with all my might. I managed to open it, but Mama was still asleep. Frustrated, I began slapping her cheeks, only it didn't work.

"Wakeup, Mama!" I shouted over and over. I began pushing her with my feet, my back braced against Papa in the driver's seat. Finally, Mama fell out of the car.

I began helping Papa next. His car door had been closer to the impact and wouldn't open. I crawled out of the car on Mama's side where I turned back towards Papa. With all my strength, I grabbed him by the shoulders trying not to look at his mangled right leg that was gushing blood. I couldn't possibly move him, could I? He was too heavy, but then he stirred awake, and I helped him out the door too. He looked back at his sons, but we both knew he couldn't help. He turned to Mama instead, forcing her to wake up.

The smell of gasoline began to overpower me, but I didn't care. I had rescued my parents, but they couldn't help. It was up to me. I would have to get my brothers. Tashunka had hit Papa's seat. It was easier to pull him from the car.

I focused on Hotah. He had hit the windshield head on, rebounding into his seat. But everybody else made it and so would he, I knew!

Only, he didn't respond. His cold eyes bugged out of their sockets, staring straight ahead, his mouth opened in a silent scream. I gently rocked his head back and forth. Wake up! Wake up! But he didn't stir.

The smell of gas became overwhelming, and I heard my family screaming for me to leave the car. I checked for Hotah's pulse the way I had learned in school. Nothing. I leaned over, kissed his cheek, and left the car.

Moments later, after I crawled to join my parents and Tashunka, the gas tank caught on fire. We watched in horror as Hotah's body burned inside, smoke and the smell of charred flesh filling the air.

***

As Chetan's memory of the events restored, her mom began twitching; Chetan sensed that the end was near. She somehow knew her mother had waited for her — waited to help bring her daughter some peace. Her mother's heart monitor began beeping loudly, prompting Nurse Renu to ease Chetan away from the room.

Chapter 18

Suzanne Harper knew she had to remain strong. Today was David's funeral. Cindy had been buried the previous day. Friends and family, formerly united in supporting the soon-to-be married couple, now had to choose. Speculation ran amok, with each group blaming the other spouse.

The service for David was being held at Our Lady of Hope Roman Catholic Church, located on a sprawling campus in Sterling, Virginia. Children playing soccer on the church's new outdoor field and guests visiting the picturesque gardens looked up at the small convoy of cars that barely filled the first two rows of the parking lot. Guests dressed in black and wearing sunglasses dabbed their eyes as they piled out of their cars, SUVs, and minivans, beginning a slow strut towards the church.

A heavy breeze, followed by darkening clouds, thunder, and lightning, forced the few relatives that dared to show to walk faster, some of the women stumbling on their high heels. Word had leaked about the FBI's questioning of Suzanne Harper. She hadn't been named a suspect, simply a key witness, although nobody knew for sure. Others had also been questioned, including Suzanne's husband, George.

Suzanne wanted to attend for closure and on the off-hand chance that she would learn something new. She realized the fallacy of the second possibility as soon as she entered, eyes boring into her from all directions.

The stares continued even after she sat with George on a pew in a row towards the back. He tried to comfort her, holding her hand as she glanced upward for inspiration. The gaping open footprint of the church with its sloping ceiling of dark-brown wood sloped taller until climaxing at 40 feet above the chancel. Glossy wooden pews allowed for ample seating, needed for the holiest days, but not today.

The priest – an overweight man in glasses, his balding head sprouting thin whisps of white hair – dryly led the congregation through prayers. "We thank you for what you have given us through David Grigorio. We now entrust ourselves to you, just as we are, with our sense of loss and of guilt. When the time has come, let us depart in peace and see you face to face, for you are the God of our salvation."

Most of the words meant little to Suzanne. *How had David's and Cindy's time come? And, to die together? Did the Lord have a plan for that?* It didn't help that the words were partially drowned out by the heavy pelts of rain striking the church's roof and windows.

Agents Proctano, Harmon, and Ridley sat in the back on the right side, studying everybody, looking for telltale signs of somebody knowing more than he or she should: a faint grin, clenched jaws, eyes darting about. An elderly lady sitting next to Suzanne made a fuss inching away as the priest began his sermon. A man sitting two rows in front of the Harpers abruptly turned around to scowl at them.

Suzanne and George left as soon as the congregation finished signing *Morning Has Broken* and the priest had spoken his obligatory concluding rites. The rain miraculously ended just in time to allow the Harpers to escape.

Chapter 19

M r. Winestone, walking his dog, waved at Suzanne and George like a petulant child trying to get their attention as George's Tesla entered their driveway after the funeral. Suzanne looked the other way. Had she looked, she would have seen the dog squatting near her prized rosebushes.

George and Suzanne's car disappeared into the garage. After the car rolled to a stop, she scampered out of the vehicle, ran towards the bedroom, and slammed the door – George's cue to leave her alone.

Two minutes later, George heard several vehicles approach, and when he looked out the living room windows, he witnessed about a dozen agents surrounding the house. Agent Proctano marched up the steps with his agents, Harmon and Ridley, flanking his side, guns at the ready.

George opened the door to Agent Proctano, Agents Ridley and Harmon behind him.

"We're taking her in," Agent Proctano proudly announced, shoving an arrest warrant in George's face. "She either comes now and leaves quietly, or we barge in and make a scene."

"Let me call her lawyer first."

"No."

"Why not?"

"There's no negotiation here. Not a fireside chat. Her choice."

"But…"

"There are no *buts*."

Suzanne approached the door as Agent Proctano finished talking. George handed his wife the arrest warrant, which Suzanne began reading.

"Let me call her attorney," George pressed.

"Sorry, but she's coming with us now," Proctano replied.

"But…"

"Last chance – we do this the hard way or the easy way. Your choice."

Before George could respond, Suzanne replied, "It's fine, George. Making a scene will make it worse. Call Sheila after we leave." She turned her attention to Agent Proctano. "If I go quietly right, can we avoid the handcuffs?"

"Yes," Agent Proctano responded.

George and Suzanne embraced before Suzanne walked with the agents to the unmarked Chevy Suburban in their driveway.

A tall, skinny, pale man watched the scene as he stood with a group of gaping reporters. He was wearing a hat and holding an umbrella, ostensibly as protection against the rain that started to fall again.

***

Later that day, George stared at Sheila like a prize fighter in a ring, only instead of being separated by a referee, they were held apart by the kitchen island at Harper's house.

"How did this happen?" he asked bitterly.

Without waiting for any answer, he began a barrage of questions.

"Arrested without warning? What about due process? Why didn't you do anything to stop it? What are we paying you for?"

Sheila wisely let him vent without interruption. When he finished, Sheila quietly suggested they sit and talk, calmly. Sheila began by reviewing what Agent Proctano told her about David's suicide note. George already knew about the note, of course, but he also remembered from his time at NSA and the military that you must understand the attacker before you can plan a counterattack.

While neither of them knew for sure what the FBI discovered in its search of Earthcare, they both agreed that the evidence must be damning. Sheila surmised that the evidence lurking in the computers established the probable cause needed to arrest Suzanne. This would either have been before or after a grand jury proceeding. The FBI may have discovered not only the program or traces of it, but potentially evidence tying it to starting the fire. If the search didn't reveal any evidence, the FBI would have waited to establish probable cause. The confession of a dead man wouldn't have been enough by itself.

"There must have been something you could have done, Sheila! She's innocent!" George continued his rant even though he knew the answer.

Sheila calmly explained that grand juries meet in secrecy, with only the prosecutor presenting evidence. The purpose of the proceeding is to decide whether probable cause existed to bring a case. If the grand jury agreed, it would issue a written indictment leading to the suspect's arrest and eventual trial. The next step would be the arraignment and a bail hearing, which Sheila would attend.

George touched the fingers of each of his hands together under his chin, listening and thinking. At one point, he even closed his eyes while Sheila waited.

"This all seems to have been started by David. I knew David, or at least I thought I did. He wasn't a bad guy. Something must have happened. I just know it."

"What do you mean by 'must have happened'?"

"I meant it doesn't make sense. Does it make sense to you?"

"It's hard for me to say. I see people do strange things all the time. Let's explore this though. You said David wasn't a bad guy, but how well did you know his fiancée?"

"Not as much as David, of course. But I've met her a few times at office functions. We even went out a few times as couples."

"Did they seem happy to you?"

"On the outside, they seemed happy, yes. But you never know, right? They both were a bit off to begin with," George said, immediately regretting his characterization. "What I mean by that is that he was a computer nerd and not the most social person. He was friendly enough but quiet. Cindy was even quieter, and it wasn't just because Suzanne is – or was, I should say – his boss."

"I understand what you mean. I know people just like what you're describing."

"This doesn't make any sense, Sheila. Suzanne wouldn't be involved. No way. And if Suzanne's not guilty, then neither is David."

"Which means…"

"That somebody framed both of them," George said, finishing Sheila's thought. "I'm going to find out why and how."

"I agree, George. It needs to be investigated. But not by you. You are *way* too close to this. How can you *possibly* act rationally as an investigator?"

"But she's my wife, and I can't sit still, letting it play out. Besides, I have a lot of investigative experience. You *know* that Sheila. You seriously think I can back off and let you hire some two-bit investigator? Nope, not happening. Sorry," George said defiantly.

George knew Sheila had a point. But he also felt confident that he could maintain his cool. His long career in the military before rising to being Deputy Director at the NSA had put him in compromised positions before.

He told Sheila about another situation involving two friends who had sold secrets to Russia. He successfully investigated the cases, putting initial doubts and personal feelings aside.

Also, like many former top government officials, he continued to consult with the government even after retirement. That allowed him to maintain connections that could prove valuable. He also still had a security clearance, allowing him access to valuable databases and resources.

Sheila asked, "Do you have an idea about where to start?"

"Yes, I do. Yes, I do."

"Good, because I need to concentrate on her defense and process."

"How does that play out?"

"Well, an initial hearing should be held within the next seventy-two hours. The judge will read the charges. I'll then request that she be released after posting bail, pending the trial."

"*Request?* That's ridiculous," George harped, raising his voice. "An innocent person? How could they do that?" George knew the answer of course, but he said it anyway. He had personally seen it happen to violent criminals, but he couldn't imagine it happening to his wife.

Sheila waited for George to cool down.

"Do you have any reason to doubt she'll make bail?" he asked.

"No, I don't, but I don't want to make any promises, either. As you know from your own work, it happens in situations where the suspect's a danger to the community or is a flight risk."

"I understand, Sheila," George paused, then said, "I would like to see her. When can I visit?"

"Let me find out, and I'll let you know. She first needs to go through intake and get processed. Maybe tomorrow, since it's getting late already and visiting hours are limited."

"Got it. Let me know. I still can't believe this." George looked down at his feet.

***

After Sheila left, George pulled up the lid on his laptop, powered it up, and began his search. So many resources were at his disposal. It was only a matter of time.

He began learning everything he could about David's background as well as Cindy's. Only his searches didn't seem to reveal anything useful. Nothing stood out, both subjects proving to be even more boring than he first thought.

David had been raised in Montclair, New Jersey, by an Italian father and a Polish mother. His parents were still married, living together in the same home. David excelled in computer science even as a child, earning a medal in an International Olympiad in Informatics competition by designing a program to estimate the amount of methane gas released by cows burping and farting around the world.

Suzanne had previously told George about the importance of tracking this information. At first, George had laughed, but Suzanne playfully hit him in the stomach before explaining that the bovine gas was a major contributor to greenhouse gases, accounting for about fifteen percent of worldwide emissions. How dare he laugh at an issue as important as that? The two of them then cackled together about the absurdity – maybe developing world farmers needed to stop feeding their cows beans?

But it wasn't a joke. Suzanne already knew the solution: improve the quality of feed and their diet by using seaweed and other supplements, but without tracking progress, it would be hard to garner support. Hiring David and his bovine gas model made sense, and she had been thrilled when David approached her so early in Earthcare's history.

George remembered the exchange as related to him by his wife. "Somebody with your MIT pedigree and established credentials could get hired anywhere," she had said. "Why us?"

David explained that he wanted to join a new organization on the ground floor. He also knew all about Suzanne's connection to the Rainbow Warrior and liked her *chutzpah*. A legend! How inspiring!

Although interesting information, George frowned with the realization that he hadn't learned anything relevant. As with David, Cindy's background, revealed through the Internet, provided nothing relevant. She had grown up on a farm in Iowa, helping her parents raise crops and milk cows, until she escaped to Marymount University near Washington DC, where she trained to be a nurse and met David through eHarmony.

George needed to rest his eyes. He thought about taking a walk outside, but he didn't want to run into creepy Mr. Winestone or anybody else.

He poured himself three fingers of Maker's Mark over an ice ball, took a sip, and extended his desk chair, thinking about where to look next. He asked himself the same questions. *What happened to him? How did he turn?*

His cellphone rang, offering him a brief reprieve. Recognizing Sheila's number, he answered and received instructions about visiting. Sheila suggested that he arrive the next morning at 9:00, the beginning of visiting hours.

***

Suzanne was being held at the Arlington County Jail, a modern building with an off-white façade and small windows that were impossible to see into from the outside. Homeless on the busy street outside used the windows as a mirror.

George sat down on a metal chair, facing a room where he knew Suzanne would sit. They would be separated by a thick glass window and would speak through a phone. He waited, nervously shaking his right leg up and down. His heart pounded rapidly.

The door to the room where Suzanne would sit opened. He watched as his wife approached, noticing signs that she was wearing down. The shine in her blonde hair had disappeared, replaced by a shaggy replica, her olive skin looked a shade paler, and her blue eyes looked tired, bags appearing beneath them. *I can't imagine what she's going through*, George thought.

George kissed his hand and placed it against the glass that separated him from Suzanne. She did the same. They both teared up and mouthed, "I Love You," before sitting on the metal chairs.

They talked about the conditions in the jail, food, guards, other inmates before turning to more serious matters. Suzanne suggested that she was doing well, under the circumstances, but George could tell she had been faking it.

"I need to ask you a few questions about David. I'm trying to figure out what happened to him, why he would suddenly turn on you and Earthcare. Any ideas? Something that could have triggered his change?"

"I've been thinking about that a lot. But nothing comes to mind." Suzanne shook her head in despair.

George stared at her in disbelief before asking, "There must be something though. What was he like? Did his attitude change before he..." George considered carefully how to complete his thought. "Killed his fiancée and then himself? Did he say or do anything strange?"

"No, nothing I can recall," Suzanne stammered. "It makes no sense, as I said. I only know that he came in on Monday, the week before he died, and then he didn't come back the rest of the week. He said he was sick and would be working from home."

"Did he?"

"No, he didn't come back in," Suzanne said, before quickly adding, "but that's not unusual though. Like a lot of other companies in this 'new age,' people can work from home. We've even begun talking to our landlord about reducing our square footage."

"Did he have to report in, the rest of the week?"

"No, not him. He's been with me forever, George, and he's the CTO."

"Did you hear from him during that week?"

"No, I didn't. But again, that's not unusual. Except that, come to think of it, Nat – one of our program directors – told me David missed a meeting.

He said it to me in passing, and it seemed as if his presence at the meeting wasn't that important."

George instinctively stroked his beard as he reflected, thinking his wife had trusted David too much. Should she have followed up? Would it have made a difference? Maybe, he thought. But probably not. He would talk to Nat, but it didn't seem that important.

A heavy-set female guard rapped her fingers on Suzanne's door and said, "Five minutes left. Wrap it up!"

"Can you think of anything else?"

"No, but I'll call you if I do, and Sheila said she thought I'd make bail at tomorrow's hearing."

"You should, she's right. Calling you a danger to the community or a flight risk is like calling Mother Theresa a criminal."

"True, but then again, I never imagined being thrown in jail in the first place."

They then both stood, mouthing, "I love you."

As George turned towards the door, he looked at a camera above his head, pointing in his direction.

Suddenly, an idea popped into his head.

Chapter 20

Naomi Johnson spotted him in the late afternoon light as she scanned the park at Farragut Square on her way to the Metro station. The thick humid summer air, even after 6:30, made her armpits sweat. She would have to delay her return home.

The man sat on a bench, dressed in a rumpled brown suit. He had been eating a sandwich next to his brown briefcase that looked as if it had been run over twice. He looked like a black Forrest Gump sitting at a bus stop, except that he looked anything but content.

She wanted to comfort him, but instead, she turned away when he looked up at her. The man quickly finished his sandwich, stood, and walked in the opposite direction.

Naomi walked around the block, careful not to look in the direction of where the man went. She knew what to do next. Twenty minutes later, she sat down at his table in the back corner of a dimly lit, narrow Mexican restaurant on the edge of Georgetown, in a position where he could see her approach him, as well as anybody else that decided to enter.

**

George made a show of looking at his watch as his sister approached, her long straight hair flapping behind her on every step.

"Took you long enough, Sista."

Naomi frowned at her brother, motioned for him to stand, and gave him a long embrace. Unlike her brother, who no longer exercised, she maintained her delicate figure by running at least twice a week. Her clear complexion, tight abs, and long legs made her look like a track star.

As they sat down, George glared at the men gawking at his sister. She effortlessly ignored the stares, focusing instead on the nachos already on the table. George knew how to appeal to his sister's sensibilities – feed her nachos smothered in cheese, beans, guacamole, shredded meat, and hot peppers, and provide fresh margaritas for her to wash it down. Watching his sister enjoy the food and sugary drink, he marveled at how she managed to stay in such great shape. Offering her a treat was a routine George had used since retiring from the NSA when he needed information from her but didn't want to show himself.

"I'm so sorry about what's happening. It doesn't make sense."

"Thanks, Sista," he paused, gesturing for Naomi to eat. "I know I said tomorrow, but I couldn't wait. There's been a development in Suzanne's case. The judge denied her bail this morning."

"Oh, my, George. I can't believe that."

"Neither can I. He called her a flight risk, stressing the seriousness of the charges. Blah, blah, blah. Sheila, Suzanne's attorney, couldn't believe it. But the judge wouldn't listen. Claimed she's a flight risk because of her previous work overseas for Greenpeace. Imagine that. My wife, a flight risk. What a joke! He also agreed with the prosecution, saying that she could have another copy of the program to cause another tragedy."

"How's she holding up?" Naomi asked while carefully raising an overloaded nacho to her mouth.

"Not good, not good," George replied, shaking his head as tears formed.

"I'm sorry," she responded. She looked around to make sure nobody could hear and leaned in close. "I managed to access the SCIF to review some *resources* that we have."

Naomi worked for a contractor to the NSA and had a top-secret SCI clearance, allowing her access to the contractor's secured area.

"As you know, when the satellite sweeps North America, there's only a few shots taken within each geographic area. It took a long time to zero in on the location you provided. I found an image that you should review."

Naomi grabbed George's hand and stared into his eyes. "George, don't get your hopes up. It may not lead to anything. You know how this works. You'll find it in the usual place, like you taught me years ago."

"Thanks. That's a big help, Sista. I can't thank you enough. It's too risky for me to try and use my own credentials. They're probably watching me. I might be a suspect too."

"You're being paranoid, George. What could you be blamed for?"

They talked for a few more minutes before Naomi left, leaving George by himself. He went to the bathroom after finishing his margarita and ordering the check.

By the time he returned, the waiter had delivered the check. He opened his wallet and grabbed his credit card; he then intentionally dropped it on the floor. As he picked it up, he found the thumb drive that Naomi had taped to the underside of the table. George dexterously used the underside of the table to press the thumb drive onto a piece of double-sided tape that he had placed on the inside of his shirt sleeve.

He paid and left, eager to get home.

***

The picture on the thumb-drive disappointed George. Although he didn't expect Naomi to single-handedly absolve Suzanne, the picture showed only a white van, not even a license plate or image of a human! Naomi had warned him that the picture might not be helpful. Still, George pounded his fist on the table in frustration.

George tried to calm himself. He knew the clue might indeed unravel the entire mystery. An important date was revealed on a time stamp. July 18 had been the day before David had arrived at work, then left early — never to return to work again.

115

The image was blurred, not unexpected since it had been taken from space. However, he noticed a discoloration that could be a logo on the commercial van.

George next hacked into the traffic camera system of Loudoun County, a simple task for someone with his cyber-espionage background. He spent the next several hours watching the cameras to identify the route that the van had taken. Starting with the house, he backtracked to the nearest camera. If the van didn't show, he changed routes until he located the van on a different camera.

In the end, he traced the vehicle to a local strip mall. It appeared as if the driver had made a mistake, looking up at a street camera before turning into the mall. A snapshot exposed his blue eyes, pale skin, lips, cheeks, slender body frame, and size. He rocked back in his desk chair, thinking about what he had learned.

The van had a Washington Gas logo, but George's Spidey sense told him that the driver didn't work there. Although the darkness of the night reduced the clarity of the pictures of the van, he found two that were helpful. Both were in the direction of David's and Cindy's house. The van must have returned to the house. *But why?*

Chapter 21

George's high spirits were quickly dashed the following day. Washington Gas refused to tell him whether the house had been serviced.

"We can't reveal that information, sir. You'll need a warrant," the nasally voice responded to his telephone inquiry.

Neither Naomi's nor George's contacts were of any help in deciphering the partial identity. He needed a new plan.

***

George swam at least two days a week when he stopped running. Shaving off a few unwanted pounds turned out to be a secondary benefit. The real benefit had been a Zen-like calm that relaxed his mind around the tenth lap. And with a calm mind came his subconscious telling him something important, causing case-solving thoughts bubbling up from the bottom.

George jumped into the pristine pool offered by Yorktown High School to Arlington citizens on the weekends. As usual, the water jolted him, even at 82 degrees, prompting him to speed up the first two laps until his body adjusted to the temperature. Sure enough, around the tenth lap, an idea popped into his head – the fire. He may have been looking at this all wrong.

After showering and changing, he drove home and fired up his computer, ready to find and digest any information he could find about the Techno House fire. Some of the available information came from watching news footage. The blaze had been one of the most devastating and deadly fires in state history, earning coverage over several days.

Two people piqued George's curiosity – Chetan, the chief investigator for the Oakland Fire Department investigating the fire, and a man George noticed in the crowd in multiple clips, staring at the rubble, watching the investigation unfold.

It took two more meetings over nachos shared by George and his sister to solidify the lead. He then visited with Suzanne, updated Sheila, and boarded the next plane for California.

Chapter 22

For Fred Turner, it all started with his great-grand father, Tito. Tito had been a teenager when he worked as a roughneck on an oil rig on the Gulf of Mexico in 1947, the very first rig of its kind.

Tito left the company several years later to form TMJ Enterprises in 1956. The "T" in TMJ stands for Tito's first name. "MJ" were his wife's initials. Mary Jane, who agreed to marry him a few days before submitting the corporate paperwork to the state of Delaware. Family lore tells that he held up on submitting the documents to form the company, waiting for MJ's affirmative response to his proposal.

The company had been an instant hit, improving upon the tender assist drilling unit Tito worked on before he formed TMJ. TMJ's new technology could be used in deeper waters, drilling deeper, faster, and safer. The company prospered for the next several decades, making enough money to fund its own research.

By 2001, the year that Fred took over as Chairman and CEO, the company had grown its revenues to almost half a billion dollars with expanded operations throughout the Gulf of Mexico, the Pacific Coast, and several states in the Southwest. Profits were poured into research and development. Fred continued to make the process as environmentally sound as possible to stave off threats from renewable energy, believing that continuing to rely on old techniques would be short-sighted.

The company remained relatively small and inconspicuous compared to industry giants such as Exxon/Mobile and BP. Fred earned a reputation as a smart leader, willing to invest the resources necessary to ensure future success.

That is, until the accident in June of 2009 changed everything.

***

Johnny McGovern, a thick-bearded welder with tattoos of the American eagle and flag covering his right bicep, enjoyed his morning coffee mixed with a shot of espresso, sitting on a chair on the top deck of the rig. He could see the construction cranes building a hotel in the distance in Panama City, Florida. Like him, they had to work the early morning shift.

McGovern took in the sea air, relaxing before his hectic day began. Only it wasn't pure sea air that he smelled on this June day; he could detect a whiff of mercaptan, the chemical that smells like rotten eggs prevalent in natural gas.

The smell didn't bother him at first. It was a common smell on an oil rig. A few minutes later, however, he began to smell more sulfur than sea air. Then, he smelled all sulfur and no sea air.

"Frank!" he shouted, clicking the button on his black walkie-talkie. "Come in, please!"

"Yes, go ahead," Frank squawked.

"I'm smelling a *lot* of natural gas up here on the top deck."

"Sure, Johnny, sure. Still miffed the operator wouldn't address the seal issue on the riser?"

McGovern tried to dismiss his boss's ribbing. He had complained three months ago that the seal protecting against an influx of gas through the riser showed signs of a crack.

"I'm trying…" were the last words McGovern uttered before a horrendous explosion blew him into the sea.

***

Fred Turner received the call an hour later after arriving at the penthouse floor of the 28-story modern glass building in downtown Houston. He listened to the rig manager scream into the phone and tried to get in a few words of encouragement. When that proved impossible, he hung up.

Rig accidents were not uncommon, and he knew to remain calm. If he panicked, everybody would panic.

Turner contacted his liability insurance carrier. Tom Harden, TMJ's insurance agent, tried to break the news softly. He had talked to Candy Victrola, TMJ's risk management officer, yesterday after she called crying about letting the insurance lapse by accident. There was no grace period, and it wasn't possible to cover any resulting claims, Tom had remarked.

After listening to the agent, remaining calm was no longer an option – his luck had run out. Everything would change. This was a disaster. Tito would roll over in his grave.

"Hopefully, any damage and injuries will be minimal," Tom said evenly before hanging up.

In the end, five workers, including McGovern, died in the accident and oil marred eleven miles of the pure white sands on the Emerald Coast. Tourism suffered for several months. Lawsuits and claims totaling over one hundred million dollars engulfed the company.

None of the claims were covered by insurance. Bankruptcy loomed. Then one day, Fred received, at his house of all places, a check to cover the entire amount – and more. The mysterious payor had somehow known how much to pay and then multiplied the amount by 150%.

Fred thought for a long minute about whether to cash the check, drawn off a bank located in the Cayman Islands. The only clue about the source of the money had been the name of the payor – The Oilmen Trust – signed by Harry Smith as trustee.

Cashing the check could cause more problems, he realized. The internet yielded no clues as to the identity of The Oilmen Trust or Harry Smith. He dialed his attorney but hung up the phone before the call could be completed.

Did he really want to look a gift horse in the mouth? Maybe he had a benefactor in the oil industry, a zillionaire from a kingdom in the Gulf to whom $150,000,000 was a mere afterthought.

Destiny had intervened. Fred had been saved. Tito could rest easy in his ageing casket six feet underground.

A year later, in 2010, Fred received a mysterious call. The person invited him to a meeting to be held in Istanbul. Although he didn't understand all of what he heard, he knew enough to realize that attending the meetings was mandatory.

He had been attending four times a year ever since, and more in the event of an emergency, nervously twisting his Aggie ring each time before boarding his private jet.

Chapter 23

Chetan slept fitfully the night after she and Zonta returned to Oakland from burying her mother. Thoughts of Hotah, her mother Kangee, and the Techno House filled her head. She still had a nagging feeling about the fire; images of Trudy LaMonte and *The Scream* haunted her.

But she knew she had to move on. After washing her shiny black hair and braiding it tight down the center of her back, Chetan fired up a pot of steel cut oatmeal, which she had learned to like. An acquired taste, much different from the greasy eggs, bacon, and cheese breakfast she routinely ate growing up. Zonta watched Chetan cook from her perch on the countertop.

The doorbell rang. Chetan lowered the flame and walked to the front door. There, she looked through the peephole at a middle-aged black person staring back at her. He had bags under his eyes, and his black coiled hair looked greasy and messy. His beard looked recently trimmed, revealing to Chetan that he wasn't always a hot mess. And his right hand held a suitcase. *What is with this guy?*

Chetan slowly opened the door as far as the chain allowed without unhooking, wary of what he wanted. The neighborhood had its share of homeless, and the building didn't have any security. Anybody could take the elevator or stairs to the second floor. He could be a beggar holding his only possessions in a suitcase.

Yet, at the same time, he seemed non-threatening. Calmy speaking through the chain, he said, "My name is George. I've flown from Virginia to meet with you. Can I come in?"

Chetan considered the request. Answering his questions through a chained door was one thing; letting him into her apartment was a different matter. The man's story didn't make any sense. Horrible thoughts flashed in her mind. *Would he force his way in, tie me up and pillage my apartment? Maybe even rape or kill me?*

Before Chetan could respond, the man continued.

"My wife Suzanne's been arrested in connection with the fire you're investigating. I have some information."

Chetan relaxed her expression slowly, not wanting to tip off George that she had been scared.

"I'm not sure I can help. The case has been closed."

"Closed? I have some information you'll want to hear. I think you'll agree to reopen the case. Can I at least tell you what I learned?"

It didn't take long for Chetan to decide, thinking of Hotah, Trudy, and that horrible image of *The Scream*. She realized she had been secretly hoping the man would persist, recalling her concerns about how the FBI had usurped her jurisdiction while failing to adequately address her misgivings.

"Sure, come in," she replied after viewing his driver's license.

Chetan opened the door wider after unhooking the chain, allowing George to enter. She gestured for him to sit on the old blue couch in her living room that also doubled as her office and told her guest that she would be right back.

Chetan walked to the kitchen and turned off the stove. Her lackluster meal would have to wait. Coffee would have to do for now. She made two cups of it, one of which she then served to George sitting on the couch.

"I made you a cup. You look like you can use one. You take it black?"

"Yes, thanks. It's been a long night. I took the early flight from Dulles and came straight to your apartment before going to the hotel," George said, standing to retrieve the cup. He took a sip after sitting down.

Chetan sat on a worn leather chair, folding her right leg under her buttocks, right knee jutting out. She sipped her coffee.

"Comfortable?" George asked, making a point to look at her knee.

Chetan laughed, "I'm flexible. So, tell me, George, why are you here?"

"Do you recognize this man?" he asked, pointing to a picture he retrieved from a folder. George had snipped the picture from a magazine article about the fire. It showed a man in a crowd watching as firefighters and EMT worked to put out the fire, attended to wounded partygoers, and removed dead victims sheathed in white. The tall, skinny man had thick glasses and a black beard.

Chetan studied the picture. "I'm not sure, I was concentrating on the victims and damage – not the spectators that night."

"How about this man?" George asked, handing her his iPhone.

Chetan looked at the photo that George had snapped of a news clip. The man had the same skinny shape, but this time he wore a black beard and fedora. His skin looked pale. "The next day?"

"Yes, and I can tell from your expression, it's caught your eye."

Chetan looked at the picture from the magazine before speaking. "Think it's the same man?"

"Yes."

"Can I see the first picture again?"

After George showed her the picture, she said, "I think I remember him from the night of the fire, but not the picture on your iPhone from the next day."

"There's more," George said, handing Chetan the traffic cam picture that he had unearthed. He then explained to Chetan about David and Cindy and the apparent connection of the same man.

125

Chetan stood and paced. George had already proven to be methodical and organized. The same man at the fire bore a resemblance to the man in Virginia, outside of David's house. And David, the dead employee of Earthcare, had died within a week after the person had been seen near David's house.

But why was George bringing this information to her? Shouldn't he have gone to the police or FBI? She sat back down. Zonta jumped onto her lap, apparently eager to hear more.

George stared at her, waiting.

After a minute, she sighed and said, "You want me to reopen the case, right?"

"Yes."

"Do you have any information about him?"

"Just the pictures. I had somebody run the images through an encryption program, and it came up blank. He's managed to disguise his face just enough to not come up. He's experienced at this."

"Hmm. That's too bad. You may be onto something. Why me though? Why don't you go to the cops or the feds?" She thought about giving him Agent Proctano's contact information, but instinct told her not to.

George looked down before speaking. "I may at some point, but I need to get more evidence proving that Suzanne wasn't involved."

"David too, right?"

"Yes, of course, at least not willingly. Right now, though, I don't have enough. I'm married to the main suspect."

"You're former NSA though. Can't you go there?" Chetan asked, recalling information in the case file.

"Maybe, but not right now. They'll be even more hesitant to get involved without more evidence, fearing that an inspector general will claim that they intervened."

"I see your dilemma, George. I really do. But I'm not sure I can press my boss to reopen the case without more. You don't even know if they're the same person. Sure, they look similar, but what does that prove? I need more before sticking my neck out on a look-alike."

"It's the same guy. I mean, look!" George said, raising his voice while thrusting the images at Chetan.

An image of Hotah flashed across her mind. *It's not the same*, she told herself. *I couldn't have saved you.* Although she didn't really know if this was true.

"I'm sorry. I really am." She stood, hoping George would do the same.

George sat for a long minute before standing. "Well…that's disappointing, Chetan, but I understand. I'm just frustrated. Can we talk again if I find out more?"

"Yes, of course."

They shook hands before George left for Virginia. Chetan's stomach began to gurgle, and she wasn't sure it was because she hadn't eaten.

Chapter 24

George couldn't believe that Chetan wouldn't help him. He had provided her with a solid lead. *What a disappointment! She could have at least looked into it further!* He would have to move on without her. He had to. Suzanne could spend the rest of her life in jail waiting for the bureaucrat to do her job.

George poured a healthy serving of 86 proof bourbon, courtesy of Old Forester. Not in the mood for dilution, he omitted his usual country club ice ball. He would either drink his troubles away or use the stiff drink to brainstorm. Half-way through his second serving, an idea took root.

***

An hour later, Naomi sat across from George on a chair around his L-shaped island. George had swept his house for bugs before she had arrived.

"You want me to do *what*?" she asked rhetorically.

"I know, but I'm at a dead end. It may be Suzanne's last hope. Doesn't Jeff, excuse me *Geoffrey*, work in that department?" George asked referring to Naomi's on-and-off-again boyfriend for the past five years who worked as an Intelligence Analyst at NSA. George didn't like him. Not only had he been afraid to make a long-term commitment to his sister, but the pompous ass had the gall to correct George's Americanization of the Brit's formal given name.

Naomi sighed, "Well, I guess I can take him to dinner, but *not* anything after that!"

"Whatever it takes, for Suzanne?" George chided.

"No! Absolutely not," Naomi responded with a smirk.

***

Three days later, they sat around George's kitchen island again, this time over dinner. They were partaking in Naomi's requested food, Afghani from a local restaurant, while discussing what she had learned.

George opened a bottle of Chardonnay and let his starving sister swallow a pumpkin dumpling before holding his hands out, to signal his impatience.

Naomi smiled before swallowing her food and sipping her wine. When she was done, she announced, "Geoffrey came through." She looked down at her iPhone before standing and walking to her brother's stereo receiver. "Want me to put on some music?"

George nodded at the rhetorical question, knowing what that meant. Naomi wanted to maintain plausible deniability.

After she left, George looked at the iPhone and scrolled to the two most recently downloaded pictures. The first picture that Geoffrey datamined had been snapped, by a security camera, at 1:15 p.m. on July 25, the day after the Techno House fire. In it, a man wearing a beige straw hat, a large black facemask, white pants, and a T-shirt that said "Cuervo" exited a cab outside the Oakland International Airport.

George initially couldn't tell if the man pictured in the photos on Naomi's iPhone was the same person as the man in the pictures that George showed Chetan. *A waste of time?* Only he knew better. *No, not a waste. Naomi wouldn't waste my time with false hope.*

The second picture had been snapped at 2:00 p.m., the exact moment that TSA had forced the man to lower his facemask. The tourist pictured 45 minutes earlier had been unmasked as a tall, skinny, albino-looking man. Even better, George recognized the TSA checkpoint as the same one that he had entered after leaving Chetan's apartment a mere seven days ago. It served American Airlines and, to his recollection, no other flights.

Naomi returned and winked at Bro' before sitting down with a narrow piece of paper in her hand. She giggled as she set down the paper. Under a large green letterhead that said GROCERIES in script, she had printed a name.

Lawrence Meridian

George, who now had a name and a face, smiled as he pushed the iPhone to his sister before diving into his dish: shredded chicken in a spicy tomato stew served over a medley of balsamic rice, carrots, and raisins. The symphony of flavors melted in his mouth as jazz sprang from the surround sound system.

***

George had no difficulty figuring out what to do next. His good friend from high school, Spelling Bee, worked at the FAA. Spelling Bee's given name was Samantha, but while in the 10th grade, she won a national spelling contest. In addition to receiving a token scholarship to apply to towards college, George coined her nickname, which immediately spread to friends, frenemies, and family.

They met the next day for lunch in a Nashville restaurant. George had insisted on flying there, after explaining over the phone that it was important that they talk in person. George made sure that they sit at an outdoor table in the hot summer Nashville sun.

Spelling Bee reluctantly agreed to sit outside and understood why fifteen minutes later. George monitored her facial expressions throughout the discussion. Her initial shriveled brow turned into a wide-open mouth before becoming an understanding nod. She agreed to access the FAA's database to seek information about where Lawrence Meridian had flown.

George paced his hotel room like a caged animal, awaiting Spelling Bee's report. Two hours later, he received an encrypted email containing one word:

HOUSTON

***

George picked up the trail the next day at Houston's George Bush Intercontinental Airport. Armed with pictures of Meridian in Virginia near David and Cindy's house and six days later outside of the burning Techno House, George canvassed the airport.

He quickly discovered that the American Airlines flight from Oakland to Houston would have deposited passengers in Terminal A. From there, he located the taxicab dispatchers working on July 25, the date Meridian passed through. No luck. Nobody recognized any of the pictures.

Next, he tried the rideshare services. Again, no luck.

Two hours were spent canvassing the stores, coffee shops, and restaurants. The only sign had been a "maybe" from a barista.

In sum, he learned that Meridian may have gotten a cup of coffee before seemingly vanishing. He had a reached another dead-end.

***

George pouted, pacing like a caged lion back and forth in the baggage claim area of Terminal A, unsure of what to do. After a few minutes, he settled on a chair, not wanting to create a security incident – a psychopath loose in baggage claim. He closed his eyes in frustration. After he calmed, his eyes opened and settled on the key to proving Suzanne's innocence – walking out the door.

Chapter 25

Chetan wanted to help George, but she didn't have enough evidence to disregard the instructions of her boss. At her apartment in Oakland, George had shown her pictures of what *could have* been the same person wearing disguises. The man pictured — assuming it really was one person — bore some resemblance to the Washington Gas driver, but that didn't mean they were *actually* the same person.

There were lots of look-alikes running around. On a planet with close to eight billion people, it wasn't surprising. Still, she couldn't shake the feeling that she had been taking the easy way out.

In the meantime, her next assignment as chief inspector awaited. She needed to review a report from an underling about the cause of a house fire.

Chetan walked through the destroyed house with her subordinate. Later that day, she began synthesizing her notes, matching pictures taken to scenes, her usual method.

As she worked, a thought made her heart race – she may have missed something.

Chetan frantically searched for images of the crowd standing outside of the Techno House the night of the fire. Ten minutes later, she had located the picture. It looked like the same man as in the iPhone picture George had shown her, only in the new picture, he held a cellphone against his ear.

The date stamp on the picture revealed the time of the call as July 25 at 4:30 a.m., before she had left to go home the night of the fire. He appeared devoid of any emotion, at the scene of a fire where 36 people died.

She had seen him, two times, the night of the fire. A question surged to the front of her brain, "who was this man speaking with at 4:30?"

***

While working on the case the first time, Chetan had directed a subordinate to serve a subpoena on AT&T, seeking access to the phone calls that had passed through the tower closest to the Techno House. One of the partygoers or occupants of the house might have contacted somebody, revealing information about where the fire began, an ulterior motive, or suspicious behavior observed; perhaps a clue had passed onto a parent, child, spouse, or friend, or maybe even a co-conspirator.

Chetan had amassed detailed biographical information on each person that entered the building. Calls made were cross-referenced. Any suspicious calls were investigated.

Only that information didn't suit her purposes today; she was more interested in calls from people who may have *never* entered the building.

"Hasn't this case been resolved, ma'am?" the AT&T clerk asked, scoffing at Chetan's request made over the phone. The clerk's negative response disheartened Chetan. The clerk could object to the request, pointing out that the subpoena arguably only included records of calls made by persons *inside* the building.

"We're just dotting the I's. Request from above. Scarred from last year's Wharf fire. You remember that?" Chetan tactfully reminded the clerk of a recent debacle where the prosecutor had forgotten to review the records of calls made by bystanders.

A smart-ass defense attorney had convinced the jury to exonerate the suspected arsonist based upon a vicious cross-examination of the ex-wife of the building owner. The prosecutor argued that the owner torched the structure, seeking insurance money to pay the property settlement owed to his soon-to-be ex. Only he hadn't considered that the defense would create enough doubt by introducing a fabricated tale about the ex-wife, who had arrived at the scene after the fire began. She had been in the area shopping and watched the fire, like many others.

The defense attorney made lemonade out of phone calls that people had witnessed her making. A fable woven out of loose threads, but little actual evidence, emerged on cross-examination. Bitter hatred, a suspicious paramour. Enough doubt to convince at least one juror to let the owner off, despite overwhelming evidence that he had taken steps looking into how much he might recover from burning his own building to raise money to pay off his spouse.

"I remember that case," the clerk responded in a monotone fashion before succumbing. "Send me a request covered by the initial subpoena in writing."

Chetan breathed a sigh of relief. Thirty minutes after formally requesting the information, she had her answer. The suspicious person that Chetan noticed hanging out after the fire at 4:30 a.m. had called Fred Turner, owner of TMJ Enterprises, based in Houston, Texas.

***

The crowded San Francisco International Airport surprised Chetan, who had never flown before. So many people in one place. Some were indifferent, bumping past others, huffing while in the various lines, signs of anxiety, rudeness, and, to Chetan, weakness.

Chetan did her best to read the signs as she maneuvered through the process. Her debrief with Celina had also helped.

After landing, renting a car, and checking into her hotel, she drove to George's house in Virginia. The neighborhood, with its manicured lawns and large brick houses, impressed her. It occurred to her that she had never been in a house as large as George's, at least one that hadn't been damaged by a fire.

An elderly neighbor walking a Pitbull made their way into the cul-de-sac as soon as Chetan parked her car and walked up the driveway. The man glanced at Chetan and then stared, obviously hoping Chetan would stop and talk. She wisely refused, continuing to the door.

A black Lab barked from inside, but nobody answered. A look into the house revealed a stash of mail on a table in the foyer area.

The dog-walker shouted, "He's not home. Hasn't been for several days. Good thing somebody's taking care of Mercy, his dog, and bringing his mail inside."

Chetan shouted back, "Any idea of where he went? How long will he be away?"

"No. But I bet this has to do with his wife. She was arrested, you know."

Chetan thought she detected a faint smile. "That sounds serious. Thanks," she said solemnly.

Chetan thought about her next move after returning to the hotel. Where could George have gone? She resolved to look for him again in a few days, upset at herself for not asking for his cell phone number when he had arrived on her doorstep. She briefly thought about giving up, but she knew that wouldn't work; the same forces that took her to Virginia would rebel.

Then it came to her. She knew what to do next.

***

The flight to Houston had been uneventful for the now-veteran Chetan on her second plane trip of her life. She felt compelled to follow the lead, even if it meant using some of the $25,000 left to her by her mother. The fire department would reimburse her if the case were reopened.

As with the flight to visit George, Chetan didn't feel the need to tell Antonio where she had gone. He would never notice if she didn't stay away too long.

He might call her studio office. One missed call wouldn't be a problem. A second or third missed call could raise questions. Antonio wouldn't condone her reopening the investigation, not without substantiation to support her still-undeveloped theory.

After stowing her bags at a local hotel, she taxied to a sleek metal and glass tower that housed TMJ Enterprises. She looked up at the building and began to panic.

What now? Her only experience had been investigating fires. While that sometimes entrenched upon unwinding the hidden motives of arsonists, it never involved trailing or tracking the movements and interactions of suspects. That was the purview of detectives or spies like George, not fire investigators. *What would she say if somebody questioned her presence, much less her motives for being there?*

Doubt set in. She should return to George's house and wait for him. That was the safe play for sure. Except that the neighbor had revealed that George hadn't been to his house for several days. She had rejected his overtures and was now on her own.

In the end, it only took an additional hour. Chetan sat outside the building on a bench, wearing a white tank-top and shades, pretending to be reading from her iPad. Occasionally, she glanced at the front entrance of the building, first looking up at the sun under the pretense of feeling its rays. She periodically looked at the pathway leading visitors in between the two white fountains guarding the entrance.

An hour later, her doubt returned. *You idiot! What are you doing? What will you do if he appears? Go home. Or go to George's house and wait for him.* She bit the inside of her cheek, a technique she used to stop her subconscious from ruining her plans.

Subconscious be dammed, she thought as her suspect came into view. The man that she now realized was the same person captured in the traffic camera near David Grigorio's house and then observing the Techno House fire was walking at a fast clip on the pathway.

Only this time, he had no disguise, which made him even more terrifying. The only albinos she had seen were in movies like *The Matrix Reloaded*, playing the role of a villain. She could tell from afar that the skinny man walking down the path had platinum hair and a pale white face. Although she couldn't see his eyes, she bet they were blue.

Even scarier was that Fred Turner followed the strange man like a puppy dog. Turner did his best to keep up the pace, but a step behind. Although she tried not to show any emotion, a terrifying thought entered her mind: *Is Fred Turner even in charge?*

As Chetan looked at both, the man walking in front of Turner suddenly looked in her direction. She looked away. *He wouldn't expect me to be here.*

Chetan's phone buzzed, thankfully diverting her attention, and providing potential cover. A text message read:

Casually walk away and meet me at Café Renato two blocks down to the right.

G

***

Chetan didn't know if she should wait for George or if he was already there. She looked around, didn't see him, and sat at a table by the window, waiting.

Another text arrived. She read the message:

Never sit by the window. I'm at a table in the back.

Chetan grunted to herself before walking to the back. Although she remembered seeing the man when she searched the café upon arriving, she realized her mistake. George had disguised himself well. He looked like a businessman, wearing a dark grey suit and blue tie.

This is a lot different than fighting fires, Chetan thought.

137

George shook his head, chuckling softly as Chetan sat down, giving him a dark stare in return. Neither mentioned Chetan's close call. *Close call is an overstatement.*

The waiter came, and they ordered two coffees.

Chetan looked at George sheepishly after the waiter left.

"I went to your house, George. You weren't there! Your neighbor told me that you were out of town. I'm glad I found you here, of all places."

"Yeah, I'll bet," George said under his breath. "What are you doing here? Last time we spoke, you refused to help."

Chetan knew how it must look from George's viewpoint, but she didn't want to concede the high ground.

"That's not exactly what I said, George. I said I needed more information first. Remember? I might help if a lead developed." Chetan explained about the phone call that the suspect made from outside the Techno House that she had traced to Fred Turner at TMJ Enterprises.

"Interesting. So, you have proof that he called Fred Turner that night. That could be important."

"Yep."

"My sister, Naomi, helped identify the man you were following. His name is Lawrence Meridian. Seems to be an enforcer currently working with TMJ."

"That makes sense. But for what purpose?"

"Don't know, but I intend to find out."

"You?"

"Yes. It's my wife who's involved. I need to save her life. But you? Don't take this the wrong way, but your skill is investigating fires. You made that very clear to me last time we met. I'm going to investigate this angle. I'll share with you what I learn."

The waiter delivered a shot of espresso for George and a chai latte for Chetan, which they both began drinking.

138

Chetan took the opportunity to think about how George had texted her as Meridian looked in her direction, the person who, at this point, had been the leading candidate to have orchestrated the killing of both David and Cindy. Investigating the living was a lot different than staring at burnt debris.

George seemed to understand. "Look, I know you mean well and want to help. I'll keep you in the loop. I'm fighting for my wife's life here. Besides, it looked like Meridian saw you. If that's the case, then you've already been compromised and could be in danger."

"Don't think so, George. The monster looked towards me, but we didn't make eye contact," Chetan said, intentionally downplaying the risk.

George shrugged. "Still, be careful. I'll call you if I learn anything of interest."

Chapter 26

George reflected on what had just transpired. Chetan had shocked him, showing up at the same baggage claim area at the Houston airport just as he had reached the deadest of ends. Following her to the offices of TMJ Enterprises was another surprise.

He thought about forming a partnership of sorts with her. George's Googling of her name revealed an impressive bio with flashes of real heroism. She had saved five colleagues who were trapped in a burning cabin with a roof that had collapsed. They would have died if it hadn't been for her heroic action in entering the cabin, saving them.

Still, while she may be a brilliant investor, she had a lot to learn about spying. Her cover may have already been sacrificed, discovered by Meridian. *If I hadn't pulled her away, she might even be dead!* George couldn't blow any chance to save his wife.

It had taken George years to master the tradecraft necessary for fieldwork, trailing people, breaking into offices, etc. He would work alone. Sending her home had been necessary, especially for what he was about to do.

***

After meeting with Chetan at Café Renato, George trailed Turner from TMJ's headquarters in downtown Houston to his unlisted house in the suburbs. He drove his Honda CRV rental car, disguising his appearance by wearing a wig with long brown hair and attaching a bushy mustache to his face. He had learned a long time ago how to look innocuous, dressed like a general contractor early for an appointment visiting a neighbor's home to provide an estimate.

As he waited, he pretended to look at his phone and review his contractor paperwork, acting like he was making appointments. Only he wasn't. Instead, he used an application on his cell phone to snap pictures of Turner and his house via his high-definition, zoomable mini-dash camera.

He spent the next several days learning the patterns of Turner's movements. Looking for something he could exploit, he discovered that Turner usually made a stop at a dated, four-story office building on his way to work.

Turner would emerge from his house at 6:45 a.m., dressed in sweatpants and a T-shirt, carrying a briefcase and a large gym bag. George suspected that he would go to a gym, only he didn't. Instead, he stopped at a commercial building with no signage, beyond the address and name of the property management company. George needed to investigate this building further.

The next day, George took an even closer look. Instead of driving by, he parked and slumped down in his seat. There, he watched Turner enter the building.

Next came the waiting and wondering for the zillionth time in his career whether there was a better way to observe a target. Turner finally emerged at around 8:25 a.m., nearly 90 minutes after entering, wearing navy slacks and a white and light-blue striped shirt, holding the same briefcase and gym bag.

George tailed Turner to his office building, where George waited about an hour and left, deciding to return to the building that Turner had visited earlier in the morning. He entered the lobby, an area that looked like it hadn't been updated since the building had been built. The grout in the off-white flooring bore chips in several places, and the brown painted walls looked chipped and faded in spots.

He scanned the tenant directory that he found next to the two metallic elevators. There were several faded spaces which George imagined had been filled prior to the pandemic. He took a picture of the listing with his iPhone, returned to his car, and Googled the name of each tenant.

There were no private fitness trainers or small gyms, much to his surprise. A yoga studio on the second floor seemed the only possible destination.

George returned to the building, using the staircase to walk up, thinking about his disdain for people using an elevator to exercise. He and Suzanne liked to compare the number of steps each of them travelled through the course of a day.

After entering the studio, a cute Asian woman with short-cropped black hair greeted George from the reception area with a cheery, "Namaste." She looked to be in her mid-twenties.

Memories of his time in a similar studio nearly thirty years ago returned. He couldn't recall if a more formal response was standard and decided upon a neutral but weak greeting of, "Hello."

George introduced himself as Steve, and the woman reciprocated with her name, Hannah. He explained he had recently moved to the area. Could he look around?

Hannah shrugged her shoulders and said, "We welcome visitors. Feel free to look around, but you cannot go into the locker rooms without someone from our staff accompanying you."

The establishment appeared to have two studios. The largest was enclosed in glass, upon which the words "Bikram Yoga" were stenciled. Mirrors lined the walls. The second had a door that was closed and labeled "Meditation."

In addition to two bathrooms near the reception area, George discovered three other rooms, the smallest of which had a door that was ajar, revealing that it held supplies. A second room had a window panel revealing a desk, computer, and files. He couldn't tell the purpose of the third room located opposite the bathrooms near the reception area. He tried to turn the doorknob as the receptionist restocked a display case, but it wouldn't open.

George approached the receptionist area and asked Hannah for a listing of classes. She handed him a sheet of paper, remarking, "This is a great place to take classes. The bottom of the sheet describes our introductory package. Take a look."

The Bikram Yoga times were 90 minutes long, the first class beginning at 6:30 a.m. each day. The meditation classes were 45 minutes each but were slotted after the Bikram Yoga classes, enabling the same instructor to alternate teaching both. The first one began at 8:30 a.m.

"Do you have to bring your own mat to the Bikram Yoga class?" George asked.

Hannah replied in a teasing but amiable tone, "Of course you need one. If people didn't use a mat, then it'd get pretty gross in there."

"And if I don't have one? Can the studio loan me a mat if I sign up to try it out?"

"No, I'm sorry. We decided a long time ago to not offer that service. Didn't want to have to clean the mats and take responsibility for sterilizing them. Try Harry's Sporting Store two miles east on Route 8. Or you can get one on Amazon."

"Do you offer any other classes beyond meditation and Bikram Yoga?"

"No, sorry, just the two."

"OK, thanks. I'll think about it. You've been very helpful," George replied before walking out.

George thought about the studio as he drove back to his hotel. Something didn't add up. Turner had arrived at 7:00 a.m. this morning wearing sweatpants, and he left at 8:00 a.m., a routine that seemed to fit a daily pattern. Except that the timing didn't fit with the actual yoga class, since that began at 6:30 a.m. and ended at 8:00 a.m., or the first meditation class that began at 8:30 a.m. He remembered from his own previous Bikram Yoga classes that you can't arrive 30 minutes late, missing the crucial warmup period.

He also knew that sweatpants were not appropriate attire for hot yoga. Men wore bathing suits and some of the women wore bikinis as instructors maintained a constant room temperature of 105 degrees.

***

The next morning, George arrived with his long blue mat from Harry's Sporting Store. He had taken off the plastic wrap in his car, releasing a slight odor. George signed up for a trial Bikram Yoga class, wearing a green bathing suit, flip flops, and a white t-shirt.

Hannah flashed him a warm smile as he paid, saying, "I'm glad you signed up, Steve! I wasn't sure about you." She chuckled before adding reassuringly, "Excuse me for saying it this way, but we get a lot of people your age. We also get a lot of people that haven't done this in a while. You'll see. You'll do fine. It'll be good for you. Just stick with it and do what you can. Don't be afraid to lie down if it becomes too much. See you in there. I double as the instructor for the early morning class. Lucky you!"

George started to walk away but turned around when Hannah shouted his name. Hannah pointed to a wooden rack by the front door and said, "You need to leave your flip flops in this rack. I'm going to lock the door once class begins."

Mild panic entered his mind thinking about how Turner would get in. He could keep coming for the rest of the week, but he really didn't want to fry too many days in a row. Maybe Turner had a key or somebody else arrived after the yoga class began to meet and let him in.

144

George entered the studio and managed to secure a spot up by the front where he could view the room with the locked door by peering through the entrance to George's yoga room. Fortunately, only the true diehards sought the front positions, near the instructor, making George an outlier in that regard. His shiny new mat contributed to the awkwardness, creating an embarrassing separation noise as he uncurled it for the first time on the studio floor.

Class began with breathing exercises that George remembered and could handle, but he knew it would be a train-wreck from there. Hannah introduced George to the class, using the name he signed up with: Steve. A few of the other participants said hello, waved or nodded, but most ignored him.

A half-hour into class, George noticed Turner arrive. Watching in his peripheral vision, he noticed Turner glance into yoga studio while waiting for the door to his room to open. The door opened and quickly closed.

Fifteen minutes later, George told Hannah that he needed to go to the bathroom. She shot him a nasty look. But George didn't even see it as he had already passed her on the way to the door.

George feigned going to the bathroom. Hannah focused on her class, ignoring George, allowing him to listen at the door to the locked room. Nothing. No sounds, at least nothing he could hear.

He returned to class, and at 8:00 a.m. he noticed Turner leave and walk towards the bathroom, where George assumed Turner showered and dressed in his work clothes. Five minutes later, a tall athletic-looking woman emerged from the same room, wearing black nylon tights and a simple white shirt. She locked the door behind her. George guessed that she was at least a generation younger than Turner.

After the class, George left the studio, but not before making note of the studio's email address used for general inquiries. A plan began to germinate in his head.

George walked to a small room with a table and three vending machines near the studio, the building not large enough to warrant a full cafeteria. From there, he used a tool masking his email address to send a query about upcoming classes to the studio's general information email address.

With the first part of the plan now complete, he drove back to the hotel. It began raining, first lightly and then harder, triggering a twinge of regret for what he had done and was about to do, until he thought about Suzanne wasting away in her holding cell. By the time he arrived at the hotel, the rain had turned into a downpour, pounding the street and his car.

A howling wind caused the rain to swirl, reminding him of a time when he and Suzanne hunkered down in the basement of a bed and breakfast at which they were staying while a tornado passed through the town. The sky normalized soon after the tornado ventured elsewhere.

George parked in the hotel garage and entered the lobby. He passed by the remnants of the free continental breakfast. The partially congealed oatmeal, more starch than oats, dry and hardened eggs, and watered-down coffee were not appetizing but provided a quick fix for his hunger.

After the rushed meal, George walked into his room, placed a do not disturb sign on the outside doorknob, and powered up his laptop. Hannah, the studio's obvious jack of all trades, had responded to the email George had sent earlier from a fake email address. Her reply included a listing of classes that George ignored.

Instead, he used another tool accumulated from his days mastering spy craft to decipher the IP address of the studio's computer. The IP address allowed George to infiltrate and obtain information about the studio's firewall, including the availability of any inbound ports. An hour later, he had infiltrated the server. Soon he was downloading dozens of emails between Amy Genser and Fred Turner.

George smiled as he read the catch, revealing what Turner and Amy had been doing behind the locked door. Amy provided him with massages several days each week, although he doubted that described the full story.

And indeed, it didn't. While the two were normally careful in their almost daily communications, a few slipups told a more complete story. Amy apparently had been encouraging a provocative relationship, one which Turner welcomed.

Many of her emails contained GIFs with links enticing Turner to click on to activate a tempting picture of Amy touching herself or posing seductively. She obviously had led Turner into accepting happy endings after a brief massage, which George imagined came with a big tip. George smiled before proceeding to the next step.

He established a Yahoo account using a username he would remember for this purpose. He then masked the identity of the account, making it look as if any emails being sent would be launched from the yoga studio's domain name in the username assigned to Amy.

Next, George prepared an email to Turner that would be masked to look as if it came from Amy's account. The email used Amy's phrasing and language patterns, including a note to press on a GIF for a glimpse of Amy giving another woman a massage. George wondered if Turner would be suspicious, but he felt his target wouldn't think twice.

After clicking the "Enter" button, he eagerly waited until Turner accepted the bait. His computer alerted him an hour later that Turner had clicked on a Trojan horse virus file George had sent using Amy's information.

The virus enabled George to gain access to Turner's email system by obtaining the login credentials. George also had been able to intercept and fulfill any two-factor authenticating requirements. Six hours later, he discovered the answer to what had rescued Turner after the oil rig disaster and how his behavior had changed since. George booked his flight home and spent the rest of his time making plans.

But first, he needed to talk to Spelling Bee about a plane.

Chapter 27

Antonio lived in a modest ranch house in a wooded area in Folsom, California. The town is best known for California's Folsom State Prison, which would have remained innocuous if not for Johnny Cash. Cash and his U.S. Army mates were killing time watching the movie, *Inside the Walls of Folsom Prison*, when he decided to write his most famous song, *Folsom Prison Blues*. Later, he traveled to Folsom to play the song at an iconic concert for the inmates.

Living near the prison made housing affordable, enabling Antonio to buy a larger lot than he could nearly anywhere else in the overheated California real estate market. He lived with two best friends– his older German Shephard, Cowboy, and his spry, marble-colored Sheltie, Blue – neither of whom minded wearing a red, white, and blue checkered bandana.

***

Meridian watched the two dogs play in the yard from a large, thick oak tree that he had climbed — a skill he learned hunting deer. Nestled in an ensemble of branches, he lay in wait for his prey.

Only a fool would dress his dogs in matching bandanas the color of the American flag, he thought. Meridian had watched Blue run circles around the slower Cowboy while their owner took a leisurely nap in the middle of the afternoon. *The pandemic has ruined American life*, he mused. *Civil servants are now paid to stay at home and sleep. It's a societal crisis!*

The dogs pranced around and ate poop, no doubt dripping trace elements onto their American-flag bandanas. *How disrespectful to our founding fathers! Home of the brave, not dung sniffers,* he sneered.

He thought about wiping everybody out now. Instead, he watched and waited.

***

Cowboy, no doubt worn out from his adventures, disappeared inside the house for a drink, leaving the young lass alone. Meridian slithered down from his position, with his scalpel, which he had polished for the occasion, and a special treat.

In position behind two thick bushes, he placed the bloody body of Temerity in front of the bush. Temerity was the name he cleverly gave to an audacious squirrel who had confidently climbed near Meridian in the tree. As punishment, he had the rodent drawn and quartered while balancing on the branches fifteen feet in the air. Talent knows no bounds, he thought.

Cowboy appeared in ecstasy after spotting the mangled mess, running to the spot, tail wagging uncontrollably. Meridian raised his scalpel, ready to strike.

"Cowboy, come get your snack!" Antonio shouted outside.

Snack? Meridian had to use his highest Zen power to control himself as dusk began to take hold.

***

The next morning, Antonio awoke at 7:30 a.m., showered, and dressed before entering the kitchen. There he set out two bowls of Kibbles 'n Bits, knowing that the dogs would come running from the sunroom. While Blue promptly arrived with her tail wagging for food, Cowboy didn't show. Was he outside? Did the older pooch need to pee again? Antonio had installed a doggy door that allowed both dogs to come and go as they pleased, which for Cowboy also meant not having to hold it in as long.

Antonio whistled to no avail. Cowboy remained AWOL. He searched the house first and then began looking outside. Cowboy was nowhere to be seen.

Fifteen minutes later, Antonio's worry rose stratospherically, especially after Blue stopped eating, her tail no longer wagging. She uncharacteristically left her food, joining Antonio to search the yard.

Antonio spotted it first. A bloody mess at the base of a large oak tree. Blue looked up at her owner and began to whine.

Somebody had slit Cowboy's throat, Antonio determined. It looked like a straight line from which blood had spilled. *Who would do such a thing? And why?*

He looked at the bandana. The edge of a white piece of paper stuck out, away from the wound. Antonio removed and read it:

Your little Indian girl is misbehaving. You need to rein it in, or Blue's turn will come next.

***

Antonio and Blue consoled each other, both beginning to cry in their own way. Antonio with tears and cussing, and Blue by tucking her hind legs under her bottom, head laying in between her front legs. After a while, they walked to the house for Antonio to retrieve a blanket to cover the body.

After returning to the house, Antonio poured himself a glass of cold water. *Killing Cowboy to threaten me? How dare he! He'd find the person who did this. Reporting Cowboy's death to the police would accomplish nothing.*

He took a sip of water. *What did Chetan learn after being told to stand down?*

***

Meridian called Turner, not looking forward to another conversation with the simpleton. Turner was a white-collar owner of a business who had been forced into the criminal world – unlike Meridian, who had practically been born into it.

"Well?" Turner asked impatiently, as if Meridian had been a mere robot.

Meridian bit down on his tongue before relaying the good news.

"It's done. You don't have to worry about the Indian or anybody else at the Oakland Fire Department."

"Good."

"And the husband, shouldn't I just take him out? Why keep him around?" Meridian asked.

"We've gone through this before. He's *not* expendable. Too many friends in high places. It would raise too many questions."

Meridian didn't like that answer, but he had little choice. He had already tried to convince Turner before to let him use the full array of his awesomeness, and Turner had given the same answer. He could continue to argue but knew better. Turner would tell his real boss, the man referred to as the Benefactor, and Meridian didn't want the troublemaker label. His career could suddenly be over in a flash. Maybe even in a more traumatic way than the pooch he had just slaughtered.

Chapter 28

Chetan's iPhone rang. The name Antonio Gonzalez flashed across the home screen.

"Hello, Antonio," Chetan answered cheerfully.

"They killed Cowboy!" Antonio shouted back.

"Cowboy?"

"Yes, one of my dogs."

"Sorry to hear that, but why are you telling me?"

"Because it's your fault!"

"Come again?"

"Look at your phone!"

Rage filled her as she inspected the images of the dead dog and of the note. She knew she wasn't *really* at fault, but there was no denying the simple fact that if she hadn't disobeyed Antonio's instructions, none of this would have happened. On the other hand, she couldn't let it go, either. A horrific fire had caused the death of dozens of people, and she now knew for certain that it had been intentionally set.

A lengthy discussion ensued. First came the statements of rage, sorrow, and hatred. The police seemed out of the question. They would probably assign a rookie as a hazing exercise. The person who committed the heinous crime would laugh at the futility of the "investigation" and might then kill Blue for sport.

With the preliminaries out of the way, the discussion turned towards Chetan and the investigation. The note left on Cowboy's bandana meant that she had become a threat. Both were adamant that she continue the investigation without letting anybody else at the office know in case of a mole.

The fire department's slush fund controlled by Antonio would be accessible by Chetan for any reasonable expenses, including any travel costs. Agent Proctano would be updated but only about any important developments.

***

Chetan began by looking into Fred Turner's background. He seemed to be an ordinary businessman, although she didn't really know what that even meant. Turner began running the family's deep water oil exploration business in 2001 and then ran into difficult times. Difficult times turned out to be an understatement.

An oil rig exploded in June 2009. Beaches were ruined and people died, which was not much different from other environmental mishaps. But this one seemed different. An article in the *LA Times* pointed out that the company's insurance coverage had lapsed, and Turner had to pay all claims from the company's own reserves, an unusual occurrence on this scale and even more rare for the business to have survived without filing for bankruptcy protection.

A cartoonist for the *Seattle Times* depicted the employee who let the policy lapse, Candy Victrola, being hung from a green and white candy cane. Fred Turner, depicted like the grim reaper, loomed over the hanging with a caption that read: "No more candy for you!" The article that accompanied the cartoon marveled at how Turner had somehow pulled the company from the brink.

Oil, one of the most important three-letter words, resonated over and over in Chetan's mind. *What is the connection?* she asked herself.

Then it hit her like a hammer, as in Benji Hammer. Chetan had created detailed notes in a file about all people near the Techno House on that infamous day. Something about Benji had always troubled her. She didn't know why until now.

At the time that she had compiled the initial information, he didn't stand out. Benji, in his mid-forties, lived and worked in the area, and lobbied on behalf of the oil industry.

Another interesting discovery occurred about an hour later. Chetan located a picture of Benji in a suit posing for a picture in the U.S. Capitol. Three senators were in the picture, with Benji in the middle. Fred Turner posed behind them, standing tall in order to be seen.

Chapter 29

Chetan brooded, thinking that she had let everybody down – the fire victims for not solving the case, George for not absolving Suzanne, and Antonio and his beloved pooch. Although she didn't have any proof, she *knew* Meridian had killed Cowboy to ensure that the investigation remained closed. Meridian and Turner obviously didn't want anybody – not Chetan and certainly not George or the FBI – to discover them.

Chetan no longer believed they were guilty of causing the fire nor the deaths of so many people. But who had been behind the framing and for what purpose?

Chetan called George and told him about Cowboy. His interest perked, but he cut off the discussion in case his phones were tapped. George told Chetan that they would meet at the same place they met the first time. She immediately understood the message, and the meeting place certainly was convenient for her.

George arrived at Chetan's door the next morning, bearing donuts as an olive branch. He held his right index finger to his lips as she peered through the peephole.

She let him in without saying anything. He removed a black gadget from his luggage that looked to Chetan like a mix between a walkie talkie and an old handheld radio. She remembered seeing the older Lakotas use them, listening to a baseball game or talk radio. George searched the entire apartment, and ten minutes later, he gave the all-clear.

"Think my place is bugged?"

"I'm not sure. You never know. There's something about Meridian and Turner that's bothering me. I'm glad you called."

Chetan frowned. She had a feeling that it didn't end with Turner and gestured for George to sit in the living room.

"Same flight as last time? Coffee?" she asked.

"Yes, and *definitely* yes. I don't like the early morning flights. But there are not that many options for direct flights, and I wanted to get here."

Chetan walked into the kitchen. Once there she poured him a cup of coffee and retrieved plates for the donuts.

They settled in the same spots as before, creatures of habit: George on the couch and Chetan on a leather chair, right leg folded under her buttocks.

Zonta jumped on her master's lap, signaling that the discussion could now begin.

"Why don't you begin, Chetan? Tell me what happened."

"There's not much to say. Antonio discovered Cowboy with his throat slit and a white sheet of paper sticking out of the dog's bandana. It had been placed in a position where it wouldn't get soaked by the blood."

Chetan showed him a picture of the note that Antonio had given her.

"Fingerprints?"

"He's checking on that, but don't expect anything."

George examined the picture. "Any other investigations that somebody would've wanted you to leash?"

"I'm sure there's nothing else," Chetan said. "Well, I suppose it's possible but unlikely. It's got to be the Techno House fire. Nothing else."

"That makes sense. You claimed in Houston that you thought he didn't see you, but it looks like he may have. It fits. You agree?" George asked.

"I suppose," Chetan said reluctantly.

"Good, and don't feel bad about what happened. These are serious bad guys. Their heads are on a swivel all the time," George said before pausing to reassure her. "Solving these cases is tough stuff. Let's start with the fire. The FBI believes that Earthcare's computers triggered it, that people died on the other side of the country because of something that David and Suzanne did. I don't even know how that's possible!"

Zonta purred and looked up, her cat ears standing at alert as George vented. Chetan bristled but understood the hell that he and Suzanne must be going through.

Chetan responded, "Here's what I think happened. As you know, it all started with the program being launched from Earthcare's computers..."

"But not by Suzanne or David!" George exclaimed.

"Yes, if you mean *intentionally*," Chetan said.

"Good point. Suzanne told me that David went to work on Monday but was not himself. My theory there is that Meridian was holding Cindy hostage, forcing David to do this. The murder-suicide that happened after the fire would've been to eliminate the key witnesses."

"Makes sense," Chetan replied.

"So, David launches the program from his computer..." George continued.

"Not exactly," Chetan interjected. "Proctano told me that they discovered digital footprints of the program on both computers but that it had been *launched* from Suzanne's computer."

"That's possible," George conceded before continuing. "Although *technically* it could've also been launched from David's computer using an IP address masked to make it *look like* it came from Suzanne's computer. Either way, Turner, Meridian, and whoever they really work for wanted to bring down Suzanne and Earthcare."

"Because of Earthcare's anti-fossil fuel platform?" Chetan asked.

"Of course! I mean *look* at Turner. TMJ makes its money by operating, maintaining, and servicing oil rigs, and now we're starting to realize that this is part of a global effort. Probably with other people from the oil industry. Who knows where this ends? Could be a global cabal of some sort, probably funded by rouge OPEC members."

Zonta, who had been trying to follow who was talking, lost interest, and fell fast asleep resting on her donut-shaped bed.

"Yep. That all fits. Startling, but it fits. Anyhow, the program is launched and received by a computer that is operating grow lamps," Chetan said.

"Huh? Grow lamps?" George asked.

"Yep. Part of the burgeoning pot industry. The fire began in the basement," Chetan said.

"How did you figure that out?" George said while nodding, obviously impressed.

"The flames burned up from the junction box feeding the grow lamps. While the grow lamps and apparatus had been destroyed, the junction box remained intact because the flame spread upward away from the box. That's how I determined that it began at the junction box."

"Impressive, Chetan. Nice work."

"Thank you. I also detected remnants of a computer that appears to have been operating the grow lamps, and I looked into the system being used. There would have been four rows of lamps, each rotating, but I believe that the program launched…"

"Unwillingly…" George interjected.

"Yep! Of course. Anyway, the program turned all four rows on, causing the overload."

"Wouldn't the circuit breaker have tripped?" George asked.

"You'd think so, yes. But I noticed a thirty-amp breaker in place of where a fifteen-amp breaker should have been. A fifteen-amp breaker would have tripped the system, preventing a fire, but not the thirty-amp," Chetan replied.

"How did the fire begin then?"

"The system would have continued to flood current, which would have caused the wires near the junction box to arc. The arcing would have produced sparks igniting flammable material, like paper or boxes stored near the junction box."

"And you believe that Meridian may have switched the breakers?" George asked.

"Yep."

"How did the FBI finger David or Suzanne for that, though?"

Chetan replied, "David apparently proposed to Cindy on July 10, 2021, in San Francisco, two weeks before the fire, placing him in the area before the fire."

"And Meridian forced David to launch the program which caused the overload at a time when Benji would've been there," George surmised.

"Yep, and he probably also returned later to sprinkle accelerants like kerosene or turpentines. Just enough to act as a catalyst," Chetan said.

"Find any evidence of that?" George asked.

"Nope, but those don't always show up."

Switching angles, George asked, "How did Meridian know Benji Hammer would be there at the right time?"

"Benji apparently was a regular. He went there every Saturday night, like clockwork. Guess he just liked to unwind there after a week of work," Chetan replied.

"Makes sense and syncs with the rest. Let's go back to the *real* beginning, though."

"TMJ and the accident," Chetan said.

"Yes, I see that you *have* made progress. Go on…you're on a roll," George said, grinning. "It's a miracle that TMJ survived, with its insurance coverage lapsing by the mistake of an employee. It's all laid out in an article that I found. Let me get it," Chetan said before rising, leaving Zonta to stare menacingly at George.

She returned a few minutes later with a copy of the article from the *Seattle Times*.

After handing the article to George, Chetan said, "The paper posits that Turner had miraculously saved the company. Nobody knows how."

"Figuring that out may solve our riddle," George said.

"Any idea of how he did it?" Chetan asked.

"I do, and that's what I need your help with," George said before standing, beginning to pace, hands gesturing as he talked.

"What with?" she asked.

"I'll get to that, but first…you need some more background. The FAA has a public database, did you know that?" George asked rhetorically. "After scouring the database, I discovered that he owns a plane."

"Personally?"

"Not personally, but through a holding company he set up for that purpose."

"How'd you figure that out?" Chetan asked.

"He named it after his company! TMJ Aviation, LLC. Not smart on his part, as it made my research easier," George said, increasing the pace of his arm flailing about. "And the best part is that…drum roll… he set it up in September 2009. Remember our timeline? In June of that year, TMJ had this horrific accident with no insurance. A mere three months later, Turner has magically solved the crisis and is buying a plane?"

"Which means that…" Chetan began.

"Hold that thought. I haven't come to the best part. A friend of mine works at the FAA. Well, she reviewed the records in her system and told me that the plane filed flight plans on a consistent basis beginning in September immediately after being purchased. Every three months after that, the plane's been going to a different city in Europe or the Middle East. Like clockwork, leaving on the 15th day of the last month of each quarter – September, December, March, June, and so on – with only a couple of exceptions for an added flight in between the quarters. It's still going on today."

Chetan nodded, causing Zonta to nod at George, who smiled triumphantly.

"Must be an expensive plane to make it over the pond so many times," she remarked.

"That's what I thought! A Gulfstream G650ER. Roughly $60 million big ones. You know why he bought that one? It fits his travel pattern." George paused for effect. "It's got a range of about 14,000 kilometers, about 8,700 miles, enough to get you to a lot of places. Remember what I said before. He's been going abroad, like clockwork, every three months in the middle of the month starting in September of that same year."

Chetan began to say something, but George shooed her off while he sat down. "Two more points. First, guess how much business TMJ does overseas?" he asked.

"A small portion? Doesn't it mainly operate in the United States?" Chetan asked.

"Exactly. But not *mainly*, *entirely*, at least at what I've been able to see through the available records." George let the implications settle. Something was happening overseas. Who was Turner meeting with? And why always abroad?

"So, what do we do now? Is there more?" Chetan asked.

"Yes."

Chetan leaned forward, silently prompting George to continue.

"You never asked why I was in Houston."

Chetan nodded, eager to hear more.

"I was looking for a pressure point, and I found the mother lode," George said before describing the happy endings Amy Genser was apparently giving to Turner at the yoga studio.

"Hmm. I see. Sounds productive. I really don't want to know how you did it. Just tell me what you learned."

"By accessing his emails, I was able to find out that he's planning another trip."

"That's why you need my help? You want me to go with you?" Chetan asked.

"No," George said, "I can't take the risk. It could be dangerous. It's my fight, not yours." George said this even though he could use her help.

"I have no leads to follow besides Meridian and Turner. You really want me to follow-up with Proctano and the FBI at this point?" Chetan asked.

He needed her help and didn't want her to contact Proctano now. The FBI had taken over the fire investigation and rushed to blame Suzanne without looking deeper. The octopus's head had proven powerful and dangerous. Could its tentacles have manipulated the FBI?

He also thought about Naomi. She was helping her brother, the husband of a murder suspect, and risking her career by *persuading* Geoffrey to use NSA resources to capture Meridian's uncovered face at the TSA checkpoint in Oakland. Contacting the FBI could lead to an inspector general investigation.

But exposing the untrained Chetan also could be dangerous and foolhardy.

"I don't want you to do anything right now. Return to your job and let me handle it for now," he finally said.

"You need my help though. I have my own reasons for seeing this through. I'm sure you can relegate my role to limit my exposure," Chetan responded.

George rubbed his beard before conceding, "Thank you. I can use your help and will try to protect you, but please understand that I can't control all risks."

"Look, George, no offense. But I've been an underdog my whole life." Chetan looked down at her feet. She thought about telling George that she had never even been on a plane before the trip to his house in Washington, but she decided against it. "What else were you able to learn?" she asked instead.

"Not much. Turner was generally very careful in his emails. There were no detailed references to the meetings. But sometimes he'd slip in a hint. Like, I'm going to a meeting abroad – he'd never say where – to meet some people. Or *my group* is getting together."

"Oh, so there are others?" Chetan asked, half wondering if she should quit investigating this.

"Maybe or maybe not. Who knows? But it certainly sounds like that could be the case."

Chetan slurped her coffee, in part to break up the building tension in her stomach. She didn't know what to say. It was too hard to believe. The Techno House fire was part of an international plot?

"Interesting…"

"Indeed. Still want to help?" he asked.

Chetan thought again about Hotah and Trudy before responding with a "Yep."

"Good. But first I need to teach you some basic tradecraft."

"Sounds like fun."

George left a few minutes later, and they agreed to meet the next day at Fisherman's Wharf, dressed like tourists.

Chapter 30

Chetan arrived on time, 9:00 a.m. at Fisherman's Wharf. The Wharf and adjacent Pier 39 were crowded with a mixture of tourists, locals, and vendors selling fresh seafood, street food, and coffee. Families with young children were gawking at the sea lions resting on a platform below the pier with seagulls looking to eat. Others were straining for a view of Alcatraz. The cool air had a hint of salt and fish.

She looked around but didn't see George, at least at first.

A man bearing resemblance to George, but with a beard, smiled at her. *Is that George? With a beard?* The man was dressed in a pair of jeans, untucked blue polo shirt, light windbreaker, and a comfortable pair of K-Swiss white and black tennis shoes. He also carried a knapsack that looked as if it had room for purchases, like chocolate from nearby Ghirardelli Square.

Not only was he dressed to blend into the crowd, looking like a tourist in the usually chilly morning weather at the Wharf, but the beard made him look like a different person. *Why tennis shoes though, and not more fashionable boat shoes?* Chetan had also dressed warmly, wearing long white pants, slip-on casual shoes, and an untucked casual, dark blue long-sleeve shirt.

Chetan wondered why George had suggested they meet there. *What did the location have to do with tradecraft?*

The bearded man retrieved his cell phone from his pocket, making Chetan feel foolish for thinking it had been George. Her phone signaled an

165

incoming text telling her to meet him at a bench to her right. She instinctively looked at the bearded man, who winked at her, making her feel even more foolish.

The bench had two sides, one facing a fishery where people were haggling over prices of smelly fish. George sat on the right side of the bench, leaning back, his left hand and wrist taking up the left side. He seemed to be watching the action at the market. The other side of the bench faced a walkway filled with people walking in different directions, as if a pack of ants had dropped on a surface and scampered away upon landing.

Chetan began to sit next to George, thinking that he had been reserving the left side of the bench for her. Only he wasn't. Instead, he moved his head slightly from side to side without making eye contact. She understood immediately and sat on the side facing the walkway.

George held his cellphone to his ear, pretending he was talking to somebody. Head nodding and laughing, he mixed in soft instructions to Chetan. George was trying to make it real: teach Chetan basic tradecraft under as life-like conditions as possible.

First came technique about dead drops in case they were split up and had to communicate in secret. George explained that he didn't like to use chalk or chewing gum to signal the location of a drop. Such items were overused and out of place.

Instead, he preferred a homemade device. He sent Chetan a picture of an object that looked like an ordinary pebble, only it had a tacky substance, and he instructed her to locate five that he had placed somewhere on Pier 39. She had to retrieve all five pebbles and a larger faux rock hidden near the marker that provided waterproof storage for folded instructions, a thumb drive, and other small objects.

"We'll use *HeroBandana#9* as the passcode to open any files," George said, although Chetan winced at the unintended reference to Cowboy. "Surreptitiously put the five pebbles and rocks in your pockets by casually bending over to tie your shoe, pick up an object, brush something off your foot. One of them will have a message with instructions on where to meet me after you're done. Think of an excuse if somebody questions what you are doing. I planted a sixth one to demonstrate. Watch what I do, nonchalantly glancing to not give away my position."

George strolled to the location, casually bending over to tie his shoe adjacent to the pebble, retrieving the rock, which was holding an empty thumb drive. Chetan now understood why he had worn sneakers. *I wish he had told me that!* Not having shoelaces, she would have to pretend to knock something off her shoe and remember to wear sneakers in the future.

George looked at his watch, signaling for Chetan to begin. It took time for her to find the first two. As she bent over, she brushed off the toe of her shoe. Unfortunately, it took more time to locate the object, and she wound up brushing multiple times.

It didn't look natural and might have drawn attention had it been for real, but nobody would be the wiser in San Francisco. There were plenty of crazies walking around these parts. Although she finally spotted the object, she was embarrassed. Chetan looked back at George, seeking some security. But before making eye contact, she had the good sense to look away. She would have to do better.

What would she say if somebody questioned her? George had told her to come up with an excuse, but she couldn't think of anything at first. Then, an idea came to her. She would say she was testing out the area to geocache later with her nephews, finding clues to help locate objects that had been hidden by another person.

She performed progressively better in the final three. Instead of brushing off her shoes, she massaged her left foot as if in pain. The maneuver afforded her more time to find the object without panicking.

It became easier to fight the urge to look back at George. Instead, she casually looked around to see if anybody was watching. Securing the third pebble, she was ready to reconnect with George. Only this time she couldn't find him. She thought she saw a lookalike, but without the jacket and beard, peering from a storefront while browsing at the display.

George sent her a text. "Nice improvement over the first two. Please go to the bathroom inside the closest restaurant. Look for the large rock in the mulch outside to the left of the entrance. Instructions for your next task are underneath. Read, shred, and then flush the commands. Also delete any previous instructions from me in case your phone becomes compromised. Memorize all, keep nothing."

Chetan read the message again before erasing it as instructed. She looked at the store where George had been a moment before, but she didn't see him. Another message arrived. "Next time, only look if you need to and use mirrors where possible." It's a habit she would have to quickly break, she realized.

She slipped into the restaurant after finding the rock and instructions, feigned recognizing somebody at a table, and walked into the bathroom. There, she sat on a toilet and read the instructions.

The next two hours were spent trailing people while George looked on from afar, blending in so that she didn't notice him. Her primary objective: find out as much as possible while maintaining her cover – what the targets were doing, interaction with others, and background.

At first, Chetan felt like a fish out of water, heart racing, doubts infesting. How could she possibly learn all of this? What would her cover be if somebody said, "Are you following me?" or Why are you staring?"

The panic subsided. She could do this. Her cover: She was an Economics post-doc doing a study about visitors to the Wharf in the post-pandemic economy. Trailing did reveal clues. Where people shopped and what they liked revealed a treasure trove of useful information about their social status, level of education, and family life.

George ran Chetan through several other exercises until dinner time, when they relaxed and enjoyed Chinese food in San Francisco's Chinatown. There, George critiqued her work while praising the progress she had made.

After dinner, George taught Chetan some basic self-defense skills in her studio apartment, after rearranging the furniture to create additional space. The defense drills continued the next three mornings with the afternoons spent by Chetan driving George around San Francisco trailing unsuspecting vehicles.

At one point, Zonta, observing George's pretend pummeling of her master, began to intervene with a scary meow. Daggers stood tall in her stretched mouth. Chetan had to stop the drill to calm Zonta's nerves.

On the fifth day, George turned to operational details after satisfying himself that Chetan wouldn't be a liability. He had purposely not given her any information about the mission in case she hadn't progressed. But she had, and now she needed to learn about the plan.

By monitoring Turner's computer, George had discovered that the next meeting would take place in Barcelona Thursday, the following week. George couldn't learn any details about time and specific location or the identity of any other participants, including the mastermind of it all. He hoped to learn more by monitoring the meeting, but that meant one of them had to get inside – or at least close enough to unmask the participants.

George revealed the tentative plan in Chetan's apartment – after sweeping for bugs, of course. The following Monday, they would fly to Barcelona where the meeting was to take place. He even knew the exact arrival time, date, and location.

As he talked, Chetan became concerned. The money that Kangee left and her meager savings wouldn't pay for her full share of an international trip. She had already taken a sizable hit on the smaller trips to D.C. and Houston.

Antonio had agreed that she could investigate quietly on her own. He wanted Cowboy's killer prosecuted and wasn't going to be bullied by a creep he labelled "*some punk!*" He even agreed to cover her other assignments and offered to use fire department money for any modest travel expenses.

Still, she didn't dare ask the city to pay for the trip to Barcelona. The city has policies against international travel (even to Canada and Mexico) that require over-ride signatures all the way up to the mayor's office. *Antonio would never agree to that. I must decline*, she thought.

George must have noticed her despair. "If this is making you uncomfortable, I can go with my sister."

"It's not that, George. It's just that…"

"Well?"

"I don't have money for a trip like you're describing."

He laughed. "Don't worry. You're helping me free my wife. You've already risked your job and your life. Can you really turn down a free trip to Europe?"

"Thanks, George, that makes me feel a lot better," Chetan said, although she felt bad that she couldn't pay her way.

They debated and fine-tuned the plan over the next four hours. A nervous moment came when George asked to see Chetan's passport.

"Passport?" Chetan asked with growing trepidation, before remembering that she actually had obtained one. She and Celina were planning on going to Cancun, but Celina's mother had died two days before the trip.

After providing the passport to George for his examination, he told Chetan he would be leaving the next day to see Suzanne, but he would return in time for the two of them to fly together. Their cover: middle-aged man dating a younger woman. Not perfect, but not uncommon either. It seemed off to her, even possibly too memorable to others, but what did she know?

The couple took an uncomfortable walk outside, holding hands and trying to relax. The full moon and streetlights provided sufficient light for them to see. The crisp air felt refreshing, although their hands were both clammy, and the walk didn't last as long as it would have had it been for real.

Chapter 31

Chetan thought about the day she left the Rosebud Indian Reservation to attend college at South Dakota State University. She was the first in her family to leave the reservation, much less attend college and study forest management. She would be on her own in a strange environment, not knowing a single soul.

Chetan marshalled the strength to get through the first couple of days. Days turned into weeks, months, and years, culminating in a college degree.

That same inner strength would now lead her to Barcelona.

The trip would consist of two separate legs. First, from San Francisco to Frankfurt, and then from Germany to Barcelona – a total of eleven hours. Then, they would board a second plane from Frankfurt to Barcelona for two more hours.

Getting through security was a breeze, although the TSA officer looked at them first suspiciously.

"First international flight for you?" he asked, eyeing Chetan's blank passport before turning his gaze to George. "But not you, sir. You've been all over the place."

George took Chetan's hand and replied respectfully, "Yes, sir."

The officer smirked. "Newly married to a virgin flyer. Honeymoon?" he asked before waiving them through.

Although George had played the part of happy boyfriend on a romantic getaway, Chetan knew better. She looked into his eyes and knew he was thinking about Suzanne. The officer's comment bothered her. Would they be too memorable, a black man in his fifties dating a Native American woman in her thirties?

Chetan raised her concern with George when they were alone, walking to the terminal housing their gate.

He chuckled, "What's wrong with that?"

Chetan laughed but pressed on. "Wouldn't we stick out to the people we're observing?"

"Maybe," he conceded before adding, "but that's the genius of it. The best covers are often the ones that stick out, making it less likely to be a cover."

"Yeah, I guess so," Chetan deferred, still not completely convinced.

***

A cheerful slim blonde flight attendant greeted them with a plastic smile and an overpowering scent of perfume as they boarded, handing each an alcohol wipe. Chetan saw that she could walk in two directions – left into a cabin with recliner-bed seats or right into a more compact section with eight seats in a row and two aisles.

Chetan began to walk to the left, but the flight attendant's plastic smile melted into a frown after viewing her ticket. The woman pointed Chetan and George to the second aisle leading to the right and into the dense rows of seats.

Once seated, their fellow passengers began a game of whack-a-mole. One person would pop up to retrieve a book, glasses, or other pacifier from the overhead bin and then sit, providing a neighbor with his or her opportunity to repeat the drill.

***

After landing in Barcelona, the couple breezed through passport control. An hour later, they arrived at the Hotel Majestic for their supposed romantic getaway. George paying made it even more weird.

173

Any doubt she had evaporated as she gawked at the building. She had never seen anything so magnificent. This was better than the finest hotel in San Francisco where the uppity Suits stay. The one-hundred-year-old structure had three frontal sides that bounded a busy intersection in the middle of the city's Passeig de Gràcia – Barcelona's Fifth Avenue, a destination coveted by tourists from around the world.

The light beige stone structure had arching windows, each with an open balcony except on the edges of the second and third floors. There, the balconies were rounded and enclosed in glass. *Probably the more expensive rooms*, Chetan thought.

Flags hung from the third floor, and a string of lights hung over the entire façade. She imagined the hotel lit at night. A sign boldly announcing the name of the hotel stood proudly on the roofline. *The entire face must be impressive at night*, she thought.

George interrupted Chetan's ogling to remind her of the location's importance. Pricey but necessary. He had previously explained that Turner's meeting might take place in a tourist area where the participants could blend in with thousands of other travelers. Hotels also had conference rooms for business meetings, and so it was even possible that the meeting would take place in their hotel or, more likely, a nearby hotel. *Never sleep where you play*, George had learned early in his career.

The Hotel Majestic also had unmatched advantages for them. George explained that their room had access to one of the private enclosed balconies that she had seen from the outside — a perch where they could see thousands of tourists passing by or waiting outside Gaudi's famous creation near the hotel, the *Casa Batlló*. George could deploy his high-resolution camera on the balcony, obscured by heavy curtains that made it difficult for tourists on the street to see them.

Fabricating the email from Amy Genser, Turner's masseuse, to Turner had resulted in a trove of information. Turner had clicked on the GIF file containing the virus, thinking it contained Amy's self-filmed porn. Turner saw the X-rated massage, and George saw even more. He learned the location of the meeting in Barcelona, although regrettably not the specific venue. Not to worry, he assured Chetan. He had other means at his disposal.

After checking in, they spent the remainder of the day and the next day touring the city. To prepare for long days out of the room, they wore layers and comfortable walking shoes. The air provided whiffs of paella, patatas bravas, Iberian ham, and churros from a myriad of restaurants. This deliciousness mixed with scent of diesel fuel from buses and cars whizzing by along the main avenue.

People passed them in droves, a mixture of cheery tourists and locals. At one point, Chetan learned the hard way to be careful, crashing into a large man rushing the other way. George chuckled softly but then reprimanded her. Even small mistakes could draw attention, potentially making them stand out to Turner or whoever he was meeting. Turner wouldn't arrive until the next day, but others could already be there, including that monster, Meridian.

George and Chetan entered the Gothic Quarter, where the Romans settled their first settlement. It was protected by a high stone wall, portions of which are still present today.

George doubted that the meeting would take place there since it was easy to get lost in the winding, narrow streets, some only a few feet wide. While some density would help them blend in, congestion in that part of the city would become a nuisance.

Next, they walked along the Mediterranean Sea, enjoying the more spacious areas where street entertainers performed unregulated tricks. There were a few hotels and casinos that George pointed out, as well as restaurants that Turner's group could be using. After lunch, they ventured uptown towards their hotel, but this time taking another busy boulevard, La Rambla.

George pushed on, walking past the hotel towards the less crowded areas until both of their feet were sore. They returned to the hotel for drinks atop the open rooftop bar.

Chetan went to the bathroom, leaving George alone for a few minutes. The bar had a string of decorative lights on each side. From the balcony, George noticed the bright lights illuminating Passeig de Gràcia. Couples were walking, holding hands, some kissing in the soft warm night.

George thought about Suzanne in jail. How he wished she was here. A tear came to his eye as Chetan returned from the bathroom. She put a hand on his shoulder, trying to comfort him as best she could.

On the second day, George led her on an exploration of other parts of the city. When they returned that evening to their hotel, each felt that in the limited time there they had developed a sense of the city's layout and its different neighborhoods. They also had taken the Barcelona subway a couple of times and learned about more mundane matters, such as how to use the designated lanes to quickly find a taxicab. The next two days would be more intense, with the stakes much higher.

Chapter 32

George's hack of Turner's computer revealed that the riches-to-rags mystery man was taking his own private plane into El Prat's private aviation terminal, arriving at 1:00 p.m. on Thursday. It was showtime. George and Chetan had carefully rehearsed the next part, which was critical to their success.

The plan was for Chetan to go to the airport before Turner's arrival. George had been coy about how Chetan would get there, but that morning at the hotel, George told Chetan, "I arranged for you to drive a red Fiat sedan to the airport. It's parked a few blocks away from here. You'll need to walk there, pick up the car, and drive it to the airport in time to arrive at 12:00 as planned."

"No rental car?"

"Correct," George said coyly, without an explanation.

"How did it get there?"

"Don't worry about that, Chetan. All you need to know is that it's there ready for you to take it," George replied, handing Chetan the keys.

Chetan knew not to ask more questions. George had resources, and she probably was better off not knowing more.

Chetan sat in the lounge of El Prat's Corporate Aviation Terminal, having arrived at 12:00, and watched the charter planes arrive and depart. It was busier than she expected, not that she had any comparative baseline from which to judge. Maybe it only seemed that way because the terminal's facilities were squished into one smaller area, unlike the larger commercial terminals in Frankfurt and the U.S. cities.

Still, she managed to secure her own personal space by a large glass window that offered a clear view of the runway. Chetan carefully followed George's instructions, snapping pictures of the arriving airplanes and passengers walking from their planes with their bags to the entrance of the terminal.

George had asked to take the highest resolution photos possible of Turner, any travel companions, and his plane. This would enable later scrutiny including through a database. Chetan made sure to take pictures of pigeons and other wildlife, storing these on a separate memory card that already contained several similar photos of what she saw outside. The camera provided by George had dual memory card slots and it was easy to flip back and forth. Chetan would be at the airport for a while, as she had arrived one hour before the scheduled landing of Turner's plane.

Fifteen minutes into snapping photos, a short plump woman approached, wearing a navy sport coat with a yellow shield sewn above her left breast. The woman said in a language Chetan didn't recognize, "Ma'am, I must ask you what you are doing. You can't take photos."

Chetan responded, "Habla usted Inglés?"

"I thought so," the woman said before adding, "American? You're in Catalan country, remember that."

Chetan noticed she had a lapel pin displaying a flag she didn't recognize but that had been one of the four hanging from her hotel. She would research what it meant later at the hotel, not wanting to show her ignorance.

Chetan also sensed an underlying tension in the woman that she didn't quite understand, but she wisely shifted to her first question. Speaking more formally than she liked, Chetan said, "I work for a company that's putting together a proposal. You have a pigeon problem here. Did you know that?"

"Huh? I don't see any," the woman barked, looking around the terminal.

"Not in here. Out there. See, here," Chetan said, showing her the photos on the camera of pigeons and other birds. "Know what happens when there are too many pigeons or other birds out there?"

The woman looked at Chetan, not sure what to say until she shrugged, giving Chetan the needed confidence to continue.

"Birds can fly into the engines, causing an airplane to crash. It's happened before. In 1988, pigeons took out both engines of Ethiopian Airlines Flight 605 during takeoff. The plane crashed, killing thirty-five people! And then in 1994, ten people died when lapwings took out a Dassault Falcon 20. And the U.S. Air Force lost a Boeing AWACS aircraft, killing twenty-four people. And, at this very same airport in 2004, a 737 operated by KLM crashed on landing. And…"

The woman held up her hand. "Enough, enough. Please! I get it. You're giving me a headache. Aye. Just tell me, why are you here though taking pictures?"

"Yes, of course. I was going to get to that. You see, I work for a company that helps airports reduce their bird problems." Chetan handed her a card that said, *Bird Control, S.L* with her name listed as *Tracy Lamano*.

Chetan explained further while the airport official looked at the card.

"We're trying to expand into the Iberian market. I'm based in the U.S. My boss sent me here to survey the runway to see if you need the service."

The guard stood there, not sure what to make of this business-like American.

Chetan continued, "Here, let me show you my company." She pulled up the website of the company on her iPhone. "See here? It talks about our services. We take away some of their food sources, water, cover. We try to repel the birds with chemicals or devices that make noise. We plant objects like fake dead animals to scare the birds away. We bring in trained falcons or dogs. Sometimes we shoot them or…"

"Enough already! I have work to do. Just do what you need to do and leave."

"I'll be out of your way in a couple of hours."

"Sure, but don't cause any trouble. We get a lot of celebrities and businesspeople off those planes. I want to make sure that you're not with the tabloids. I'll be watching you," the woman said before walking away.

Chetan breathed a sigh of relief before continuing her work.

***

George didn't look like himself. He arrived at the airport by taxi at 12:30 p.m., and he was wearing a grey one-piece maintenance outfit, like one he noticed being used when he researched the airport. He had also applied a latex bald cap in a color matching his skin, installed blue contact lenses, and utilized Spirit gum to affix a black beard and matching bushy mustache.

George kept track of the different outfits he used. After all, it would be comically bad if his outfit resembled the one that he had used tailing Turner in Houston several days ago.

George watched Chetan from a distance. After catching her eye, he left for the parking lot. She seemed safe. He left, knowing his presence could cause an issue, and his role being elsewhere anyway.

He entered the parking area, but not before donning his name badge, Nicolau Bonet. The pretend maintenance worker held a litter picker upper and trash bag. In the online picture of an actual maintenance worker, he had noticed the type of badge used and litter removal tool and had successfully managed to emulate the badge and procure the same tool.

He began picking up trash, looking at the cars parked. Nobody questioned his presence.

George glanced at his watch, 1:00 p.m., and sent a text to Chetan. "Enough birds?"

Five seconds later came the response. "Not yet."

"LMK when threshold reached."

"Will do."

They repeated the drill twenty minutes later. Same response. The flight must be late, George figured.

George felt moisture building under his latex cap and beard. He couldn't stay there much longer.

After another hour and a half had gone by, George had cleaned the entire parking lot. He couldn't stay there forever. Remarkably, nobody had questioned what he was doing, but George began to think the worst. *Maybe the group changed the date or location.* He had searched Turner's server before he left and hadn't discovered any change. Still, Turner could have discovered the Trojan virus.

Presently, a silver Mercedes arrived and parked near his position. George looked at the driver, with his unmistakable platinum hair and pale face, and let loose an inward groan. *It was real, now!*

He had been on many operations before, first with the military and then while at the NSA. Operations always made him nervous. *Nerves are a good sign. They make you careful.* But this time, the stakes were larger than ever.

It made sense that Meridian had arrived in advance, to prepare for the meeting. It also suggested that the meeting would be with a larger group, requiring more complicated arrangements.

Meridian emerged from the car and glanced at George, who quickly resumed his litter removal operation, before walking towards the terminal.

George could feel Meridian's eyes bore into him, but he made sure to keep his head down and eyes on his work. *Good thing he had been dressed in a maintenance outfit and disguise.*

181

Out of the corner of his eye, George noticed the man approaching. George had to resist the urge to look up or tremble. Fortunately, his Spanish was passable, but he wouldn't pass for a native, not knowing any Catalan.

It looked like Meridian was about to speak until he received a call, distracting him. He began to walk towards the terminal.

George breathed easier and texted Chetan. "Have enough for proposal?"

"Yep," Chetan responded before adding, "Customer two hours late, but entering soon."

"Good. Purchaser on his way."

George put away his phone and moved towards the Mercedes. Once there, he fumbled some trash near the rear of the car, and while picking it up, he attached a covert GPS tracker to a piece of metal on the undercarriage. The magnet in the tracker held it in place.

Satisfied, George resumed his trash removal, and he waited for Meridian to return with Turner from the terminal.

***

Chetan received a text from George that said, "Go to the office and write proposal." It had been getting boring, watching and taking pictures. The adrenaline of her first real assignment wore off quickly.

She knew from George's text they were successful. Her reply was a simple thumbs up emoji.

Chetan disassembled her camera equipment, packed up her bag, and left, nodding at the security guard as she left. The woman looked glum but waved, no doubt relieved at seeing Chetan leave.

She drove the red Fiat, trailing the silver Mercedes carrying Turner and his driver. George had told her it wasn't important to always see the car. Her role was simply to stay in the vicinity, while following using the GPS tracker.

***

George returned to the hotel to remove his maintenance attire, shave, and transform into his next person. That began with the outfit: a flat herringbone tweed cap, checkered polo shirt, and vest. He filled a backpack with additional provisions, including a change of clothes in case it was needed. Chetan made a few simple adjustments to what she was wearing while in the car. They were now English tourists.

The tracker application on George's iPhone indicated that the Mercedes had turned onto La Rambla, a development that seemed to rule out the harbor district but little else. He hailed a taxicab.

About twenty minutes after entering the cab, George caught a glimpse of Chetan's car driving on the opposite side of the road, trailing the Mercedes from a comfortable distance. Both cars were going up La Rambla in a northwest direction. George's taxicab drove the opposite direction from the northwest, traveling southeast down La Rambla.

"Oops! I think we're going the wrong way, and I'm late for my appointment. Can you do a U-turn as quickly as possible?" George asked his driver.

"In this traffic?"

George dug into his wallet and retrieved a 100 Euro bill. Showing it to the driver he said, "Yes, please, but be quick! I'm late."

The big bill unleashed the inner-Formula One driver from his drab taxi-driver veneer. He made a hairpin turn and started dangerously weaving in and out of traffic. George hoped it wouldn't cause their car to stand out, but he had little choice. He couldn't leave Chetan alone, even if she was trailing Turner. Unfortunately, he could no longer see Turner's Mercedes or Chetan's Fiat.

***

Chetan's heart thumped as the Mercedes turned onto La Rambla. It was getting real, and she had regrets – but only for a millisecond. *Calm down!*

It's too late to back out now. She felt bad for George and Suzanne and liked George, but she wasn't doing this for them.

The uphill portions of the road enabled her to verify what the tracker indicated – that the Mercedes had continued driving up the famous street. Chetan occasionally glanced at the street performers, food vendors, and colorful pedestrians packed in the promenade separating the north from the south sections of the road. She recalled that a terrorist drove a van onto the same median in 2017, killing 14 people.

Chetan turned her attention to the Mercedes, a couple of blocks ahead. Seeing Meridian driving his pseudo-boss, Turner, in a foreign country made her stomach growl. The target slowed. The car then made a right turn onto Carrer de Santa Anna, followed in close succession by a second right turn onto Carrer de la Canuda. A few minutes later, Chetan made the same two turns, hoping that George would follow soon in his taxicab.

The traffic obscured any view of the Mercedes, although her tracker confirmed the car had not turned yet. A moment later, the car slowed. Her nerves fired alarms as the car turned onto Avinguda del Portal de l'Àngel. Almost immediately after making the turn, the car stopped, with the tracker showing the same location as before. The Mercedes either disappeared or was parked out of view. Panic ensued.

Should I pass? And where is George's taxi?

She passed Avinguda del Portal de l'Àngel, continuing on Carrer de la Canuda, fearing it would be too obvious to turn onto the same narrow street with its dearth of vehicles. She decided instead to turn onto the next street.

Turner must have parked his car, she thought.

She would have to find him and follow him on foot, where she would be more exposed. He could be going straight to the meeting or to his hotel. Either way, she couldn't lose him. Otherwise, the entire mission would be a failure.

She parked her car in a public garage and texted George. "Where are you? He stopped at Avinguda del Portal de l'Àngel. Now on foot."

A minute went by with no response.

Fuck! I must locate Turner, she told herself while frantically looking around, carefully approaching Avinguda del Portal de l'Àngel.

Chetan tried to walk casually. *Relax. Look natural.*

Chetan looked around but couldn't see Turner or Meridian. They seemed to have disappeared. *What is going on?*

Chetan noticed the black decorative posts preventing vehicles from the area where she now stood from entering the true heart of the Gothic Quarter – the shopping, mingling, tourist traps, and an eclectic mixture of Gaudi's pearls. The look and feel of the ancient dark and middle-ages to 19th century rebuilding, all punctuated by masters such as Gaudi, Picasso, and Miró.

Chetan felt compelled to enter this wonderland but resisted, and instead, she texted George again. "Target is gone. Where are you?"

Chapter 33

George received Chetan's first text alerting him that Turner's car had stopped moving. It sounded like she was following the seasoned killer – Meridian – and Turner on foot. That *definitely* wasn't part of the plan. He had wanted to protect Chetan and not put her in a position where she could be recognized. Meridian had already spotted her once and could again, despite Chetan's disguise and being halfway around the world.

He also didn't want to send her back to the hotel. He would need her soon, for the next part. While thinking about how to respond, George received Chetan's second text explaining that she had lost the trail. *Great! Just Great!*

George texted Chetan. "Stand down. Go inside a store and stay out of sight for now." Hopefully, she would listen, giving him time to think.

With Chetan seemingly pacified, he decided to enter the Gothic Quarter, speculating that Turner and Meridian had gone there. Since they had parked their car and not a lot of time had elapsed, they couldn't have gotten very far. The area felt like a maze. People were packed into the area like sardines, even more so than yesterday.

He looked around but couldn't see any sign of Turner, Meridian, or anybody else that looked suspicious. *Damn!*

He saw only the sights and sounds of the area, but there was no trail to continue. The streets were made of grey stone, some areas restored with different shades for replacement pieces, giving the roads a mismatched look. People were walking everywhere – in the middle of the wider streets and in and out the wide selection of stores, bars, gelato shops, bodegas, and coffee bars. Some of the streets and alleys were not more than a few feet wide, while others had space for roller skaters, cyclists, and street performers. Black, waist-high decorative bollards separated the pedestrian-only areas from vehicle traffic.

Staying in the Gothic Quarter posed a number of risks to the meeting participants. They would all be unfamiliar and have difficulty navigating the maze of narrow streets, some only a few feet wide. Even worse, the crowds would be a nuisance, making it hard to conduct any counter-surveillance, and there may have been reluctance to be situated close to a lot of people so soon after the pandemic. George had the same concern, although he still had confidence that his vaccine would protect him from any serious infection. Chetan had also assured him that she had been fully vaccinated.

Of course, the same disadvantages to having a meeting in the Gothic Quarter also made the location fitting. It is hard to pursue a rat through maze under the best circumstances. It is even more difficult with thousands of other rats filling the maze. George's stomach ached thinking of two especially dangerous rats turning on their pursuers.

Chapter 34

Meridian parked the Mercedes on the first level in a garage near the Gothic Quarter, close to the vehicle barriers. Since Turner's flight landed two hours late, they had to hustle to make the meeting on time. Meridian had left the hotel after making the arrangements to retrieve Turner, and the Benefactor would blame him if the meeting couldn't start on time.

He knew not to disappoint the Benefactor.

By the time they had arrived at their hotel, Turner had only twenty minutes to prepare for the meeting. He barely glanced at the hotel's Art Deco features. Had he paid attention, he would have noticed the hollowed-out middle of the hotel in the shape of an octagon, allowing visitors to see all five floors from the lobby. Each floor held a unique pastel color, and a white staircase could be seen weaving through it all.

Of course, Turner wasn't interested in any of that. He didn't have time to focus on such mundane matters.

Meridian took Turner's luggage to his room while Turner washed and changed into more formal clothes for the meeting. It was Turner who noticed the mistake first – he had left his carry-on briefcase in the car. Although he shared the blame, he yelled at Meridian as one would reprimand a child, causing Meridian to dream of employing his surgical tools. After all, it had been Turner who had forgotten to take *his* briefcase.

While Meridian walked back to the car, Turner took the elevator from the fifth floor down to the second floor. He interrupted a waiter as he was serving one of tables, demanding that he direct Turner to the meeting room. The waiter paused and scowled at Turner before pointing towards a hallway on the left-hand side of the room.

***

Turner knocked before entering the room. Angel, a lanky woman dressed conservatively in a navy suit and white shirt, opened the door, and immediately administered the retinal scan test. She handled administrative matters for the Oilmen, but she had obviously been pressed into double duty because Meridian was retrieving Turner's forgotten luggage.

Turner dressed Texas style, with his brown Stetson hat. A splintered toothpick hung from his mouth – a habit he had formed when he quit smoking years ago. The large man with hands strong enough to crush walnuts surveyed the attendees, looking for a place to sit at the oval, mahogany table.

The impeccably dressed suck-up, Ming Rong Zhang (also known as Mr. Perfect to Turner), sat right next to the conference room speaker on side of the table closest to Turner. *As if the Benefactor could see who was sitting closest! I bet he sat in the first row at school.* Turner thought that Ming had whispered something into the speaker phone, but he couldn't be sure.

The European representative, a Norwegian man with thinning blond hair and a pale completion, sat next to Ming. Noah Rosdahl, outwardly nice but a bit pompous, didn't bother Turner like the rest of the lot. He greeted Turner with a friendly smile and wave.

Cristiano Sousa, the Brazilian South American representative, glared at Turner from his position sitting next to the speaker on the far side of the table. Although Sousa joined the Oilmen in 2014, five years after Turner, the Benefactor seemed more deferential to the Brazilian than the other members. *Did that have anything to do with Sousa's accountant?* He had heard rumors. Couldn't be, he realized.

The short plump man with bronze skin, dark eyes, and deep eye sockets spit a brownish liquid into a spittoon as he observed Turner.

I'd rather sit next to my ex-wife than him, Turner thought to himself, knowing that the Benefactor would take out any anger on somebody sitting next to Sousa rather than Sousa himself. A glass of water in front of the chair next to Sousa signaled that the weak-bladdered tall Nigerian had occupied that seat, giving Turner a better option.

He whispered hello to Turner as he entered the room, damp hands touching Turner's exposed skin on his right arm. *Ugh! Why does he drink all that water if it just sends him to the bathroom?*

Turner sat next to the clean-cut Norwegian as the Benefactor's non-descript, obscured voice boomed, "Ah! Nice of you to join us! Don't be late again."

How did he know I had just arrived? Turner thought as Mr. Perfect smiled at him. *That prick must have whispered something to his master.*

"Now that we're all *finally* here, we can begin. We have a lot to discuss. Let's get right to the outlook report."

One by one, each person provided a report, updating the participants about the energy sector, fossil fuels, and then the dreaded renewals. CO_2 emissions had declined, a byproduct of less travel during the pandemic, and this was a development nobody wanted as it meant less demand for fossil fuels. The group feared environmental groups seizing the opportunity to keep emissions at a lower level.

The six representatives of the Oilmen nodded in agreement – not that they had a choice. Although the Benefactor couldn't see the participants, somebody could earn points by reporting a non-compliant member. Fear mongering kept participants in line. *Unus pro omnibus, omnes pro uno. One for all, all for one*, a phrase the Benefactor had drilled into each member from the start.

When it was Turner's time to speak, the Benefactor interrupted him immediately. "Any chance of Suzanne Harper being exonerated?"

"I…wouldn't expect so," Turner waffled.

"Well, what is it? Don't hedge with me. Tell me what you know!"

"The evidence is strong against her. Linking the program to her computer was a stroke of genius. The judge apparently also believes she's guilty. Suzanne's been denied bail, ostensibly because she's a flight risk. But I doubt the judge would have denied bail if he thought the case was weak," Turner replied.

"Good. And the husband, George?" asked the Benefactor.

Turner shifted uncomfortably in his seat. Should he mention Chetan spotting Meridian in Houston? The Benefactor had asked about George but not Chetan. However, he also knew that Meridian had discovered that George had flown to Oakland twice to meet with Chetan and that they were probably working together.

Hoping to pivot the discussion to Chetan so that he could provide a more complete response, Turner replied, "He's looking into the case, as you might imagine he would, given his background. Meridian's trying to keep tabs on him. We also know that he's working with Maka."

"The fire inspector?"

"Yes…well…she's more than that. She's the chief investigator reporting directly to the fire marshal. She may be the worst threat," Turner said.

"How so?" asked the Benefactor.

"Meridian spotted her in Houston, watching him – and me."

"And you're letting me know this *now*? You could have reached out using the chat room," the Benefactor said, referring to an online chat room that was checked every day after 9:00 p.m. Access to the forum requires a username and password to a website reserved ostensibly for Chess

Grandmasters – except that unlike other similar websites, this site was closed to anybody but the Oilmen.

"I...thought...it could wait for our meeting today."

Sousa, Ming, and the other members of the Oilmen tried unsuccessfully to suppress grins.

"And my guy, Meridian, he agreed to that?" asked the Benefactor.

Turner squirmed in his seat. "Yes, it was only a few weeks ago."

"What!? *Only* a few weeks ago? Are you fucking serious? The two of you are imbeciles! Why did I assign Meridian to help you if this is what I get? And you, a few weeks is a lifetime! And maybe even longer in your case."

Turner gulped before pivoting. "I think we need to eliminate both of them."

"You *think*? I don't pay you to *think*! *I'll* tell *you* when it gets to that point. If George is eliminated, then it'll tip off his friends within the government, including that sister of his. It could also force Proctano to reopen the case. He'd lose any cover he has. How did the inspector get involved again? I thought the case was closed."

"It was, but she somehow got connected to George. They've been talking," Turner said.

"Hmm. And my guy, Meridian, I assume he's monitoring that?" the Benefactor asked.

Turner thought about Meridian killing Cowboy. It appears as if the Benefactor didn't know about Meridian's slaughter. Although that would be more a problem for Meridian than Turner, Turner realized that revealing the plot now would send the Benefactor into an apoplectic fit. And nobody would be safe if that happened.

"She's getting closer though. That's why I'm concerned."

"Concern? Didn't we just discuss that? Drop the issue, or you'll get dropped. Do I need to go over that again?" the Benefactor screamed the rhetorical question into his microphone.

"No...thank you... I understand," Turner said softly.

It was then that the Benefactor introduced a new topic. Nobody could have imagined what the Benefactor would say – a rarity for those gathered, who had, by this time, thought they had heard it all. The timetable was being accelerated, with the *coup de grâce* to happen soon. Details to follow...

Chapter 35

Chetan didn't know how to react to George's text. *Stand down?* George must have a good reason, she knew.

Chetan trusted George, but this was her investigation as much as his. She would continue and had an idea.

She would follow the tracker to where she lost the Mercedes. Turner probably didn't know that he was being followed, she surmised, otherwise he would've directed Meridian to continue driving. He must have parked near where Chetan had parked. *Could I discover a clue looking into the Mercedes, like a note left on the dashboard or seat?*

She began walking towards the intersection of Avinguda del Portal de l'Àngel and Carrer de la Canuda, scanning every direction as she walked. A parking garage emerged in the distance – and then it hit her. The garage had two entrances, the one where she entered and parked on Level 2, where the grade had been higher, and the one where the Mercedes must have entered on Level 1.

She entered Level 1 and walked up an incline before spotting Turner's silver Mercedes. A light fixture hung above the Mercedes, illuminating it.

Chetan looked around. Trash, including cigarette butts, were visible, and some light bulbs flickered or were completely broken. The air smelled stale and dank. Only a few empty spaces remained, and a couple of cars had gathered dust, indicating they'd been there for a while. Two people speaking in a language that she didn't recognize walked up the ramp to Level 2.

When the two other people were out of range, Chetan used her phone to snap a picture of the car before gingerly approaching. Once in position, she peered into the car, hoping to get a glimpse of a receipt, paper, or note. A briefcase was nestled in between the back and the driver's seat. A Post-it Note hung from the middle of the dashboard, but she couldn't see the contents from her vantage point.

She strained her eyes, hoping to be able to read it, but the writing wasn't clear enough for her to make out. The note seemed important, and it made sense that the name of the hotel or another telltale sign would be affixed to the dashboard, but the words evaded her. Disappointed, she walked around the car looking for a better angle. Nothing.

Desperate and not wanting to let the potential clue remain undetectable, she began to size up a picture of the note using her phone when she heard a voice, distant, but discernably English. It was a lone voice, perhaps speaking into a phone. After snapping a picture, Chetan wheeled around, footsteps sounding nearby.

What she saw made her want to jump over the railing onto the level below. *Did he see me? If I jump, he'll see that for sure, and I'll be trapped. Meridian will kill me, like David Grigorio and his fiancée, Cindy.*

She cursed inwardly and resisted the urge to panic. Chetan quickly minimized herself by collapsing onto the dirty ground in between the Mercedes and an old boxy red car with faded paint. She crawled under the red car closer to the side opposite the Mercedes. Facing the ground, she put her hands under her torso, minimizing her body further. The confined space – trapped under a car – made her think of Hotah, causing her spirits to plummet even further.

Meridian's footsteps remained steady. A good sign. Chetan heard him fiddling with the trunk latch, which then opened and quickly closed with a "Goddammit," mumbled under Meridian's breath.

Meridian took a few steps towards the back seat. Chetan held her breath, even as she realized the futility of it.

Instead of Meridian looking under the car, Chetan heard the back door open. A briefcase had been placed on the ground by Meridian's feet. *He'll take the briefcase and leave! Phew!*

But Chetan's celebration proved premature. Meridian dropped his keys! The key chain had been dropped so close to the car that one of the keys lay underneath the car, a foot away from Chetan's head. *He's going to bend down and see me for sure*, she thought.

She saw his hand fumble to retrieve the keys and she thought of trying to flee, but she was cornered like a caged animal.

Just then, she heard other footsteps approaching. Suddenly, the image of Sungmanito, the Lakota Wolf Spirit of war, came to mind. Before she could figure out her vision, she heard a woman's voice.

"Hola," it said.

Meridian grunted hello while casually picking up his keys.

The other footsteps continued, sounding more distant until they disappeared deeper into the garage.

Chetan heard him chide himself for being clumsy.

Then, at the worst possible moment, with Meridian still nearby, Chetan's phone rang.

Fortunately, she had left it on vibrate, and she pressed her body against it, hoping to stifle any noise. But did she dampen the noise enough? Maybe not, she feared when Meridian seemed to stop any movement.

Chetan prepared to shuffle out from under the car to defend herself. Maybe she could kick Meridian in the balls and escape.

As soon as the threat materialized, it ended. A higher power was protecting her for sure. Meridian closed the trunk and walked away carrying the briefcase, pushing his key fob and locking the trunk.

She waited under the car until she thought the danger had receded. *Is he tricking me though? Maybe he's waiting for me to emerge.*

But it wasn't a trick; she could see his backside and the briefcase fade into the distance.

With the emergency evaporated, she turned her cell phone from vibration to silent mode and texted George.

"Meridian spotted by garage near Avinguda del Portal de l'Àngel and Carrer de la Canuda. Following on foot. Text, no calls."

"OK," George quickly responded. "Be careful. Try to find out where he's going."

"Duh!. What else would I do?"

Fifteen minutes later, after following Meridian from what she had hoped to be a safe distance, she saw the man enter the Hotel Barcelona Catedral. The exterior of the hotel was unlike anything she had seen in the San Francisco area. The hotel's pink stone exterior had wrought iron balconies, seemingly held up by gargoyle statutes. Interesting figurines wearing formal wear stood on the balconies, a funky nod to the new and old.

She texted George the good news. She had discovered where they were staying.

George texted back. "Great work. I think I know where that is. Walk towards the Barcelona Catedral but do not look back at the hotel. I'll find a nearby café for us to meet. Follow my lead if you see me."

***

George, holding his backpack, turned from his position deep inside the Gothic Quarter to walk towards the hotel and look for a café or other shelter suitable for scouting the hotel. The 15th century cathedral came into view across from a public square.

Closer to the hotel, he found a restaurant that offered outdoor seating with a view of the cathedral to the right and the hotel entrance to the left.

It wasn't perfect, as the view of the hotel was blocked by densely packed planters, but they would make it work.

A nearby street sign pointed to different monuments and streets in the area. One of the signs provided George with a strange sense of encouragement: "Spain: A Real Dictatorship." He knew from a previous trip about the people of Catalonia and their quest to remain free from the efforts of Franco's fascist government a few generations ago.

George sat at an outside table, placing his backpack beneath it, positioning himself in view of the hotel's door. He ordered two espressos, water, a plate of jamón serrano, and a serving of patatas bravas. Chetan joined him a few minutes later.

They discussed the plan. George would take touristy pictures of Chetan with the hotel entrance in the background while surreptitiously scanning the area. Posing as tourists wouldn't be a problem, but they needed to strain for a clear view without blowing their cover.

George smiled at Chetan as she sat with her back towards the hotel's entrance. After the waiter delivered the food and drink, they drank and ate while George watched the hotel door from his position. George also used his phone to locate a schematic layout of the inside. They studied it while they waited.

Only a few people entered or left the hotel over the next two hours, mostly people with families or other obvious tourists, no single men or women who looked like they were there for a business meeting.

To be sure, George photographed the more likely candidates. But after looking through the pictures, he shook his head in disgust.

"Something wrong?" Chetan asked.

"I would've thought they'd have left the hotel. That they'd go someplace, not meet where they're staying," George explained.

"Jet lag?"

"He flew on a private jet. They're posh. Besides, people traveling for business usually don't come here to sleep off their jet lag, at least not right away. Sleeping when you arrive is counterproductive. It's better to get on local time," he said.

"What do you think is going on then?" she asked.

"I don't know. But they should have come out by now, or we should have seen others enter. Unless…"

"Unless he flew in the day of the meeting, or the others were already there waiting," Chetan said completing George's thought.

"You might be onto something. Time for Plan B. Can you order me a shot of whiskey?" he asked.

***

George took his backpack with him to the bathroom of the restaurant. There, he removed his wool cap, checkered shirt, and vest, transforming himself into a proud Ghanaian. His brown shirt had a bright yellow and orange collar with frayed decorative material running down from the neck of the shirt to his midline. A green, red, and yellow stole hung around his neck like a scarf. His pants were black, and he wore a traditional cropped black hat with gold trim. He topped off his attire by splashing cheap cologne over his clothes and body.

Chetan, wearing a simple blue floral dress, smiled at him when he returned, receiving the backpack from George.

"How do I look?" George asked with a straight face.

"Traditional," Chetan responded, handing him the shot the waiter had delivered.

George swished the shot around in his mouth, dribbled some of it down his cheeks, and drank the rest before saying, "Good. I packed the clothes and your flower in the bag for you. We discussed this possibility. We're on to Plan B. On my signal, as we planned. Questions?"

Chetan responded nervously, "No, not at all. Good luck."

She thought about what lay ahead. It made her stomach turn. Her experiences in fighting fires and investigating arson cases proved she could handle stressful and dangerous situations. Heck, she had even rescued her entire family, except for poor Hotah, from a burning car. Still, she had never done anything like this.

***

George walked out of the restaurant and entered the hotel's lobby a couple of minutes later. All five of the hotel's magnificent levels were visible from his position on the bottom floor. Looking up, George felt he was trapped in a kaleidoscope with all levels hollowed out in the octagon center.

But his attention immediately turned to the floor above, which he presumed to contain the check-in area, restaurant, and, hopefully, the meeting rooms. George slowly walked up the staircase, looking around at the Art Deco-styled second floor like a tourist would. Black and burgundy walls painted with a glossy finish, a brightly lit white tray ceiling, and an artistic chandelier in the shape of an open umbrella with individual lights in lieu of metal points provided a funky, decorative look.

A waiter working the tables near the hotel bar asked if he could help, suspiciously eyeing the drunk African gentleman. One table contained used dishes, silverware, and mugs but no occupants. A second table had been occupied by a young American couple holding hands across the table, the wife or fiancée admiring a sparkling ring on her left ring finger.

George slurred to the waiter in a practiced Ghanaian accent, honed from years of military attaché service.

"I'm *heeere* to look *arooound*, mun. What a gooooorgeous hotel this is."

"Sir, you can't just look around. This is a private establishment."

"Private? What, because I'm an African? *Yoou* don't like Africans?" George raised his voice as he spoke.

"Sir, please calm down. You know what I meant. Do you have a room?"

"*Nooooo*, mun," George answered with a deep haughty laugh, looking around the floor. "Do *yooou* have one?"

"Sir, I'm going to have to ask you to leave then."

"*Leaave*, what about all of them?" George asked, panning around at a growing group of people gawking at the scene. "Yoooou haven't even asked me *whyyy* I want to look around, mun. My company is planning a retreaat! *Shoooow* me your meeting rooms, like you do with your *other* guests, mun."

"Okay, sir. Just calm down." The bartender nodded at the waiter, which, to George, meant he would get his way.

"Right, this way, sir!" the waiter said, with emphasis on the word *sir* as if mocking George. "We have three rooms that your *company* could use."

The first room, vacant at the time, looked like it could only hold a meeting of about ten people.

George barked loudly, "*Tooo* small, mun!"

The second room was occupied.

"I can't take you in there, there's a meeting going on."

White curtains were drawn for privacy, but a gap in between allowed George a peek at some of the occupants. People sat upright at a table; the mood seemed tense. George could only see the faces of two people sitting around a brown, oval mahogany table. He saw the backs of two other people. He didn't recognize anybody and couldn't see if anybody else was in the room.

The third room was vacant. George briefly looked inside. *Maybe they're not at the hotel*. There was something about the second room that made him pause.

The waiter turned to George and began to say goodbye, before abruptly turning around, hurrying back to his station.

George followed the waiter and began to shout, "Hey, youuu, mun. I want to go inside. Now!"

The waiter either didn't hear him or ignored him, not bothering to turn back. George followed, shouting louder as they returned to the lounge area.

"Hey! I want to seeee the roooom. Let meee look inside, mun!"

The bartender rushed over from behind the bar and confronted George, with the waiter standing at his side.

"Sir, please keep your voice down. There's a meeting going on in that room. You can't go inside."

"But I need to seeeee it. Why can't you open the doooor, mun, and let me seeeee?"

"I'm afraid that's not possible. Call back tomorrow morning and make an appointment with Marcella Bonella. She'll take you."

"Nooo. That will not work. I will not be heeere, mun, and my boss is going to be upset. Let meee just see." George began walking towards the room.

"Stop!" the bartender yelled after him.

Only George wouldn't listen. He did slow down though, not wanting to cause an issue close to the room.

The bartender grabbed his right arm from behind, and the waiter followed his lead, grabbing his left arm.

George complied as they escorted him out of the hotel, all the way protesting, "But I just want to seeee the room!"

Once outside, he continued to resist as a small crowd began to gather. The hotel employees continued to hold George as he continued his threat to return to the hotel. As the crowd looked on, George caught Chetan's eye and gave her a slight nod meant only for her to understand.

Chapter 36

Chetan collected her thoughts. Before leaving the restaurant, she had deployed George's bag of tricks in the bathroom, emerging as a new woman. The basics were black pants and a white button-down shirt.

The next object was a little out there, but George had convinced her of its necessity. A disgusting, large black mole with three strands of black hair hanging from the middle to be affixed to her right cheek with glue.

Mole, nice to meet you. Oops, don't say mole... George had said, laughing as he used his best Austin Powers impersonation when Chetan had practiced wearing it at the hotel.

It reminded Chetan of her mother once sewing a button on Chetan's blouse in a hurry, forgetting to clip the end of the thread. George had explained that the mole would draw attention away from other features of her face.

Best of all had been the grand prize that George had already affixed to the shirt pocket above her right breast: a long-stem daisy with a yellow bulb and white petals. A dark brown wig topped off the ensemble. Chetan tied her ponytail high and tight to her head, covering it with the wig.

Chetan used George's distraction to slip into the hotel entrance behind the crowd that had gathered to witness the spectacle of the drunken Ghanaian being thrown out of a hotel. She knew the location of the meeting rooms by studying the layout while at the restaurant with George. She also understood that she didn't have a lot of time.

Once on the second floor, she located the same bar that George had been to moments before. With the bartender and waiter occupied outside with George, she calmly filled eight glasses with water before placing them on a small brown circular waitress tray. It took a few precious minutes, and she worried the entire time that the bartender and waiter would return. *Would they throw me out of the hotel like George? Or worse?*

But they didn't return, at least not until Chetan had left the bar area and walked towards the meeting rooms. After locating the only occupied meeting room, she pressed a button in her pocket, activating a tiny video camera hidden inside the daisy's yellow bulb, and knocked, at first tentatively, afraid of the looming danger, but then louder after reminding herself of her many other obstacles that she'd already overcome.

Meridian, who moments before had handed Turner his briefcase, cracked the door open and beckoned the waitress to enter with the water. Seeing him up close for the second time that afternoon made Chetan want to run.

Luckily, Meridian couldn't stand to look at her. The mole worked as intended, drawing his gaze, causing even the sycophant to impulsively turn away.

He rudely removed a glass from her tray and opened the door wider, letting her enter.

This was going to work, she said to herself. That is until she saw the retinal scanner. *Am I going to have to pass the test? Had the* real *hotel staff been pre-cleared?*

Chetan didn't wait to find out as Meridian didn't force her to use the scanner. *Is this a trap?* Ignoring the looming danger, she set out the glasses in front of the six occupants seated around the table, making sure that the daisy's front pointed once at everybody's face.

Chetan then left the room and took the stairs at the end of the hallway down to the lobby. She couldn't fully suppress a sigh of relief as she walked out. Forty minutes later and still alive, she retrieved her red Fiat from the garage and drove to the Hotel Majestic. While in the car, she pulled off the wig and ripped off the mole, leaving a small bloody mark on her face that she wiped with a wrinkled napkin from the glove compartment.

Back in her room, she changed and went to the bathroom to wash her face. But in the process, she saw something that caused her heart to shudder – a greasy smudge just below the wig she had worn – looked back at her. She realized then she had soiled her face while hiding under the car in the garage. Maybe she wouldn't get away with what she did after all, although Meridian would surely have stopped her at the hotel if he had recognized her. Unless...

Chapter 37

Meridian thought about the woman he had let into the room. She looked vaguely familiar, although he was certain he would have remembered her, especially from that hideous mole on her face.

The more he thought about it, the more it bothered him. If he had a mole like that, he would have had it removed. Heck, he could have done it himself! She also had a small greasy smudge on her forehead. She was not repairing a machine at the hotel; they had engineers and maintenance people do that.

And something else bothered him too. Her hair had been a little *too* perfectly shaped on the sides. No loose strands. Yet, it stood unnaturally tall on her head. The woman had the same body shape and height as...Chetan! She had had a ponytail, he remembered.

Could it be? In Barcelona? Why not? She was working with George, after all. *Maybe killing the mutt backfired.* The thought scared him, especially since he didn't run the killing by the Benefactor first. Killing a dog wasn't the same as a human, he had thought at the time. He needed to clean this up himself, without anybody finding out.

Meridian left the room and approached the bar, overhearing the bartender talking to a waitress with blonde hair. Although Meridian didn't speak Catalan, they seemed upset, and he heard the word "Ghana". The waitress also didn't look like the woman who Meridian had let into the room to serve water.

"Is there another waitress on staff?" Meridian asked the bartender.

The sheepish bartender shook his head side to side.

"What did the Ghanaian look like?"

"Like an African," he replied meekly.

Meridian felt like choking the bartender. "Can I see your security footage?"

The bartender furrowed his brow at Meridian and again asked, "Why?"

"Why? Because you've been had, you idiot! The African led you outside, clearing the way for an imposter to invade our meeting." Meridian didn't add that he too had been at fault.

"It's broken," the bartender replied with a smirk. "Security camera is broken."

"Yeah? Well, how about this?" Meridian said before punching the smirking young man in the nose. "Broken like that? Listen, asshole, I'm holding a sensitive meeting now. You want me to take this up with management? Tell them that you allowed a fake waitress to invade our meeting?"

The bartender looked like he was going to call for help, but then he quietly ushered Meridian into a back room where they scanned the footage.

"See?" the bartender said triumphantly, pointing out the Ghanaian.

"Sure, I see. Here comes your fake waitress. See that?"

* * *

George met Chetan at their room and immediately emailed the pictures to his sister, Naomi. It was time to leave, and fast, in case Meridian or the others had discovered the connection between George's drunken Ghanaian act and a fake waitress.

They quickly checked out of the hotel, loading their gear into the car. George drove them to Zaragoza, thinking that if Meridian was now looking for them, he would guess a closer destination like Andorra. Both locations had international airports.

Chetan sat in the passenger seat, doing what she could to remain useful. She fidgeted in her seat while they both discussed the possibility that Meridian had figured out what had happened. Neither was particularly worried though, thinking that even if he suspected something, he would think she had planted a bug or poisoned the water. At worst, he might sweep the room for bugs and order new water. Surely, he wouldn't abandon his post at the meeting to chase a hunch. Right?

***

Meridian did abandon his post, however, to briefly interrogate the bartender. He had learned about the apparent diversion created by the Ghanaian and the mysterious waitress who had entered the inner sanctum to serve water. He now realized that the imposters were George and Chetan. He had to find them – and fast!

Meridian had carefully checked the room as soon as Chetan had left it, ruling out the possibility that she had left a bug in the short period of time there. He couldn't think of anything that would have spooked her. So why did she leave? What did she accomplish?

The daisy had been an unusual choice. Why would she have worn it?

Unless… Of course! *That bitch took pictures*! *I need to get them before they leave the city.* But first he had to update the Oilmen, since he could be gone for a while.

He needed to learn more about the waitress who had served them water. She couldn't have learned anything of importance about what had been said at the meeting since she wasn't there very long and didn't leave any listening devices. He would report back as soon as he learned anything.

The room turned deathly quiet. *Is this the end?* Meridian thought. As a child, he loved watching James Bond movies. Images of the Frankenstein-looking Jaws grasping Roger Moore by the throat, throwing him like a rag doll, and then trying to bite his neck as a vampire would came to mind. Or the movie – he could think of more than one – where a hole in the floor opened above James Bond, threatening to send him into a quiver of snakes, or was it sharks?

Meridian snapped out of it when the Benefactor spoke.

"Disturbing. Failure at all levels. Meridian! You better act fast before they get away! Meeting adjourned. Watch your secure portal for the other matter we had discussed earlier."

Meridian knew he didn't have much time. Then an idea formed in his head.

***

Meridian entered the parking garage minutes later. A teenager with a face covered in acne was watching the FC Barcelona vs. Crystal Palace game on a small television behind the pay counter. Meridian thought about quietly slipping past him or using his medical tools, but knew that would cause more issues than it would solve.

Instead, he pounded his left hand on the counter to gain the attendant's attention.

"Excuse me, but this is an emergency. My car, parked on Level 1, has been vandalized. I need to see your security footage. You have cameras. I've seen them."

"Hmm. Sorry, but I can't do that. I'm just a cashier. You'll need to contact my boss, Ms. Borges."

"I just want to look at today. Do we really need to bother her? You can watch me. I'll pay you for your time. Easy cash for you," Meridian said, handing the clerk a 100 Euro bill.

The clerk paused but then pocketed the bill, waving Meridian on before turning his attention back to the game.

It took ten minutes for Meridian to locate the Mercedes and spot Chetan taking pictures of the Post-it Note before he had arrived. As Meridian approached, he saw Chetan hide under the car parked next to the Mercedes. He felt like a fool.

Something told him to look further. Chetan wouldn't have known where he had parked unless she had used the same garage. She may have even followed them to the garage. Twenty minutes later, he spotted Chetan leaving a red Fiat, parked on Level 2.

He noted the number of the parking spot, nodded to the clerk on his way out the door, and walked to where the Fiat had been parked. It was gone. Now he had to figure out how to gain access to Barcelona's city camera system.

***

The road to Zaragoza was long and would take George and Chetan about three hours. First, they made a stop. George explained to a confused Chetan the reason, and he knew from her smile that she understood.

On the way to the airport, they weaved through the lush countryside, viewing rivers, mountains, and green spaces. Chetan fell asleep in the passenger seat while George stared straight ahead. They were making progress, George driving as fast as he could, thinking about Suzanne but also Meridian, who was probably chasing them. He wanted to board their plane back to America – in a passenger seat, not a casket in the cargo bay.

***

Meridian sent a text message to a mailbox monitored by an intermediary for the Benefactor.

"Need access to Barcelona traffic cam grid."

He had wished to avoid seeking help from his boss but at least he had some progress to report.

Meridian contacted the Benefactor through the usual means – by leaving a message on a portal that would be passed onto his boss once validated by an intermediary. It took only twenty minutes for the Benefactor to respond, rewarding him with a return message: "Meet courier wearing blue cap at the north steps to the Barcelona Cathedral."

Meridian arrived at the steps a few minutes early, preferring to see the courier with the hat before the person saw him. A bespectacled man with a blue hat approached. The courier handed Meridian a piece of paper, which Meridian read before giving it back to the man. The courier then walked away. The entire exchange took less than thirty seconds, during which time neither man spoke.

The paper given to Meridian by the courier directed Meridian to the offices of Marina Catala. Marina worked as a route planner for Transports Metropolitans de Barcelona, known locally as TMB, the agency responsible for the public bus system. *Perfect!*

Meridian had no difficulties entering the city government building, a tall modern structure that stood out like a sore thumb. In a city with ancient buildings made of stone and decorated with gargoyles and other statutes, this building had a curious red façade that looked like scaffolding from a distance.

Marina, a tall woman with shiny black hair, greeted Meridian with a frown after he entered the foyer area of her department on floor three. Marina coldly escorted him to her office, which Meridian perused as he entered. The young woman had pictures of two twin girls on her wall. No husband was pictured, however. *Divorced? Kids a product of a one-nighter?*

Meridian put aside the idle musings and concentrated instead on the woman's certificates. She had passed two route planning and traffic monitoring courses (Level I and Level II). *Perfect! The Benefactor had truly worked a miracle.*

With no time to waste, Meridian immediately hopped into her seat. Fortunately, the room had no windows for inquiring eyes.

Meridian rasped his fingers on the desk and bounced his knee up and down as he strained to view the camera shot that Marina had cued up for him. There it was, Chetan's red Fiat driving out of the garage in the Gothic Quarter on the computer monitor.

Next, he had to trace the movements of the car. Although the program was simple to use, he had to check cameras at various points in time. The painstaking work took time that Meridian didn't have.

He eventually traced the car all the way to the Hotel Majestic. A traffic camera at the intersection outside of Hotel Majestic captured the Fiat as it pulled up to the valet stand.

A valet parked it, and then a short period of time later, he spotted it driving out of town. Meridian raced out of the building, hotwired a nearby silver Renault, and sped in the direction of the red Fiat.

***

Chetan continued sleeping in the passenger seat, head slanted towards the door in a sharp angle that, to George, looked uncomfortable. Although he wanted to turn on the radio, he didn't want to disturb her.

They had made progress, George thought to himself, proud of the way he had worked with Chetan. They had marched right into the den of some very bad people, their actual meeting. Everything had gone according to plan.

Naomi now had the images of the participants and would help them identify the group. They would then dig into each person's history, hoping to unearth information that could be used to spring Suzanne and locate who had killed David and Cindy.

Until they came face-to-face with his worse fear.

***

Meridian raced his hotwired Renault on the highway in hot pursuit of the red Fiat. He knew where they were heading; they were running away, rats scampering away with stolen food, towards an international airport that would take them back to America.

He didn't have a lot of time to close ground. Racing the car as fast as he could, he prayed that the police weren't out for speeders. It was a risk he had no choice but to take. The Renault would soon be reported as stolen by the owner, but Meridian guessed he had enough time to capture or kill George and Chetan and flee the scene before the risk materialized.

An hour into his journey, he spotted the car. Meridian drove behind the car, put on a black hat he found resting on the passenger seat, and began flashing his lights.

The car pulled over to the side of the road. Meridian smiled. The Benefactor would hail his accomplishment. Sure, there had been a lapse in security, but he had acted decisively. The threat would end – permanently.

Killing them in Europe would delay any investigation from the American authorities – a big bonus. Weeks would pass. The Benefactor had already accelerated the timetable for the final act. They would have enough time.

He pulled his car beside the red Fiat, angling it towards the road like an undercover cop.

He drew his gun and approached the car.

***

The acid in George's stomach began to boil when he saw the Renault behind him, flashing its lights. The driver looked like Meridian. He had found them. George didn't have time to wake the sleeping Chetan, still slumped down in the passenger seat.

***

Meridian knew something had gone terribly wrong before he saw the driver's face. The driver wasn't George. And Chetan was not in the car. Instead, a large muscular man with jet black hair and tattoos on his neck rolled down the window.

The man said, *"He fet alguna cosa malament?"*

What language is he speaking? Meridian asked himself before realizing it was Catalan. Meridian could only say the basic greetings in Spanish but nothing in Catalan. Unable to communicate, he instead thrust pictures of George and Chetan from his phone into the man's face.

The man responded, *"Qui són ells? Què vols?"* ("Who are they? What do you want?")

Meridian tried again with the same result. He had no choice but to let the man go.

***

George relaxed as he passed the Renault, which had pulled over a red Fiat. Meridian looked furious standing at the side of the road. The countermeasure had worked, George thought, as Meridian's figure fell out of range in the rearview mirror.

Having his local asset (a former CIA informant who had initially delivered Chetan the red Fiat) take back the Fiat had been a stroke of genius. They instead drove a white Volkswagen, rented using a false name. Had George still been in the NSA, he would have bragged to his colleagues about leaving his assassin standing dumb faced on the roadside.

Chapter 38

A maintenance issue delayed the flight out of the Zaragoza airport by an hour. George watched the entrance like a hawk, waiting for Meridian to arrive. Part of the idea behind having his tattooed contact drive the red Fiat on the same road as George and Chetan had been to fool Meridian into thinking that Zaragoza was a mere diversion.

Meridian would hopefully switch directions to get to the airport in Andorra. After all, Andorra was closer to Barcelona, and it would have been the more natural destination to begin with. Meridian could simply flip around and go the other way, reaching the airport there a couple of hours later.

George didn't voice his trepidation to Chetan, just as he didn't tell her about Meridian racing past them to interrogate the man with the tats. She had been sleeping, missing the excitement. He wasn't usually a man for cliches, but he believed in letting sleeping dogs lie.

While thinking it through, George kept a wary eye on the entrance to the boarding area. Meridian never appeared, and they boarded after the mechanics repaired the wheel. The plane took off, allowing George his first smile since before his wife had been arrested.

***

With George and Chetan having escaped, Meridian had no choice but to contact the Benefactor. He used the same method he had used earlier in the day.

It had been Meridian's responsibility to safeguard the meeting, and he had failed. Now, he would be the bearer of horrible news – two failures in one day.

Meridian sent a text message to the same mailbox as before, noting simply: "They escaped." Fear overwhelmed him while waiting for a response.

"Explain…no, check that – you imbecile! I'm calling you now" came the response.

It was a bad sign that the Benefactor wanted to talk. The incoming call displayed as Unknown Number. Meridian picked up immediately, paused, and said, "Hello."

The obscured, unisexual voice responded, saying, "Tell me what happened."

Meridian explained the events of earlier in the day.

Halfway through, the Benefactor lost patience, saying, "That's enough! Blah, blah, blah. One more chance. That's it. Don't blow it."

"What do you want me to do?" Meridian asked.

"I've finalized our next step. There's a meeting coming up, and I need you to plant something for me."

"Where?"

"Zurich."

"What am I planting?"

"A large device."

Meridian wanted to know more, but he knew not to ask.

"When?"

The Benefactor ignored the question, responding only with, "I'll have it delivered to you with further instructions. And Meridian?"

"Yes?"

"You're out of chances."

The phone was cut off before he could respond.

Chapter 39

Naomi picked up George and Chetan at Dulles Airport after their flight from Spain landed. They cleared customs and retrieved their bags. Naomi made a point of having Chetan sit in the passenger seat of her light blue Prius.

"It's the least I can do. Suzanne is family to me," Naomi said, as she drove to George's house. Chetan had agreed to stay there instead of a hotel.

As the women began talking, George waited for his opportunity to change the topic. She seemed chipper, even though he knew she must have spent virtually all her time investigating the video after receiving it.

"Any luck?" he asked eagerly.

"As a matter of fact, yes! I searched our database and talked to a colleague. Eager to help you, George. Off the record of course."

"And?" George piped up from the backseat.

"I pulled together information on three out of the five members of the group besides Turner, whom you already know about. As for the other two, I couldn't find anything."

"Any pressure points on the three?" he asked.

"Nothing on two of them. The third person may be useful, though."

"Good!" George crowed from the back seat, behind Naomi.

"First, before I talk about him, I discovered the name of the group."

"They have a name?" Chetan asked.

"More like a corny rock band – the Oilmen – than a criminal enterprise."

"Catchy," Chetan said.

"Yeah, a colleague heard a rumor about one of them joining a group called the Oilmen," Naomi added.

"Interesting," George said while Naomi paused to gather her thoughts.

"Yes, it is. They're led by a person, not even sure if it's a man or a woman, that they refer to as the Benefactor."

"What are…eh…the Oilmen trying to do?" Chetan asked.

"Sorry. My contact didn't know anything else about the group itself, and I couldn't find anything else on the organization."

Naomi stared straight ahead at the road as she navigated the turn from the off ramp of the toll road onto the bottleneck before the merge into Interstate 66.

Naomi discussed two of the individuals for whom she had background info — an American, Fred Turner, and a Norwegian, Noah Rosdahl. The information about Turner confirmed what George and Chetan already knew. Rosdahl by comparison seemed like a boy scout. The three of them chuckled speculating how the Benefactor must have used porn to entrap him. Naomi's voice became chipper as she turned her attention to the third.

"His name is Cristiano Sousa. Interesting character. Lives in Rio, and it looks like he's been involved with the Oilmen since sometime around 2014. Is that when the little band started?" she asked.

"No, we're pretty sure that Turner was coopted to join in 2009. That's when his company, TMJ Enterprises, almost went into bankruptcy because of a horrific oil rig explosion, only to mysteriously rise from the ashes like a phoenix," George explained.

"What's so interesting about Sousa?" Chetan asked.

"Good question. And I think he's someone to focus on. Brazilian, politically connected, Runs his own fiefdom in Rio. Best of all is — drumroll please — I figured out how you can get to him."

"How's that? Sista, please!" George pleaded.

"The usual — through his accountant!"

218

Chapter 40

On March 29, 1996, Pablo Espinoza graduated from Universidade de São Paulo, one of Brazil's best public universities. He looked for his grandmother — Nana — in the crowd as he walked to the podium standing tall wearing his brown cap and gown. The moment lasted one minute but the wide smile on Nana's face would make it last a lifetime.

Espinoza's mother had died from breast cancer when Pablo was two. Nana and his father, José, raised him, until the next tragedy hit.

José was a police officer investigating the Red Command, a large cocaine trafficker. The cartel fought back. A corrupt internal affairs officer planted 10 bricks of the drug in the Espinoza household when Pablo was twelve. José died a year later in jail, shanked in the neck in the bathroom.

Nana now had to raise Pablo alone. She inundated the grief-stricken child with love, God, and strong values. Receive a good education and leave this godforsaken place, she said repeatedly. And so, when Espinoza and Nana made eye contact at graduation, he felt as if both deserved the honor.

Only Espinoza didn't want to leave Rio. He was not ready to start over in a strange city.

***

The idealistic man longed to tackle systemic corruption in government and business which had consumed his father. He had read about it in the Panama Papers, learned about it in school, and had even taken an oath to fight against it upon passing his Chartered Certificated Accountant exam. And today he would take his first step in achieving his goal.

The dark-haired accountant, devoid of any muscle or fat on his six-foot-six slender frame, lumbered into the sterile conference room. It was his third interview at Campos and Fontes, a reputable accounting firm with offices located in Rio de Janeiro.

The firm's hiring partner met him in the lobby with a wide smile. The man escorted Espinoza to a corner conference room where an older woman stood as Espinoza entered.

Espinoza had not met them in his first two interviews and didn't know what to think. *Another interview with two more people?*

As they sat down, the hiring partner said, "I'll get right to the point. You've impressed a lot of people here. We think you'd make a fantastic addition."

Espinoza took a deep breath trying to remain calm. Respect and modesty, traits drilled into him by Nana. "I can't thank you enough. Your firm has always been my first choice," he said.

"Great," the woman said. "Starting pay is 45,000 reals and you're eligible for bonuses too."

"When do I start?"

**

For the first seven years after joining Campos and Fontes, Espinoza worked on routine audits of large companies in the banking, petroleum, construction, and insurance sectors. The work was tedious, but he had learned a lot and liked the work.

One Monday in January, the senior partner of Campos and Fontes promoted him to partner. He would now begin making serious money if the firm did well, which it always did.

He would replace a partner who left Campos and Fontes leading a financial audit of Laredo Industries. Laredo sold machine parts needed by oil producers. He had heard about Laredo from talking to his co-workers, but he didn't know that much about the company.

Espinoza read as much as he could about his client's contact, Laredo's Chief Financial Officer, Cristiano Sousa. Like Espinoza, Sousa had risen through the corporate food chain culminating in his current position. A gossipy trade press article described him as having an insufferable personality, but Espinoza chalked that up to jealous colleagues who had been passed by like a Lamborghini zipping past a Honda.

The rotund, diminutive man scoffed at Espinoza's extended hand when he walked into Sousa's office for the first time. Sousa barely looked up from his papers, spitting tobacco juice into a spittoon, as he blindly gestured for the accountant to sit.

Espinoza looked into Sousa's deep eyes after sitting, waiting for the meeting to begin. He sat, as directed, on one of two chairs facing Sousa's large, flat desk filled with papers, some in piles, others scattered.

"You're the new partner in charge, eh? The last guy didn't last too long, so hopefully you'll do better," Sousa warned.

They talked for about an hour about the business before leaving.

***

The first hint of a problem came the first year when an accountant working under Espinoza questioned the price of equipment sold by Laredo to Petróleo Brasileiro, better known as Petrobras, a business owned by the Brazilian government and one of the largest petroleum companies in the world, owning oil refineries, power plants, terminals, and pipelines.

"The price is 150% of the market rate!" Oscar Lamonte, a newly minted accountant, announced, grinning.

Espinoza contemplated the high markup. *I was like that when I first started. But it's difficult to establish an accurate market rate these days. My hands are tied without evidence of any fraud, kickbacks, or misstatements.*

"150%? Are you sure you're comparing apples to apples. Have you accounted for included services and inflation? I need more, *much more*, to raise alarm bells."

In the end, Espinoza signed off on the financial statements, certifying the veracity of the company and its dealings with Petrobras. Campos and Fontes rewarded Espinoza with a bonus for completing the audit, a small portion of which paid for a lavish dinner with Nana.

Over the next five years, Espinoza certified and approved the release of five additional financial statements. Each year, he would receive a bonus, significantly larger than the amount received in the previous year, after releasing the current year's statement.

***

Naomi's Prius hummed east on Interstate 66 after making it through the bottleneck. The D.C. area's infamous traffic returned to about eighty percent of pre-COVID volume.

"I assume Espinoza crashed down to Earth at some point," George said, interrupting his sister's tale.

"That's an understatement," Naomi explained. "Turns out Espinoza's a minor pawn in one of the biggest scandals in Brazilian history – and perhaps the world. Sousa was one of many players, although a large one at that. The scandal – named after Petrobras – netted roughly $2.1 billion to businesses, including Laredo, and politicians. Espinoza, for his part, received twenty years in jail. He's one of many low-level fall guys rotting in jail. The real culprits, like Sousa, got off scot-free."

"You said billion?" Chetan asked.

"Yes, billion with a *B*!"

"Petrobras has assets of close to $200 billion USD and annual revenues of roughly $50 billion USD. So it wasn't that difficult to hide the money over a number of years."

"Is this the one that Lula got caught up in?" George asked, referring to Luiz Inacio Lula da Silva, the former and current president of Brazil.

"Yes, and in return for looking the other way, part of the overpayments was used to buy votes for Lulu and others in his Workers Party, creating a self-perpetuating circle of corruption that lasted years."

"And Sousa?" asked Chetan.

"He apparently cleaned up millions, and, as I said before, he wasn't even charged." Naomi responded.

"How does this help us? Do you think that the Benefactor bribed somebody to let him off and that's what ties Sousa to the Oilmen?" George asked.

"I really don't know, but it's possible. I couldn't find any information about why Sousa wasn't charged." Naomi said before adding, "but I did discover something interesting…"

Chapter 41

Brazilian prisons are horrible places to live, even on a temporary basis. With the third largest prison population – only China and the U.S. imprison more people – prisoners cram into spaces half the expected size.

Chetan read about riots and deaths occurring in addition to rapes and even a bizarre case of cannibalism that almost caused her to forgo the trip. In one riot at the Altamira prison in 2019, sixty-two inmates died, and that is just the *official* number.

George and Chetan flew from Dulles Airport into Rio de Janeiro, checked into a hotel, catnapped for two hours, and left for a privately run prison thirty minutes outside the city. Chetan's heart pounded as she walked into the boxy, grey structure.

Institutional black and white linoleum tile lined the walkway leading to the security checkpoint, where a smelly guard groped up her legs, vaginal area, and chest purportedly feeling for weapons and communication devices. Chetan had been through this before, back on the reservation, and knew that protesting would only make it worse.

After they were released, they walked on the same linoleum tile to a waiting area, where they sat in metal chairs waiting to be called. The room was filled with anxious relatives, including some women with loose-fitting shirts, desperate to see jailed spouses and partners.

A woman in a booth barked out words in Portuguese that neither of them understood. A dozen or so people stood and walked towards the exit. Chetan and George stood and approached the exit, but a male guard blocked their path, pointing towards the people that remained seated. The message was clear, even if the language wasn't.

The drill repeated an hour later, but this time the guards let George and Chetan into a large room. The area was filled with metal tables and chairs and roving guards wearing bulky body armor, some with guns and others with menacing German Shepherds. Everybody seemed to stare at them as they entered, especially at George.

A man with long, bony limbs sat at table waiting for them to arrive. His face looked tired, his eyes sagged, and his black hair looked greasy.

Next came the most important part.

"*Você fala inglês?*" George asked in choppy Portuguese.

The prisoner laughed and said, "Yes. Speak English. Good for you."

The next five minutes were spent establishing bona fides. George and Chetan were posing as reporters working for an American newspaper. Pablo Espinoza told them about his background as an accountant working for Campos and Fontes, culminating in his promotion to partner heading the Laredo Industries audit.

With preliminaries out of the way, George got straight to the point.

"Any comment on why you're in here and Sousa's out there, running free?" George asked.

Espinoza looked at them, thinking about how to respond.

He's scared, Chetan thought.

Espinoza leaned in and asked, "You American?"

George nodded yes.

Chetan watched Espinoza closely. Espinoza's right-hand seemed to slip into his pocket. Espinoza then stood, causing Chetan and George to stand.

"I sorry. No can help." Before walking away, he said, "Thank you for coming. You were the first visitors since the burial of my sweet Nana many years ago," and shook the hand of George first and then Chetan. A guard separated them and escorted their prisoner away, leaving the stunned Americans standing by themselves.

***

Chetan and George climbed into their yellow rental car. Chetan began to talk, but George ignored her. Ten minutes later George pulled off the road.

"He gave me this when he shook my hand," George said. The slip of paper had one word.

Nana

"But she's dead. She died during the trial. He has no family," Chetan said.

"Poor guy. Stuck in jail, no family," George said, thinking about his own wife.

"*Nana*. What could that mean?" she asked.

"She's apparently his grandmother, from what I read before we left the States. She's buried at a place not too far from here. Read that too," George said.

"Buried? Interesting you say that," Chetan said before speculating, "If you were Espinoza, fall guy in a large scandal where the top perps made fortunes, what would you do?" Chetan asked.

"Especially, if you were…"

"An accountant."

"You'd have records," George said.

"It sounds like he was allowed out for the funeral," Chetan pointed out.

"Maybe he left something…" George mused.

***

Two hours later, they found it. A key underneath a partially buried rock adjacent to the headstone.

***

"But how do we gain access to it? We can't just waltz in with a key," Chetan said.

226

"I've been wondering about that too. He must have planned this out though. Maybe he has a friend there?"

"Only one way to find out," Chetan said.

An hour later, they walked into the glass front stand-alone structure which said:

Banco Comunitário do Brasil.

A man wearing a brown tweed jacket with blue slacks and a silver nametag that said *Francisco* stopped them as they approached an area protected by metal bars. George and Chetan could see a black granite counter in the middle of the square room and safe deposit boxes on each of the three walls. Bright lights illuminated the room.

"Help you?" Francisco asked, apparently guessing that they were Americans.

"Yes, you can, thank you. Our friend, Pablo Espinoza, gave us his key and directed us here."

"Please," Francisco said extending his hand out.

Chetan, who had been holding the key, looked at George, who nodded. *What choice do we have?*

"Excuse me, por favor. Wait over there," Francisco said. He pointed to four empty chairs before disappearing.

Francisco returned thirty minutes later.

"Close door when leave. Maybe need this," he said, handing them a bag. And he was right.

"Wow, the motherlode," Chetan said after opening the box and placing the contents on the table. "Are these what I think they are?"

"Yes, indeed," George said, smiling. "And if these contain what I think they do, it'll be time to go into the devil's den. Deep inside a favela."

"A favela? Sounds like food," Chetan said.

"It's not. Definitely not."

Chapter 42

In 1896, peasants living in Canudos - an impoverished settlement in the backcountry of Brazil - attacked the town of Joazeiro. They demanded that local merchants deliver wood needed in Canudos to build a church. Brazilian troops were summoned to quell the fighting, but the tenacious Canudos peasants prevailed, armed with little more than tools used to farm and old muskets, embarrassing the troops.

Initial humiliation gave way to rage. The Brazilian army returned, only to be defeated a second time. Then came the heavy artillery and the eventual slaughter. During the war, the Brazilian soldiers lived in shacks on a hill inundated by spiny flowering favela plants.

After the war, the soldiers returned to Rio. With little money, they settled in temporary housing in the hillsides surrounding the country's storied coastal city. There, they waited for the government to honor its promise of permanent housing, which never arrived. The temporary housing turned permanent and grew, spiraling out of control like a raucous weed.

The shanty towns, named after the plant that had started it all, became crime infested, dirty places. Rats and crime bosses competed for influence in the favelas.

Outsiders inadvertently entering the slums got lost, robbed, or killed. Tourists watched the mayhem from the safety of a road above the fray, but they were specifically warned not to enter.

The same danger that kept outsiders out of the favelas drew Sousa, his family, and his militia into the shanty town. Sousa established a haven that he could rule like the Godfather - earning profits dwarfing what he had made during the Petrobras scandal. And the Benefactor, who had protected Sousa from the pesky prosecutors, would be paid back in spades.

***

Sousa sat watching his workers perform magic down below. From his perch on his second level bay overlook, two glass paneled windows afforded him the three S's: seclusion, security, and superiority. When fully staffed, Sousa's team of eleven worked like a well-orchestrated Premier League soccer team.

Five members of the team worked at Sousa's offsite facility - a plantation the size of a hectare located in the Amazon, protected by bribed military officers. The remaining members worked in the favela in a four-structure compound connected by an underground tunnel. On the outside, each had an aluminum roof and flimsy, uneven painted wood for walls, fitting in with the neighborhood slums. The exterior was all for show, of course, as a proper wooden roof lay underneath the fake aluminum roof, and thick insulated walls held it all up.

Sousa spit tobacco into a cup. His mouth now clear, the short, pudgy man reached for his walkie-talkie.

"Hector, how's last night's batch?" Sousa asked in Portuguese, referring to a shipment of four barrels of unrefined cocaine that had arrived the previous night.

"Good enough. Most of the jungle soup has been filtered sufficiently. The purification process can continue here."

"Good, we need to hit our targets ASAP," Sousa replied.

It had better be good enough, Sousa thought. The Benefactor had been pressing for more sales of the powdery white drug, concentrating through newer distribution channels into the burgeoning European market.

The other members of the Oilmen hadn't yet learned that most of the funding came from Sousa's drug trafficking operation, set up as part of his deal with the Benefactor. The Benefactor had helped clean up the implosion that had occurred in 2014 in the wake of the Petrobras scandal. Underlings – in Sousa's case, Espinoza - took the fall, relieving public pressure enough for the senior operators to escape any real punishment.

In exchange, Sousa became indebted to the Benefactor. However, as often occurs in such arrangements, the share demanded by the Benefactor recently began to increase.

***

George and Chetan pulled to a stop at a switchback near the top of a mountain in Rio, overlooking a large favela. There, they looked down at the favela. What they saw made them more nervous than before.

Thousands were living in filthy living conditions. It was a dangerous place for many reasons – one being it was ripe for another COVID-19 outbreak. Brazil had been hit hard during the first wave of the COVID-19 pandemic and again because of the different virus variants.

Dressed in simple worn-out clothes purchased at a local consignment shop and wearing cloth masks, George and Chetan boarded a bus filled with tired workers heading back to the favela. Once there, the workers would spend a few precious hours with their families eating rice, potatoes, and, on payday, a small amount of chicken. Sleep would come fast but only for four or five hours, before the schedule would repeat the next day, starting with a heavy dose of Brazilian coffee.

Some of the workers looked at the strangers. George and Chetan sat together on the dirty seats, heads down, keeping quiet.

As the bus drove, the road turned from pavement to potholes to packed dirt with craters. Chetan recognized the stop and, not wanting to speak, gently elbowed George. He nodded and pulled the cord, letting the driver know to stop. They were a few blocks away from Sousa's street. They disembarked, ignoring the stares from the others, and walked up the street to Sousa's four-shanty-house structure before knocking on middle one.

A small square at eye level in the door opened, revealing protective glass. Tiny perforations allowed a bodyguard, with a tattoo on his neck that Chetan could barely see, to ask what the visitors wanted.

George told him they were there to meet with Sousa. Using contact information dredged up from his sister's contacts, George had arranged the meeting after dropping hints about the information that he and Chetan had unearthed to get through Sousa's gatekeeper. The tall guard grunted something that made George look at Chetan, who responded by shrugging her shoulders. He then pointed to George's wallet, the top of which was visible in George's front pocket.

Chetan figured it out first. She withdrew her vaccine card from her pocket to show the guard. George did the same, revealing that they were up to date in receiving their COVID-19 shots. The guard grunted again before shutting the square, leaving George and Chetan to wonder if they had made the trip for nothing. A minute later, the door opened, exposing a second bodyguard, this one short and stocky.

The guard with the tattoos was tall and thick with two tattoos visible on his neck – one with a cross and wording that Chetan didn't understand and the other a clock with no hands. *Never ending jail time.* Chetan had seen it at Rosebud from people who had served a lot of time in prison.

Each guard wore a white shirt exposing a Glock visible at their waistlines. They patted down George first while Chetan looked on with anticipation. When it was Chetan's turn, the short bodyguard felt her breasts while the tall one laughed.

If he does that again, I'm going to kick him in the balls. Second time this has happened in two days. The goons at Cal Fire weren't even this bad.

George took a protective step towards the short guard but stopped when the tall one punched him in the chest.

George gasped, bent over, and then stood upright. Chetan touched his arm tenderly and said, "It's all right, George. Let's just get this over with."

***

Sousa walked into the room after the guards had finished, closing a metal door to the right side of the security room. He looked like the man in a picture that Naomi had shown him: short, plump, with bronze skin and eyes that were hard to see. The room became tense as *O Chefe*, the boss, scolded the guards in Portuguese.

He gestured for his guests to enter the living room and sit on a small but plush yellow couch. A Sony flat-screen television hung from the wall opposite the couch, and a marble coffee table sat in between. The ceiling was low, and Chetan and George had to descend into the room.

Sousa had done his best to obscure his protective cocoon, but he had to sacrifice some comfort in the process, George mused.

Sousa stuffed a wad of chewing tobacco in his mouth immediately after settling into a chair to the side of the couch. He pointed to his watch and said in English with a thick Portuguese accent, "You can begin by telling me why I don't let the vermin who live in my slums have it out with you two."

Chetan spoke calmly before George could respond, "I suggest you hear us out first. Maybe it'll change your mind. You can always kill us after."

Sousa stared at Chetan, worrying George. Then, Sousa looked at George.

After what seemed like an eternity, Sousa chuckled and said, "I like this one!" He spit into his cup, after which he sternly added, "Tell me what you got, and be quick about it."

After retrieving her iPhone, Chetan played a short clip of Sousa talking to Pablo Espinoza in Portuguese. George and Chetan had used Google

Translate to carefully select and memorize the clip to be played at this pivotal moment:

Pablo: I can't sign off on these. It looks to me that you've overcharged Petrobras by at least $50,000,000 Reals this year alone!

Sousa: That's none of your business.

Pablo: It's my job!

Sousa: Well…even if true…you've signed off in the past.

Pablo: Not at this level. It's now clear to me, and will be clear to my partners later today, that you've established a pattern of illegal price gouging. You're required to offer the government-owned Petrobras your standard rates for goods and services.

Sousa: [an audible spit can be heard] Don't give me that! You're in too deep enjoying your fat bonuses. I know where you live with your sweet Nana. Do you even know who you're talking to?

[An audible sound of a door slamming is heard ten second later.]

After the clip played, Chetan said, "We sent you only part of what we have."

George tried his best to suppress a smile. Chetan had come a long way.

"I've been hearing these allegations for years, yet nobody's touched me. Because nobody can." Sousa looked at his watch and spoke softly. "I'm busy. Leave now or get to your point quickly," he advised and, for emphasis, over-spat his cup, coming close to where they were sitting.

Chetan looked at George, who nodded, before she said, "Look, Cristiano, we know all about you. Not just your corrupt past, but why you haven't been charged when others have, including Pablo."

"I've had enough of this already. Same old shit. What makes you think I care?"

"Maybe we should release it then," Chetan replied.

Sousa shrugged.

"You might not care, but what about the rest of your group – the Oilmen and your secret benefactor? Wouldn't you become expendable, a liability?" Chetan asked.

Sousa scowled at Chetan and then at George before turning his gaze back to Chetan.

"Let's talk about that," Chetan said, handing Sousa pictures of the Oilmen she had taken in Barcelona.

Sousa feigned a look and shrugged. He looked at her intently.

"It was you! You were in the room. You served us water and had a flower on your chest. Camera?"

"Yep, and your boy, Meridian, failed to catch us."

Sousa looked surprised.

"You didn't know, did you?" she asked.

"He's not my responsibility," Sousa said.

"Thought so. Even you are in the dark," Chetan said triumphantly.

"Why don't you just tell me what you *think* you know?" Sousa said.

"Everybody has a similar story of reincarnation and redemption as you," George said. "Each living in different parts of the world. Your skin was saved from one of the largest corruption scandals in Brazilian history, and that's saying a lot for Brazil. Turner, the North American representative, was bought off by the person whom you all refer to as the Benefactor, saving TMJ Enterprises from near extinction after a 2009 oil rig explosion.

"Then there is Ming Rong Zhang. His bitumen mining company dominated its competitors by blackmailing local officials into revoking their business licenses. Internal affairs were about to arrest him when, like you, the Benefactor magically caused the charges to disappear. Don't you see a pattern?" George asked, not talking about the other two, who he didn't know much about. He continued after receiving no response.

234

"You all have the same benefactor. Everybody doing his dirty work. Yet, you don't even know who he is! Heck, I could be him for all you know. We want to know about him," George said.

"Or *her*," Sousa said after a long pause.

"True, the Benefactor's voice is obscured," George said.

"You tell an interesting story, but it's all based upon wild conjectures. I don't have to listen to this anymore. What is it that you want? Money? Information?"

Chetan drew a deep breath. "Information. We want to know about this Benefactor, who he *or she* is. And what is the purpose of all of it?"

Sousa played along. "Why should I answer these questions?"

"Good question. Finally, a relevant one. The answer is obvious though. We talked to Espinoza. He gave us the tapes. How do you think we know what we know? If you answer our questions, we'll try to help you when the time comes. And, obviously, if anything happens to us, our associate will release the tapes," Chetan said.

"Immunity? Is that what you mean? No, thanks. I'd be dead by then," Sousa said.

"Nobody must know. We met you inside the favela. Nobody followed us, certainly not on a bus into the favela," George said.

Sousa considered this. "I can't help you, and you can't really help me. You need to leave now." With this said, Sousa stood.

Chetan tried one more time. "How about plausible deniability?"

Sousa laughed hard and then sat back down. "You're a tenacious little bitch, aren't you? Especially for an American."

He stood again and walked into the next room. Chetan and George looked at each other, unsure what to do.

Sousa walked out of the room, leaving them with two guards. One pointed a rifle at Chetan. The other pointed a pistol at George.

Sousa returned ten minutes later. "You have three minutes to leave, otherwise we'll kill both of you and serve you to my hungry neighbors." While Sousa's actions terrified them both, their eyes were drawn to a newspaper article from the *Daily Mail* that Sousa had set down before them after retrieving it from the inside of a book on his bookcase.

"Three minutes and you leave me alone. Agreed?"

"Agreed," George replied.

Sousa left them alone under the watchful eyes of his bodyguards.

Chetan skimmed the article while George snapped a photo of both pages. It appeared to be about a man named Roberto Schwartz, who seemed rather ordinary at first glance.

"I think he's toying with us," Chetan said, throwing her hands up in despair.

"You didn't see anything useful?" George asked.

"Not really. It's talking about some guy that lives in London and goes to Oxford. The person grew up poor in the industrial part of Birmingham, but the school awarded him a full scholarship, giving him a free ride."

"There must be something in there that's useful, no? Otherwise, why would the *Daily Mail* have published the article in the first place?" George asked.

Chetan continued to read but then paused, shrugging her shoulders and frowning. "I don't see anything. The end talks about him meeting a Mahdi Salman and describes their relationship. They apparently became friends, very good friends, as a matter of fact."

George, who had finished taking pictures, elbowed in so that he could read along with Chetan.

"Maybe *more* than friends. See the picture on the second page? A paparazzo must have snapped it while they were at the park. Walking side by side, Roberto's right hand is reaching for Mahdi's left," George pointed out.

"So, what's wrong with that? Even if they're gay, who cares? I still don't get it."

"It says here that Mahdi has royal ties," George said, ignoring Chetan's retort.

"Royalty? English? Queen Elizabeth?"

"No, much more interesting. Saudi. This is about to get interesting. *Real* interesting," George replied with raised eyebrows.

The two of them walked out of the house, and George caught a glimpse of Sousa nodding before exiting through the door.

Chapter 43

As a child, Mahdi Salman knew he was different from other members of the royal family. His parents – Abdullah and Fatima – tried to isolate him in a vain effort to protect the family image. Abdullah's father, Muhammed, ruled Saudi Arabia with steel nerves, a sharp temper, and an unforgiving demeanor. Cross him and you might wind up in a wooden box, shrouded in a *kaftan*, body positioned with your head towards Mecca.

But Mahdi was deemed too soft for the crown, despite being technically in line after his father, Abdullah. His parents knew that the Allegiance Council would never select him as the king-in-waiting, the next Crown Prince.

As a toddler, Mahdi preferred butterflies and birds to oil and money. By age twelve, he demonstrated a capability for math years beyond his peers, especially compared to his royal relatives, who had little reason to study hard. By age fifteen, a family doctor made a fatal mistake of explaining his belief that Mahdi was "on the spectrum." It would be the last diagnosis the doctor would ever utter, even though everybody knew he had a valid point.

King Muhammed Salman happily agreed with Abdullah's decision to ship his outcast grandson to study in England. London had become a popular destination for Saudi money and power, with the elite developing two lives: reserved in public, especially in Arabia, and extravagant, risky, and playful – many times with European mistresses – when in London.

England would serve Mahdi well, an opportunity to foster his interest in secular disciplines. He would still learn the Qur'an, but he would also be able to continue developing his exemplary skills, first in math and then in engineering.

One night after studying, he met Roberto, who had been fishing for change to pay a cashier for his lunch at a fast-food restaurant. Mahdi was behind him in the line.

Instinct propelled the young Mahdi – with olive skin, cropped black hair, and a neatly trimmed mustache and beard – to help Roberto. There was something about the man that intrigued Mahdi, a connection, although he didn't know why. And, not that this mattered, but like Mahdi, they both had a skinny frame with slim arms and legs.

Mahdi felt liberated and freer living in London, with more choice in how he dressed, looked, and acted. He placed his hand on Roberto's left arm and said, "I got this," before walking to the cashier.

After paying, Roberto said, "Thank you. But you didn't have to do that." He continued to look in his pockets, but coming up empty, Roberto said, "I must have left my money in my room."

"Don't worry about it. It's nothing. A few pounds, that's all."

The two spent the next twenty minutes eating together, and then another hour walking around Oxford's campus. An unlikely friendship was born between the scholar from a working-class family, first in his family to study at a university, and the Saudi royal. They became best friends, and some would speculate, even more.

A year later, they shared a flat off campus. That's when the *Daily Mail* published its piece as a "good news" story, touting the unlikely, and possibly homosexual, relationship between Mahdi Salman, grandson of the current king, and Roberto. It would have remained a piece relegated to the newspaper's gossip column, if not for Sousa locating it years later.

A few years after graduating from Oxford at the top of his class, Mahdi began to excel on an international scale. He worked for a large multinational company specializing in tunnel boring technology for deep, intricate, vital tunnels used to allow travel through mountains, waterways, cities, and other obstacles.

Mahdi discovered more efficient ways to make wide-diameter drills capable of digging through dirt, passing the material behind the drill, and laying down concrete shafts in place of the freshly removed dirt, all the while staying deep in the ground. The older "dig and cover" method requires digging from the surface down to where a tunnel is needed. The process sometimes causes complications, including disrupted pipes and utility lines that then need to be rebuilt and relocated. An infamous example is Boston's Big Dig that finished 220% over budget.

Soon Mahdi found himself in places like China, Chile, Spain, the Middle East, Switzerland, and France, proving his technology on actual projects. Mahdi preferred to work on ventures that helped the environment, including diverting water for more efficient use and creating tunnels for trains that used magnetic levitation technology to transport goods and people, using less energy in the process. He shied away from opportunities to trade on the value of his name in favor of staying in the field in a hands-on role.

His success should have been enough. Gradually, though, he began to pine for more. How many hours would he have to labor as a service provider to make even close to what his lazy family made from the luck of having giant pools of oil in the ground? He would never receive the privileges they enjoyed on the outside looking in, and to top it off, they were about to blow it all.

He had heard whispers that some – including his uncle Ali Salman, viewed as a likely candidate to be ruler one day – were open to exploring the need to diversify away from Saudi reliance on fossil fuel. The fools had neither the intellect nor capacity to understand such complex matters.

By the grace of Allah, we have inherited the biggest oil reserves in the world. Even thinking about diversifying away runs counter to our core beliefs. Reducing market share in exchange for unproven alternative sources of revenue? Never.

Even worse, Mahdi saw through their false facades, fast cars, and paramours. Deadbeat hypocrites who abstain from pleasures of the body, mind, and soul, *except* when visiting private discotheques in Marbella, Barcelona, Dubai, and the Red Sea. Showcasing Hermes scarves and Rolex watches overseas while covering up in the presence of Wahhabis at home.

As Mahdi's doubts grew, so did his desire to enhance his position in line for the throne. And so, he began to plot methodically. He mapped out a complex algorithm of events, building a network of like-minded people through bribery and trickery. The group would be referred to as the Oilmen, with him being the anonymous Benefactor. Quarterly meetings were arranged and held with absolute secrecy. One day, he would return to Saudi Arabia, and when he did, he wanted to be prepared.

***

Sousa had long suspected that the Benefactor hailed from the Middle East, an area of the world that controls much of the world's oil yet is suspiciously unrepresented in the Oilmen group. He had always thought that the Benefactor might be the secret representative of the Middle East and further speculated that Saudi Arabia, putative head of OPEC, was the most likely country to head the activity.

The next clue came when the Benefactor talked to him privately in his shrouded voice about how Sousa's compound in the favela would be constructed. The Benefactor demonstrated an unusual expertise in construction techniques and tunneling technologies. It didn't take long after that to theorize that the Benefactor might be Mahdi Salman, the grandson of King Muhammed Salman. From there, he read about Mahdi's life, knowing that one day it could come in handy, and that is when he happened upon the *Daily Mail* article.

***

241

Years later, in 2019, came Mahdi's big break – an opportunity he never imagined would come without him having to use force. He couldn't believe his luck.

Ali Salman summoned him home. At first, Mahdi thought about protesting. Was he ready to return? Were his plans far enough along? But he knew he wouldn't get another chance. Returning to the lion's den would be risky, but he was ready.

The Allegiance Council had chosen Ali as the Crown Prince in line to replace King Muhammed when the time came. And the time had come, with the King having died of a heart attack. Ali knew that Mahdi had no illusions of becoming king and would temper any aspirations of Abdullah.

Being brilliant was a bonus. The perfect middleman, that's what Mahdi had become.

Only they were tragically wrong. He had become so much more…

Chapter 44

King Ali Salman walked in late to the 2019 OPEC meeting being held in Vienna, Austria. Better to keep the subordinates waiting. Several years ago, well before his death, Ali's father, King Muhammed Salman, had appointed him to head the Kingdom's most critical department: the Ministry of Energy. Being the de facto head of OPEC was a key, albeit tedious, perk of the job.

His official title as the Saudi Arabian Minister of Energy had changed over the years. The name of the ministry used to be Ministry of Petroleum and Mineral Resources; then it changed in 2006 to the elongated Ministry of Energy, Industry, and Mineral Resources. Three years ago, the name changed again, this time to the simpler Ministry of Energy.

Changing the names did little to detract OPEC's growing problems. Getting fourteen separate nations – located in the Middle East, Asia, South America, and Africa – to agree on production quotas proved to be nearly impossible. Worse, even when the disparate countries agreed, cheaters quickly reneged.

For a time, Saudi Arabia acted as the swing producer, cutting its oil production when needed to make up for the charlatans. Additionally, by 2014, American oil production had doubled, approaching that of Saudi Arabia, further shrinking OPEC's global reach and authority.

***

The minions inside the large conference room at OPEC's Secretariate building in Vienna, Austria, hushed as King Ali Salman walked in with his trusted subordinate, Mahdi Salman.

Ali knew some were wondering why he hadn't yet appointed a new head of the Ministry of Energy. The replacement would serve on OPEC's Strategic Conference, wielding Saudi's one vote and outsized influence.

Laughing to himself he thought, *These fools. There's too much that happens in the back chatter at these meetings to trust a subordinate, even my brilliant, pawn, Mahdi.*

Ali looked around the room, wondering for the umpteenth time why OPEC had designed the space to resemble the sleek spacious look of a Washington, D.C. subway platform. Some clown must have returned from a trip to America's capital before thinking about how to design the room.

Elegant smooth white panels lined the vaulted, curved ceiling. A corridor through the room lead to the head table, where the minsters sat on a podium in front of a row of flags. Each side of the corridor contained a long light green table upon which sat microphones, flowers, and small table flags for the delegates. Assistants sat behind the envoys.

People stood and clapped for the new king as he entered, some offering King Salman an awkward mixture of condolences because of the recent death of his father and congratulations for taking his place. Others simply clapped, afraid to say anything at all. The louder ones Ali knew as the suck-ups.

A large imposing man before his appointment, now he made people nervous. Ali dressed in a traditional red and white checkered keffiyeh draped over his head and down each shoulder, held to his scalp by a thick black agal. He wore a traditional white collared shirt with a brown thobe with gilded gold-colored edges. The only body part showing was his olive brown face with its thick black mustache and bearded chin.

The king took his place at the end and gestured for Mahdi to sit at the table lining the corridor. He gaveled the meeting to order.

Each minister in the universal language of English, took a turn discussing the oil revenues in their country for the current year and the projected revenues for the upcoming year. The room became quiet by the end as everybody contemplated what they had heard.

Nobody was surprised. Revenues were declining as people and industry had begun to shift towards alternative fuels. King Salman brought up the question nobody wanted to honestly address: "What can we do about the decline?"

The minister from Kuwait said, "More production cuts in order to boost the price?"

The representative from Venezuela scoffed, "Cuts? Is that our answer for everything? How much more can we suffer?"

Sousa, using his deep connections to many of the key players to gain admittance, watched in disgust.

King Salman began to protest, thinking about how Saudi Arabia traditionally bore more than its fair share of any reductions. *How much more can the Kingdom absorb?*

But Ali held his thoughts after noticing Mahdi's slight head shake once he caught Ali's eye. He wisely accepted Mahdi's advice, staying silent, instead eliciting more comments from the floor.

"What about Russia? They never do what they promise. Why should we?" the minister from Iraq chirped.

"Here, here," said the ministers from Angola and Iran.

"Is there a new approach?" an assistant to the Algerian minister asked from the back. The room went silent, waiting for the anticipated berating of the assistant.

The Libyan minister obliged, chiding his junior colleague, "Like what? Switch to solar power?"

Everybody laughed, except the assistant, whose face developed a reddish hue.

The assistant continued to press his point calmly saying, "I'm talking about something else. Is our problem public relations? Can we change the debate? Start a campaign to build support for oil?"

"How do you propose we do that?" King Salman asked.

"Simple. By directing our worldwide network of public relations firms to develop public relation campaigns for television, print media, and the Internet touting the benefits. I'm talking not just preserving jobs, but environmental benefits. I bet you most people don't realize that increasing oil production decreases reliance on coal, which is *the* real nightmare from an environmental standpoint."

"Hasn't this been done before?" King Salman asked.

"Yes, but not in a long time. It's almost like the environmentalists have made us afraid to speak. We live in fear that raising the issue will backfire," the assistant said.

"I see. Let's think about it. We have a lot to cover in this meeting, and we need to move on. It's certainly something to consider."

King Salman pivoted to the next topic.

***

Mahdi watched his boss carefully as he handled the questions from the bold assistant from Algeria. Based upon his interactions with Ali prior to his becoming king, Mahdi knew that Ali didn't like distractions from a set agenda.

Still, Ali hadn't displayed, at least outwardly, any annoyance and didn't immediately pivot. Something the assistant said had caused Ali to pause.

Mahdi thought he noticed his boss suppressing a smile. Pivoting, even slightly, to a more environmentally friendly façade, seemed to intrigue the ruler of the most prominent oil family in the world. He was about to warn his boss about the dangers of opening the floodgates to the scum environmentalists when Ali wisely moved on.

Chapter 45

Meridian's blue eyes looked at the computer as he logged into *Chess Masters*, at 9:00 p.m. The albino man clenched his jaw and pursed his lips together as he waited for the website to load. He hated the Internet, like all the other things he couldn't control.

Slow connection, fast connection. Who knows what will happen and when it will happen? If the Internet had a brain, I'd give it a lobotomy.

He wasn't there to play chess. He did not even know how to play chess. The Oilmen used the chatroom as a drop box for coded messages. Meridian had been logging on every day since leaving Barcelona.

Meridian knew that the other members of the Oilmen also would be logging into the chatroom. One bound, everybody bound, collective knowledge made everybody more loyal to the cause. At least that's what the Benefactor thought, although Meridian had his doubts.

A message appeared, making him smile. *Shit is getting real!*

Meeting with patient to occur October 1 in Zurich. Dr. M to prep for emergency brain surgery on October 3.

He clicked on a link next to the message, bringing him to a page describing the upcoming October 3 meeting of the United Nations Climate Change Conference. To Meridian, the roster of attendees looked impressive. *Not!* The more he read, the more excited he became. Best of all, the pesky Greta Thunberg would be speaking last, as the keynote speaker.

Meridian realized that the Benefactor had planned for something massive. Decoding the message was simple. The Benefactor directed Meridian to plant a bomb on October 1 to devastate the environmentalists.

Boy, it's going to be a blast!

Chapter 46

George returned to Virginia the day after his adventure with Chetan in the slums of Rio. The trip was surprisingly successful. Layers of the onion peeled, and they had avoided any tears, so far, at least.

It began with the fire at the Techno House. George knew that Suzanne, David, and Earthcare had been framed for starting the fire. A computer program may have lit the match by causing the electrical overload, but it certainly didn't happen at Suzanne's or David's behest.

George and Chetan, working on their own at that point, each learned about the connection between the man — known to them at that point as Meridian — and Fred Turner of TMJ Enterprises, located in Houston. The onion needed more peeling, however

George had successfully hacked into Turner's computer, discovering the meeting in Barcelona. There, he and Chetan had successfully infiltrated a meeting of the Oilmen. In the brief time there, Chetan — playing the part of a waitress — had taken pictures of the participants, noting that the ringleader had orchestrated the gathering with the skills of an opera conductor.

That took them to Rio, where they had hoped to peel into the next layer — discovering more about the conductor. And now they were close to determining the Benefactor's identity.

Despite all the progress, George knew that he and Chetan needed to peel deeper and faster. He wasn't sure how much longer Suzanne could take, being jailed for crimes she never committed. She had sounded more tired and with less hope of getting released each time George had talked to her on the phone or visited her. Although she always tried to hide her growing anxiety, George could tell. "Stay strong," he would say, "they're making progress." Which they were, but to her it would never be fast enough.

How long can she last without losing her sanity?

Another looming danger to her was the Oilmen. The more onion layers he and Chetan peeled, the greater the risk. They could reach her, threaten her, forcing George to back down — just like they already attempted with Chetan, killing poor Cowboy. It was a serious risk that worried him, but what choice did he have?

They needed to operate fast, reach the snake's head before anybody else got bit, especially Suzanne. Could Mahdi be the agitator? Or is another member of the royal family – perhaps even King Ali Salman – behind the plot. He didn't know the answer, but he intended to find out.

Despite progressing into the onion's core, he couldn't shake the feeling that the involvement of the royal family signaled something deeper, more troubling: a power struggle, and probably within the Kingdom, one of the most powerful nations in the world.

This was getting more complicated. He needed help. But first, he wanted to see his wife.

***

The guards at Suzanne's prison had a horrific time during the ebbs and flows of the pandemic. Worries of a devastating outbreak and staff shortages made their normally stressful job even more concerning. The prisoners spent more time in isolation making them even more jumpy when encountering other inmates. The many stresses made the prison a simmering cauldron.

Which is why Suzanne quickly became a favorite, behaving as a model prisoner, treating the workers with respect, being patient with delays and shortages, and not holding any of the workers in disrepute. She even had a knack for discussing environmental issues, like recycling and efficiency, in a friendly manner, even with those with whom she had disagreed.

George, for his part, had also developed a rapport with his wife's jailers, asking the guards about their interests, how they and their families were doing. He brought small boxes of chocolate for them to share.

Suzanne smiled at George as soon as she saw him. George looked at his wife and, seeing through her brave facade, noticed signs that she was wearing down: the bags under her eyes, pale skin, shaggy hair.

He kissed his hand and placed it against the thick glass that separated him from Suzanne. She did the same. They both teared up and mouthed "I Love You" and then sat down on the metal chairs.

George updated her about the case, speaking through the perforated holes in the glass. She nodded and held a big grin as he talked. He and Chetan were making progress, having unmasked the members of the Oilmen and getting closer to the Benefactor.

After George finished the debriefing, Suzanne's grin turned into a frown.

"This is getting complicated, honey. Don't you think?" she asked.

"Yes, definitely. It is."

"Maybe you should get some help. Talk to Agent Proctano," she suggested.

"We may, but first we need more. Proctano rushed to judgment, and it will take a lot to convince him that he made the wrong decision," George said sullenly.

"I understand, and you do have a viable lead — Roberto."

"Yes, but how to get at him is the question," George said. "There's really only one way, but it's dangerous."

"Absolutely not! I don't want you to join me here," she said.

"No way, Suzanne. You've been framed and remember our vows: until death do us part. Right? Just hear me out."

"Go on, lay it out," she said.

George explained his idea while a terrified Suzanne looked at him intently.

"No way. Much too dangerous," she said after he finished.

"Not for me, Suzanne. Remember that I have operational experience. I just need a team."

"Are you sure?" she asked.

"Yes, I'm not letting you rot away. We're still going to Tahiti — together," he said, putting his palm on the glass again.

Suzanne relented, and they spent the next hour quietly game planning scenarios in coded terms that only a husband and wife could understand. Suzanne had resources beyond her company, trusted contacts, some dating back to her Greenpeace days, that could be used if needed, she said, before reminding George about the Boucher Boys.

She had rescued the young brother – Ronan – after the first of two limpet mines hit their *Rainbow Warrior* ship. When the second mine hit, she suffered permanent nerve damage to one of her legs in an injury that caused her lifelong pain. Cashing in the chit was long overdue.

Chapter 47

The Boucher Boys, as they were affectionately referred to by friends and allies, were the product of an Irish woman, who chose their given names, and an Italian father. Their Irish traits from Ma were mixed with Pa's roots, giving them an eclectic look: reddish nose and hair combined with olive skin and hazel eyes. Always up for an adventure and remembering how Suzanne had saved Ronan's life on the *Rainbow Warrior*, they eagerly agreed to help.

Connor, three years older than Ronan, dominated his brother, but in a kind, light-hearted way. They did everything together, beginning at an early age on their farm in Kent County, England. Fun included cow-tipping until they graduated to drinking immense amounts of beer at the local pub. There, they became local celebrities, famous for stirring up the crowd, shouting horrific imitations of John Lennon or David Bowie, or, at the end of a night, singing folk songs. Pa and Ma didn't care what time they came home, if they completed their chores on the farm.

Years later, they became activists of a different sort. The brothers employed their skills well, entertaining shipmates late at night with drunken renditions of their favorite songs. Legend has it that the drunken crew once shouted the chorus to *Whiskey in a Jar* so loud that it awoke the crew of a nearby ship.

Mush-a ring dum-a do dum-a da
Whack fall the daddy-o, whack fall the daddy-o
There's whiskey in the jar

***

Connor, wearing a Manchester United football cap, sat at a table outside a pub in Chester Square.   Sipping a pint of Young's Bitter with a small layer of foam, ostensibly enjoying the midday sun, he watched for his mark to appear. He preferred the traditional beer to the growing collection of home-style micro-beer, not understanding the fuss.

His hazel eyes were momentarily drawn to a row of white-washed stucco townhouses with black terraces containing ornamental shrubs that looked like they were maintained by Edward Scissorhands. Garden squares, international embassies, and upmarket hotels shined like beacons further down the street. He held back the urge to spit on the street, scoffing at London's excesses.

Although there is an acute housing shortage in the city, whole streets in Westminster, Kensington, and Chelsea are filled with expensive yet vacant housing purchased more as a haven by elitist foreigners to launder money than for actual residence. Since the mark lived in the ritzy Belgravia section of London, it provided an opportunity to fight back for the little guy.

After draining his beer, he stifled a burp, not wanting to draw unnecessary attention. A small slender man wearing glasses, navy pants, and a yellow sweater walked casually down the street with his white poodle.

After the dog pooped on a narrow strip of grass, the mark bent over with an inverted bag for collecting the excrement. The man turned back towards where he came from, the pooch lighter on his feet with the man trailing, holding the bag carefully, with only the tip of his thumb and forefinger touching the top of the plastic.

Connor snickered to himself. Then, he texted his brother: "Mark homebound."

***

Ronan waited patiently in the townhouse, surprised at how easy it had been up to this point. He was sitting at the kitchen table eating the mark's supply of Hobnobs and drinking his lite beer. It tasted more like seltzer than the dark stuff he liked, and immediately he regretted opening the can.

When the door slide began to move, Ronan readied his gun and put down the beer.

"Welcome home, honey!" Ronan barked as soon as the target saw him. "Have a nice day?" he added, pointing his gun at the man with his right hand, moving his left index finger to his lips, and uttering a loud "Shhh" just in case he didn't understand sign language.

The target began to protest when, suddenly, he was clubbed from behind. Connor caught him before he hit the floor.

"Hello Roberto," Connor said.

***

Connor called George, who, at that moment, sat in the getaway car, while Ronan applied a healthy dose of the sedative drug, Versed, to make sure Roberto didn't wake up while they moved him. It had been George's idea to use Versed. He was familiar with the substance from his days working for the government on a cross-agency project after 9/11.

When used in high doses and within certain parameters, the drug put patients into a deep but safe sleep. Too much of the substance could poison or even kill the patient.

George drove a black cab that Ronan periodically used to earn some extra pounds. The seats were worn down, various rips healed by duct tape. Chetan sat in the passenger seat, helping to navigate around London's chaotic streets courtesy of Google Maps.

The cab had been owned by the Boucher Boys' late mother, Elizabeth. Two years ago, Ma had fallen off a cliff into the Sjoa River in Norway. She had been taking a selfie with her husband when she slipped on a wet rock. They were walking to an embarkment point where they were to take a raft through the Class III and IV rapids. Pa jumped in the water in a failed attempt to rescue his wife. Both perished in the cold and treacherous waters.

George turned off the "TAXI" light on top of the car before nodding at Chetan. His partner then signaled for the brothers to move Roberto into the car once the street emptied of any pedestrians.

The brothers put on their European football hats, pulling down the brims to cover their faces. The ritzy area had more than its share of video cameras.

They dragged the limp body into the last row of the cab, which faced the front of the cab. Ronan sat next to the body. Connor sat in the middle row facing Ronan and Roberto.

Soon after George maneuvered the cab onto the street he asked, "Hey, Ronan. Did you blokes search Roberto?"

Blank looks from the brothers filled the car with silence. George touched his hand to his forehead in a sign of disgust.

The brothers quickly began searching Roberto.

"Careful! Do not awaken him," George admonished.

Ronan retrieved a cell phone and a watch from Roberto's body, holding the objects up for George and Chetan to see. George held his tongue while handing his wand to Ronan to check Roberto for dangerous objects.

After Ronan checked, George began driving back to the flat.

"That parking spot better be there," George said.

It was. George pulled into the spot and pointed to the flat after making sure the street was empty. Ronan returned the objects to the flat; George got into the car and drove away.

Connor looked at Ronan and slapped him on the reddish head. "You're such an idiot!" He addressed George, "Do you think we're in the clear now?"

"Yes, we should be fine," George said in a measured tone. "Even if his phone or watch had a GPS device, which is quite possible, we didn't make it very far. You should thank your brother for letting us know the truth, otherwise it would've been much worse."

"Yeah, I guess so." Ronan said dryly.

George turned onto the A2 Highway on their way to Kent County. It started to rain shortly after entering the fast-moving traffic.

In the past, this county, located near the English Channel, had staged fake armies, blow-up tanks, and landing craft made from scaffolding tube as part of Operation Fortitude South in the days leading up to D-Day. The ruse convinced Hitler to move some of his most hardened troops to defend the Pas de Calais as opposed to the Normandy beaches.

Today, the county would be the scene of a different ruse altogether: convincing King Ali Salman to provide information incriminating the Oilmen and absolving Suzanne and Earthcare in the process. Sousa had provided them with information suggesting that the king's nephew, Mahdi Salman, was the Benefactor a revelation that could devastate the family on the heels of the Jamal Khashoggi debacle. Khashoggi, a Saudi nationalist working for *The Washington Post*, had been lured to Istanbul, where he was drugged, killed, and then chopped into pieces by assassins hired by the Saudi royal family.

The *Daily Mail*'s article had provided additional leverage by discussing a provocative, and potentially homosexual, relationship between Mahdi and Roberto. Roberto was a threat that could bring down the entire royal family and would help them peel at least one more layer of the onion.

They were driving to the empty family farmhouse. Ronan had considered living on the farm, but the memories of their parents' drowning together were too painful.

They tried to sell the farmhouse, the pen for animals, and other facilities. But prospective buyers were not willing to purchase structures in need of significant updating and repair and land with overgrown weeds, fallen trees, and other signs of neglect. It had been two years since the death of their parents, and the property had yet to yield a single acceptable offer.

It was dawn by the time that they arrived, the sun barely visible beyond the horizon. George hoped they weren't making a horrible mistake. Kidnapping and drugging a person in a foreign country was a big risk.

A narrow gravel road signaled the entrance onto the Boucher property. It had pockets of water collected from the afternoon rain. They turned the cab from the gravel road onto a circular paved driveway. George eased the car to the entrance of the house.

He stopped the car and looked back at Roberto and then up at Connor.

"He's still asleep. If he doesn't wake soon, we'll have to rouse him ourselves."

Chapter 48

Kadir Khan spotted it first – an alert on one of the phones he was monitoring, a chap named Roberto. Roberto's cell phone had stopped pinging, meaning that somebody probably had powered it down. The subject, like everybody else on Kadir's list, would have been explicitly told to not turn the phone off for more than an hour, even when charging.

Kadir reviewed the program that logged the phone's movements. It had last pinged from Roberto's Saudi-financed flat in London. Perhaps, inshallah, it had run out of power by mistake or accident. A virus? Or perhaps Roberto had dropped it in the toilet. Kadir hoped for the best but feared the worst. It was his job. King Salman paid him to worry.

Kadir knew Roberto's value. He did not know why, but the subject was at the top of a list of people that the new King *personally* requested that he keep tabs on. He would have to tell his boss first, but he knew that his boss would have to call the king.

There was one other person he had to call: Mahdi Salman. Mahdi had approached Kadir several years ago, asking to be contacted if Roberto's name appeared on any report or trigger. As with the king, Kadir didn't know the reasons for Mahdi's interest, but he knew better not to question a member of the bloodline.

Before making his calls, Kadir studied the pinging pattern. He learned that Roberto's phone had taken a trip around the block – seemingly in a car, based upon the rate of speed – immediately before being powered off. That was two hours ago. Something wasn't right.

260

Kadir told his boss, which was risky because it required interrupting an eighty thousand riyals backgammon match. His boss told a more senior level boss, who was smoking a hookah at the time. The senior level boss shouted into a closed bathroom door to inform a junior member of the bloodline who carried the official title of Page to the King. The Page washed his hands and went straight to King Salman with the news. Kadir relayed the same message to Mahdi.

***

Nasir Tafuri received a call from King Salman. The King trusted Nasir. Their relationship began many years ago when King Salman was just another member of the royal family. Nasir had always handled King Ali Salman with discretion even while his father, King Muhammed Salman, had been alive. Now that Ali had been named the king, Nasir had become even more valuable.

Nasir began by using a program to gain access to the closed-circuit TV cameras on Roberto's street. London had more cameras than any other city, making it possible to follow people and vehicles by hopping from one camera to the next. Done correctly, it could also show the speed of travel.

Nasir could not believe his eyes. The camera in front of Roberto's Belgravia flat showed footage of a lifeless body being dragged into a traditional London black cab.

By comparing the time stamps of the different frames, he determined that five minutes later the cab had returned to the flat. A person with his head covered who knew how to look down away from the camera, ventured from the car into the townhouse and then back out to the cab. The vehicle then left the area.

Next, Nasir compared the time that the phone had stopped pinging to the events caught on camera. He used this information to determine that the phone had gone offline when it was in the cab. This meant that the captors had made a mistake, accounting for the trip back to the flat. The villains must have taken the phone back to the house so that it could not be traced.

Nasir tried to follow different cameras for footage of the car after it left the flat for the second time. Although he lost the car a few kilometers from Roberto's flat, he managed to see the license plate – a solid lead.

Nasir passed the information onto his liaison officer at Mabaheth, Saudi Arabia's intelligence service. Thirty minutes later, the officer called Nasir with both good and bad news.

The good news was that they now had a name: Elizabeth Boucher, a co-owner, with her husband, of a farm in Kent County. The bad news was that she died two years ago, drowning in the Sjoa River in Norway.

Nasir strummed his pen on the desk, thinking about what he had learned. A search for the surname, Boucher, revealed five families living in London or nearby. One with matching information lived in Kent County.

He and two subordinates began studying a wider scope of closed-circuit TV footage. Thirty minutes later, they spotted the license plate driving towards the southwest of London.

Where are you going? Nasir whispered to no one.

Five minutes after that, they saw the car around the A2 road. *Ah, of course! The family farm in Kent County.*

Nasir updated the King, before placing a call to activate the Kingdom's local assets.

Although Elizabeth had died, Nasir speculated that Elizabeth's children had inherited the family farm located near the A2 road in addition to the cab. And they were heading there with Roberto.

I need to get to the bottom of this immediately, Nasir thought, thinking of Jamal Khashoggi.

***

Chetan opened the door to the Boucher house. A stale odor leaked out reminding her of the gym clothes she wore in junior high school. Her mom,

Kangee, used to yell for her to bring home her gym clothes otherwise she would have kept them there until the end of the school year or the gym teacher had forced the issue.

Chetan next cleared the kitchen table and pulled out one of the six wooden chairs for Roberto.

Ronan shouted at Chetan as he and Connor dragged the still-sleeping Roberto into the kitchen, "Get some rope! It's in the garage. It's on the right, past the living room."

The Boucher Boys tied Roberto up a few minutes later. George tugged on the rope, confident it was secure. Roberto showed no sign of awakening.

"Connor, get me some cold water," demanded George.

He knew what to do as Connor handed him the glass. George threw the cold water into Roberto's face, causing him to stir.

Only the mark didn't awaken, not the first time at least. It took two more splashes for Roberto to awaken.

"You must've been *real* tired," George sneered, looking at Ronan.

Roberto looked at George and then surveyed the Boucher Boys and Chetan, eyes bobbing around like a swallowed lure. He struggled against his binds but quickly gave up.

Chetan realized that Roberto was not an operative. He looked weak. It wouldn't take long to make him sing.

Ronan waved at Roberto with a sheepish grin on his face while Connor was wiping up the water off the floor.

Roberto began struggling a second time against the rope while shrieking, "What do you people want? You've kidnapped me!"

"Good morning, sleepy head," Chetan squawked triumphantly.

George began, saying, "Now, listen carefully, Roberto. This here is..."

But he didn't get the chance to finish. *Boom!* The front and back doors to the house and the door leading into the house from the garage exploded open. George counted at least six people dressed in black with unmarked uniforms, wearing nighttime vision googles and holding large guns. They burst into the house from each of the house's three doors.

Red laser beams danced around the chests of the Boucher Boys, George, and Chetan like a game of laser tag gone awry. George approached the invaders, holding up his hands, as if to show he was not armed, trying to calm the situation. It did not work.

George watched as his partner was thrown back onto the floor, hit by a bullet. Bullets also flew into Connor, Ronan, and into his chest.

Chetan thought about her brother, Hotah, burning to death in the car fire a long time ago. Images of Trudy Lamonte and *The Scream* completed the nightmare as she drifted away, thinking about what the next onion layer might have revealed.

Chapter 49

Meridian pulled up next to the modern glass Zurich office building in a white service truck bearing the name of the Zurich power company: *Elektrizitätswerke des Kantons Zürich*. At first, the long Swiss name topped off by an unfamiliar accent gave Meridian heartburn, until he learned the moniker: EKZ.

The Benefactor had been clear with his prime directive, and Meridian knew he could not fail again after the fiasco in Barcelona. His fingernails dug into the steering wheel just thinking about it. Get the job done on October 1, the Benefactor had directed. Meridian knew that he had run out of *Get Out of Jail* cards.

Pawns within the Benefactor's network had arranged for a power outage the night of September 30. Building management would call EKZ. That call for help would be intercepted by a hacker posing as a dispatcher for the utility.

Meridian would be called instead. He didn't look forward to the mission as much as a surgical operation, but he admired the plan's genius. The Benefactor had even arranged for him to receive a replica of the utility company's uniform, a truck, and equipment from a separate operative.

He would assume the name Joaquim Müller, affixed to his hardhat and sewn on his uniform. The computer hacker had added the name to the utility company's records. The Benefactor left no stone unturned.

And so, on October 1, Joaquim Müller drove his shiny white utility truck to the ill-fated utility pole. Office workers roaming the street, no doubt pleased by their temporary leave from their mundane jobs, watched as the worker laid down bright orange pylons, keeping bystanders away from the truck.

To extend the crowd even further, the utility worker brandished wires that, to the untrained eye, appeared hot. Meridian used the lift on his truck to hoist himself, his tools, and his special package to the existing transformer. He knew to be extremely careful with the aluminum cylinder dressed up as secondary transformer. Only it wasn't. Inside, it contained nitroglycerine and a detonator to be set off when a microprocessor would be activated after receiving a signal downloaded from the Iridium satellite serving the area.

After landing on a metal platform by the transformer, he placed orange rubber mats around the wires he would soon be twisting his head into, like a snake burrowing into a hole in the ground.

A twist and turn of a bolt, screw, and wire here, there and everywhere – all for fun, of course. Next came the grand finale. Using his body to obscure the package, he placed it into position near the transformer. A few twists and turns later, he removed the rubber mats and descended back into his truck.

Once inside, he texted the operative who had hacked into EKZ's computers: "Mission complete."

Fifteen seconds later, power resumed, and life returned to normal – or at least workers from the office building thought.

A satisfied Meridian smiled as he drove away into obscurity.

Chapter 50

George awoke in a dark room. His back hurt. He was lying on a hard mattress on a metal platform that stuck out from the cinderblock wall. He had an eerie feeling harking back to his training. The military had locked him in a cold dark room for three days straight with little contact beyond a medic delivering cold soup through a slot in the door.

He shifted his focus to Suzanne and Chetan. What would happen to Suzanne now that his cover had been blown? And poor Chetan, who didn't have to help. He knew that she was all in because of her own ghosts and motivations, but George still felt responsibility for her.

Thinking about them hardened his resolve to survive. He would figure out a way to rescue Chetan, who he assumed was still alive. If his captors had wanted them dead, he wouldn't have woken up.

The floor felt hard, like concrete, even through his shoes. A sliver of light peeked through a small slit in a window to his right. His hands were drawn to a sharp pain in his chest. His pants felt damp, and he smelled his own urine.

Then he remembered. They had been in the Boucher farmhouse when they were wiped out by at least six warriors dressed in black. The fighters appeared to be highly skilled, trained professionals.

Hostage rescue team? MI6 or MI5? His foggy mind forgot which branch protected the homeland versus fighting in foreign lands. Why would they leave him in a cell stinking of urine? He should have been processed, afforded due protection. Like in America. Maybe he wasn't in England. If not, where was he?

His thoughts were drawn back to the pain in his chest. He wasn't dead, that much was obvious. He felt for the wound, but it had been covered by a thick bandage. It seemed to be only a flesh wound, and his captors had treated it. *Shot with a tranquilizer?* He hoped the others were also safe, maybe in an adjacent cell.

George stood up and approached the door. He called for the guards.

"I have a right to an attorney! I'm an American!"

No answer.

You stupid ass! Why did you say you were an American? That might make everything worse.

He listened for a response. Nothing.

He began pounding. Then he heard it. *A prayer? Where the fuck am I? Is that Arabic? Middle East? ISIS?*

His mind cleared, and he remembered the connection. Roberto. King Salman. The Saudis must have captured him. He was relieved, but only slightly. At least he was still alive.

After the Islamic call to prayer from a nearby mosque ended, George resumed pounding on the door. The guard opened a slit in the door, looked at George, and shouted down the hall in Arabic. The door opened, and two guards burst out laughing, pointing to George's pee-stained crotch.

A third man approached. Although he was smallish in stature with a thin manicured black beard, he stood proud, exuding confidence. He introduced himself as Nasir Tafuri, shooed the guards away, and held out his hand to George saying, "Salam alaykum."

George responded in kind but dryly, "Alaykum Salam."

"Ah! I'm impressed. The guards will take you to shower. Somebody will bring you clean clothes. We're going to then have a meal. Break bread together. Then we'll talk. Inshallah," Nasir said to George before walking away.

The guards escorted George into the shower. One of them gestured to a large, white, ankle-length robe called a thobe hanging from a hook. A large blue towel hung from a second hook. A pair of boxers, white pants, socks, and leather sandals were sitting on a chair in front of the thobe and towel.

George showered and changed. It took him a couple of minutes to figure out how to wear the thobe, the loose material feeling like a bathrobe against his body. He also didn't understand whether he had to wear both the pants and the thobe, taking the thobe on and off several times.

He guessed both were needed. His captors wouldn't have given him a choice. This was no fashion show.

The guards were waiting for him once he emerged from the shower room. One of them seemed to suppress a chuckle while escorting George to a dining room. There he saw Chetan, wearing a black abaya covering her head, chest, and legs, sitting at a table with Nasir.

George locked eyes with Chetan. They nodded to each other.

The dining room had white paneled box walls with decorative trim. The square room had one long table set for ten and two individual tables, each for four. Large burgundy area rugs with traditional Arabic designs dampened the lighting, making the room appear more intimate. King Salman's portrait was hung in the middle of one of the box walls.

Nasir pointed to the nicely appointed table. "Have a seat, George. Join us. Let's get comfortable first. Eat. We can talk business later. I'm sure you're hungry."

George looked at the table but first wanted assurances. "Where are our friends?"

"You must mean Connor and Ronan," Nasir said with a grin. This raised George's alarm bells, until Nasir added, "Don't worry. They're fine. I assure you. For now, at least. We're holding them as well."

"And Roberto?"

Nasir ignored his question, saying only, "After the meal, please. It's our custom."

The table had fresh dates, nuts, and thick yogurt. An assortment of plain and flavored hummus filled different containers around a small glass lazy Susan. Two waiters dressed in black thobes and red and white checkered abayas brought out dishes of grilled fish and chicken smelling of coriander and cinnamon. The food was served in round clay pots with pictures of camels resting under palm trees. A waitress, dressed in a black full-length burka with a traditional hijab veil covering her face, served iced tea.

George waited, at first patiently, but then began rubbing his stomach. *I'm so hungry! When can we eat?*

Nasir spread his hands out in front, signaling for his guests to partake. Table talk was limited to simple topics like the weather, while George and Chetan gorged themselves from two large communal trays. One contained rice and chicken filled with spices and herbs, and the second had falafel, pita bread, and small dishes with tahini, garlic paste, and hummus mixtures. A waiter served them lentil soup.

George briefly thought about COVID before eating from the communal trays. Nobody wore masks either. His deep hunger and seeing Chetan already diving into the food helped him overcome his caution. A pleased Nasir ate slower and more deliberately than his starved guests.

After the meal, George and Chetan waited for Nasir to talk business while they enjoyed mint tea and cookies.

"I've studied your files. Both of you. Interesting that the two of you are working together. How did that happen?"

Chetan leaned forward to talk, but George shot her a dirty look. He would take the lead. She had no experience in international diplomacy.

George said calmly, "*Shukran, laqad kana lazizan.*"

The startled Nasir failed to stifle a grin. Looking at Chetan, he said, "Your partner surprises me, thanking me for the meal in my native tongue. *Ealaa alrahb walsaea*, Mr. Harper. You're welcome."

Nasir took a sip of tea, paused, and said, "Now that we're more relaxed, it's time to talk. But first, I want some answers to my questions."

"Then you'll answer ours?" George pressed.

Nasir scoffed before replying, "You have a short memory. You forget that we're holding you for kidnapping somebody under the protection of the King. We could just hold you and your friends, put you on trial, and then mete out the punishment here in Saudi Arabia."

Nasir paused for effect before continuing. "Is that what you want? First, I want to know how the two of you got together. It's a gap in our understanding of this unfortunate affair."

George looked over at Chetan, who nodded at him. He considered their options. He could try to gain Nasir's confidence, explain the events that had brought him and Chetan together. Many of the facts the Saudis, no doubt, knew. Nasir had said that Connor and Ronan were being separately held. They had probably already cracked anyway.

And so, George proceeded to tell Nasir about what he and Chetan had learned in the wake of the Techno House fire, skipping over the events of Barcelona, Rio, and their penetration into the Oilmen. After covering the basics, George explained that they had conjured up a plan to kidnap Roberto. Roberto had apparently formed a homosexual relationship with the King's nephew, Mahdi Salman – allegations that would be devasting to the royal family.

George and Chetan were there to strike a deal, and now they hoped to do that.

Nasir tried to maintain his poker face. George looked at Nasir like a puppy looking at his owner, hoping Nasir would talk freely in exchange for George's candor.

It didn't work. Nasir stood, snapped his fingers, and walked towards the door.

With the guards approaching George and Chetan, George shouted, "Wait! What now? We're American citizens! You can't just detain us."

Nasir shot George a glance before turning away.

***

Chetan spent the night alone in her cell staring up at the ceiling. Ambient light shined through the bars illuminated the warehouse-like light fixture hanging from the dark ceiling. She didn't want to face the cold cinderblock on her left or take a chance of rolling off the narrow bed onto the concrete floor. Instead, she laid on her back, not her usual side-sleeper position.

Sleep evaded her as dark questions raged. Would the Saudis cut them up into pieces like Khashoggi? They would do the same to Connor and Ronan. Nobody would even know they were there.

After her panic attack subsided, she calmed, put her hand on her stomach, and used the 4-7-8 method to slow her breathing. Sleep came but only for a fleeting minute or two, as she began to think about seeing her mother the day she died.

Dressed awkwardly in blue scrubs and a surgical mask, she had entered the hospital room. When Chetan held her mom's hand at the end, Mom repeatedly said her brother's name, unlocking memories about the fire that had killed Hotah after the horrific car crash years ago.

Chapter 51

The first call to prayer woke Chetan as the sun began to rise. She didn't remember closing her eyes but felt that she had slept at least a few hours.

Two hours later, as an anxiety headache sprouted in the front of her head, two of Nasir's minions appeared. They opened the door, pointed to the abaya that Chetan had hung on a hook, closed the door, and waited for her to dress.

As Chetan obliged, she feared that surviving the night had only been a prelude to a daylight killing. *Can we escape?*

The guards opened the door again, blind-folded her, and escorted her out. Next would come the dreaded hood that she had seen on the Internet.

They led her up a staircase, opened a door, and shoved her inside.

This is the end. At least I will be reunited with my family.

Chapter 52

Sensing that the guards did not enter with her, she hoped for an opportunity. As she tore off the blindfold and readied herself, she heard a familiar voice.

"What did you expect would happen?" Nasir asked, staring at her from behind his mahogany desk.

A chandelier provided ample light to the room, which had a white marble floor. A large painting of King Salman hung on the wall behind Nasir, and the Saudi Arabian flag stood proudly to his left.

George, dressed in his white thobe, sat at a table with a large tray of juice, fruit, yogurt, eggs, and nuts. He flashed her a reassuring smile. A steaming coffee pot and the unmistakable fruity and sugary smell of Arabic coffee drowned out the competing tobacco vapor emanating from a hookah sitting on a side table adjacent to Nasir's desk.

Chetan shrugged, not sure what to say.

"That's ok, as you Americans like to say. Welcome," Nasir said to Chetan with a grandiose gesture to enter. "I'm sorry they had to blindfold you, but my office location is a secret. Your friend here got the same treatment five minutes ago. He looks comfortable now." Nasir gestured towards George reassuringly. "Please, eat and drink while I talk in private. We're going to have a busy day."

George and Chetan looked at each other, waiting for Nasir to continue.

"I apologize for ending our discussion last night so soon, but I had to verify what you told me and seek guidance from the king. He has given me the full authority to talk to you more candidly, if you will, and in the private confines of my office. I assure you that nobody's listening in. My assistant swept my office before you arrived."

Chetan stared blankly, not sure what to say, happy to still have her head but not pacified either. George looked at her patiently. They would let Nasir talk.

"You think your politics are bad, you should understand what we have to deal with," Nasir crowed, splayed hands out as if praying to a high power before continuing. "Life in this palatial building can be more cutthroat than in your White House. You know, I've worked for the current king even before his father died. I'm telling you that we believe there are certain elements that *may* be working against my government and the interests of King Salman. Those elements seem to be the same people that the two of you are looking for. We may be able to help each other." Nasir stopped and smiled bashfully.

"You're going to have to do better than that, Nasir. Explain yourself," George requested.

"Yes, of course, but first I'm going to partake in this food and encourage the two of you to join me." Nasir gestured dramatically at the spread of food before them, laid out with gilded drinking glasses and delicate silverwork on each setting. "We can talk while we eat. I was serious before when I said it's going to be a busy day."

Nasir repositioned himself at the table, helped himself to a serving of food and coffee, and gestured for George and Chetan to follow his lead. He then continued speaking.

"As I'm sure you know, Mr. Harper, King Ali Salman is my country's Minister of Energy – an important role, as you might imagine. In that role, the king represents my government at OPEC. He recently sensed a plot emerging. The more moderate members of OPEC, like the king, as you'll soon realize, want to prepare for the future by developing alternative, cleaner sources of energy, becoming a leader in the fight to curb global warming."

"Really? That doesn't seem likely," George interjected.

"Why not? If we could do so in a way that uses our vast resources to help the world and at the same time preserve OPEC, why not? Imagine the economic investment we would realize if OPEC did this. We would still sell oil, of course, at higher prices to countries that balk at renewables."

"Higher prices? Wouldn't you be undercutting demand though?" Chetan asked as she sipped her coffee.

"True, Chetan. But don't forget that we would be reducing our supply, which, by the way, we would have to do *anyway* as the available reserves begin to dry up. In the meantime, we'd position ourselves for the renewable energy market, selling products like solar panels, wind turrets, and hydropower plants. Some of the member states could even develop technical expertise to sell."

"Interesting idea," George said. "You'd not only diversify revenues, but you'd ensure your economic prosperity."

"Yes, I can feel your lightbulb going on, as you Americans like to say." Nasir stood and began pacing, using his hands for emphasis. "Your country has been squandering its advantage, leaving a vacuum for us to suck up. Your last administration's war on renewables ensured this outcome. We, on the other hand, have the resources, willpower, and work forces to invest. The Gulf countries have become hubs for the great universities. We have mastered desalination and our brothers in Dubai have created island paradises that lure Europe's wealth to the Gulf. Why can't we create renewable energy? We have more sun than anybody! Done correctly, OPEC will resurrect itself as the next great cartel."

"You sound as if you're making a political speech," George said.

"Yes, indeed. Our politics are not that different from yours," Nasir replied after returning to his seat.

Chetan scoffed.

Nasir ignored her and continued. "It's true. The old-timers aren't buying in and are actively resisting the idea. You have the same sorts of stalemates in your government – the older generation, stuck in their ways." Nasir leaned in towards George and Chetan, who sat opposite from him. He whispered the next part, "The difference is that in this part of the world, those in power have more *persuasive* tools to employ."

"That's an interesting take on this, Nasir. But why should we believe you? I mean, it could just as easily be King Salman as the bad guy and somebody else trying to make everything kosher," George said.

"True. But you're still living, right? Why wouldn't we have just killed the two of you and your cohorts, if King Salman is such a *bad guy*, as you say? You kidnapped an important asset, after all. Why am I even talking to you now?"

"To find out what we know beyond what I told you last night. Then once we tell you, all bets are off. See our dilemma?" George responded, feeling a bit calmer than before.

"Yes, I do. So, let me put more of my… chips on the table first. If I do that, will you answer my questions?"

"Depends on what you have to say," George said. "It's a bit like you're asking us for immunity. Let's see what you've got first. I also want your assurances that Connor and Ronan Boucher will be released to the care of their embassy immediately."

"That's fair. A *quid pro quo*. Popular words back in your country. Let me start by saying that the brothers have already been flown back to England and paid for their troubles in exchange for their agreeing not to disclose what happened. I also want to point out a few obvious facts, some of which you conveniently left out last night. My sources tell me that you know about the Oilmen and their leader, a chap they refer to as the Benefactor. We also know that both of you were in Barcelona and Rio."

George bit his inner lip to stifle his reaction, resisting the urge to look at Chetan. This promoted Nasir to say, "Relax, George, we are on the same side here. I think the group is working against the interests of King Salman, and we could use your help."

George looked at Chetan, who shrugged. "What did you have in mind?" George asked.

"Our sources say that the group is planning something big."

"Against the king?" George asked.

"We don't think so, at least not directly."

"What is it that you *do* know?" Chetan asked.

"Of course. I'll get to that. Our intelligence tells us that the Benefactor accelerated plans for taking down the environmentalists. We know that the purpose of the Techno House fire had been to eliminate Benji Hammer."

"The lobbyist for the fossil fuel industry? Why would that have been the goal? Wouldn't that hurt their cause?" Chetan asked, her interest piqued at the reference to Benji. The dead man seemed to be at the center of what was going on.

"Yes, yes, I understand why you think that, eh! After all, he is responsible for blocking legislation in your country that would have forced the oil polluters to pay millions for pollution credits. I think the Americans refer to it as '*cap-and-trade.*' A hero, yes? He should be celebrated, not killed. Right?"

Chetan stared at Nasir, who was grinning.

"That's what your research would tell you, right? But you wouldn't know that King Salman had just hired him to work on a solar power initiative. Now, one might think he's available to the highest bidder. Only he liked the idea. I mean *really* liked it. Besides, who better to help than the industry's assassin for higher, switching sides? I met with him myself. That's why Benji Hammer was killed at the Techno House. He was about to work with me and my boss!"

"And framing my wife for the murder killed two birds with one stone. Sorry for the over-used cliché," George said, his voice sour.

"Yes, yes! See? That's correct, but three purposes were served when you think about it. In addition to sidelining your wife and killing a traitor to the fossil fuel industry, they also tested the use of the program."

"Ah. That's interesting and very disturbing. That brings us to the next stage, right?" George asked.

Indeed. There's a large meeting of environmentalists planned in Zurich tomorrow. We think that's the target."

"Why don't you contact Interpol or your friends in the CIA or MI6 then?" asked George.

"Believe me, we tried. But there's a famous Arabic proverb that sums up our situation right now. *Whoever gets burned by soup, blows on yogurt.*"

"Ah! I know that one," said George. "Once bitten, twice shy. But what's the once bitten?"

"No comment," Nasir said curtly.

George knew what Nasir meant without Nasir having to say it. Relations with the entire world, including the Americans, had soured after Jamal Khashoggi's brutal murder and the failure to impose any real punishment on those involved. George recalled that although eleven Saudis were prosecuted and five were sentenced to death, they were later pardoned. In the aftermath, the Saudis became isolated, with cooperation amongst the intelligence services being curtailed.

"How did you find out about Zurich?" George pressed.

"The usual – eyes and ears."

"And where will the program be launched from?" George asked.

"Marrakesh."

"Morocco! Oh my. I haven't been there in years," George said thoughtfully.

"How do you know this?" Chetan asked Nasir.

"Once again – eyes and ears. Sorry. Can't go further."

"So, a potential mass murder in Zurich launched from Morocco," Chetan summarized.

"Yes, ma'am. That about sums it up," Nasir said.

"And you'd like us to work with you?" George asked.

"Yes, I do. I'm not sure who I can trust here. If word leaked that we were onto them, we would fail. But only you George, if you are willing. You have the experience. If not, then I'll get both of you home safely."

George looked at Chetan.

"If George goes, I go. I've been on this case before anybody. I'm seeing it through," she said.

George nodded at her, and then both looked at Nasir.

Nasir sighed and said, "We don't have time to debate this. I may regret this but okay. George? How about you?"

"I have two questions first. How did you track us to Roberto's house, and what is his connection to all of this?"

Nasir replied, "By monitoring his cell. It wasn't that difficult."

"Sure, but why?" George pressed.

"We can get into that if you commit to working with us. Otherwise, there's no reason to tell you."

George spoke first. "That makes sense. I'm in, of course. It's my wife on the line! But Chetan," he said, looking at her, "you've done enough. You should go home, back to your real job. You sure you want to go?"

"Thanks, George. But I'm seeing this one through. Stop asking me that." Chetan replied glaring at him.

George paused before addressing Nasir, "Looks like both in. Now it's your turn. Who's behind this? Who is the Benefactor?"

"In order to understand, we need to go back to the beginning..." Nasir said, signaling the start of a longer discussion.

Chapter 53

Nasir stood and began pacing as he talked. "Mahdi Salman, poor Mahdi," Nasir said, shaking his head. "He had it all."

"Can you sit down? You're making me dizzy," Chetan asked.

Nasir chuckled as he sat. "That's funny. Nobody ever said that to me before, but I can see what you mean. To understand Mahdi, you need to first appreciate the pressures of directly serving the House of Saud. His grandfather, of course, was King Muhammed Salman, Allah welcomes his soul."

"Yes, of course," George said.

"King Muhammed Salman had two children, Abdullah, who is Mahdi's father, and the current King Ali Salman. The Allegiance Council appointed Ali as the Crown Prince, not Abdullah. The Crown Prince is first in line to the throne, king-in-waiting if you will."

"The current king doesn't appoint his successor?" Chetan asked.

"That's right. It used to be that way, but infighting has ruined the system. In fact, it used to be the younger *brother* of the current king, not the current king's son."

"That makes some sense, though," Chetan said. "After all, a brother would have more experience than a son."

"Maybe so. But it also led to problems. Like a ruler beginning his reign at the age of 81. This happened with King Abdullah IV, who took over in 2005 after King Faud died. Fortunately, Abdullah, God rest his soul, *rahimah allah*, had the foresight to change the system. He created the

Allegiance Council, whose job it is to pick the Crown Prince from three persons nominated by the current king."

"Nice history lesson, Nasir. How does this help with Mahdi though?" George asked.

"Yes, yes, yes. You Americans want everything spoon-fed and fast," Nasir sneered. "The answer is right in front of you already. The Allegiance Council…"

"Gets to pick," Chetan interrupted. "And that means Mahdi is potentially a candidate for when King Ali Salman dies."

"Yes, exactly! Only, you wouldn't think he would be the logical choice because –"

"Because of Roberto," Chetan said.

"Officially, I can't comment on that. My *understanding* is that they're no longer *friends*."

"And you certainly don't want that subject explored, beyond that article in the *Daily Mail*," George said.

"*Daily Mail*? That trash? Writers just looking for a headline?"

"Maybe so, but it must have struck a nerve here in Riyadh. Yes?"

"Again, no comment," Nasir replied.

"Still, the government is keeping tabs on him. Must be why we tripped a wire," George speculated.

"Again, I can't comment," Nasir said, smiling.

"You must admit, though, he wouldn't be a good candidate as Crown Prince," Chetan pushed.

"No comment."

"Nasir," George began, "I understand you can't talk about certain matters. But I'm trying to figure this out. We've wasted a lot of time."

Nasir sighed before conceding, "Fair point. We believe that Mahdi is behind all of this. That he is the Benefactor, although we can't prove it.

Given the previous, dare I say, *issues* in our government, we can't risk another scandal. We are trying a different tactic."

"Yeah?" Chetan asked incredulously.

"Keep your friends close and your enemies closer."

"Seriously? You're quoting Vito Corleone?" George quipped, stifling a grin.

"Yes, I guess I am. We watch movies here too. *The Godfather* is a hit."

"I can see why," George deadpanned.

"Well...it's the best way to gather information. But now he has disappeared," Nasir admitted.

"And as you said before, his organization – the Oilmen – is trying to blow up the meeting that's about to happen in Zurich. Seems a bit drastic for just some policy differences. Don't you think?" George asked.

"Perceptive, Mr. Harper. Very good. Mahdi's motives run deeper. Much deeper. After graduating from Oxford, he helped Dragados perfect its tunnel boring technology – a superior method used to build mass transit projects, avoiding calamities like Boston's Big Dig. Technology that *reduces* the need for oil. Technically, he should be happy with the king's foresight," Nasir said.

"What do you think happened?" Chetan asked.

"A few factors. For starters, Mahdi has changed. He used to be this shy kid, a nature boy, with no hint of any interest in money or power. A doctor here made a mistake uttering the words '*on the spectrum*' when describing him. So he was banished to London to study. And then he came back a changed man, somebody who has gained fame through his own efforts. It builds confidence."

"And now he's vying to be the next Crown Prince? That's why you explained the history, how the king may choose the candidates, but the winner is chosen by the council," Chetan pointed out.

"Indeed. He's trying to show that he's got mettle and, at the same time, exposing his family for going soft with the hope that the Allegiance Council will choose him."

"He must have had this plan in the works for years though," George said skeptically. "I mean to build his network, the Oilmen, establish contacts and power."

"True. His plan has been in the works for years. Returning to the government at King Ali's request allowed him to advance his plans. A mistake, for sure, but one that seemed like a good idea at the time."

"Can I venture a guess that it was your idea as a key advisor to the king? Keep your enemies close? Only it seems to have backfired?" Chetan asked.

"Yes, good guess, Chetan. We had whispers of something for a while, but we didn't know what he was up to until recently."

"And then he disappeared," Chetan added.

"True. It turns out that his plans were further along than anybody had imagined. He had his program built, and he already had a network in place, coerced into doing his bidding. Apparently, he began planning this years ago while still in London. Killing Benji Hammer and discrediting your wife were necessary 'collateral damage' as you call it. Well, you know the rest."

"What about Zurich?" Chetan asked.

"Yes, that. Interesting, the two of you are partially to blame for that."

"Huh?" George asked.

"We believe that at some point you got closer to Mahdi, and it spooked him. He apparently has accelerated his plans. He is trying to take out a bunch of prominent environmentalists from all over the world to attend the meeting in Zurich. When we talked yesterday, you seemed to leave out some details. Care to elaborate on what might have spooked him?"

Chetan looked at George, who proceeded to explain. "We learned about a meeting of the Oilmen in Barcelona. Chetan and I penetrated it, first myself posing as a Ghanian businessman, and then Chetan, posing as a waitress."

"Did they figure out it was you?"

"Yes, they did. But not until we were on our way to the airport at Zaragoza."

"Clever. I'm impressed!" Nasir said, nodding his head. "What did you learn?"

"Information about three members of the Oilmen."

"But not Mahdi?"

"We learned that later, as you know. So, how do we stop him? You said the program is to be launched from Morocco," George asked.

"Correct."

"Why there when his target's in Zurich?" Chetan asked.

"Remember, he's an engineer, methodical and smart," George said. "It doesn't matter where he is if his program is going to launch the bomb."

"From Morocco?" Chetan asked.

"It can be launched from anywhere with a sat phone," George said.

"Very good. And the further away the better," Nasir said.

"Especially if he's in an obscure place like Marrakesh. Even better if he's inside the medina," George added.

"That's what we fear. We suspect he's deep in there. Very deep. Good place for him to hide," Nasir said.

"Ok. What's the plan then?" asked George.

"Here's what I have in mind…"

Chapter 54

Marrakesh, dating back to 1062, is one of the busiest cities in North Africa. Like many ancient cities, there are two halves - the modern part and the archaic medina.

The medina is encased in pink and sandstone-colored clay walls rising 25 feet high with fortified bastions. A small number of gates allow visitors to enter or leave an area that is so big – 700 hectares or 1725 acres –that tourists must hire guides to avoid getting lost.

A maze of tight alleyways, bazaars, food, beggars, and hagglers awaits the brave visitors that enter. With no central arteries, structures made of nondescript sandstone, and the absence of any tall central building, many visitors lose their bearings.

The same features that make it difficult for the uninformed made it ideal for Mahdi, for he was uniquely informed, having done engineering work here after graduating from Oxford. He had picked out a hiding spot in the tannery section deep inside the medina. There, he would wait for the conference in Zurich to begin. He would then launch the signal for the bomb to explode using his Iridium satellite phone.

The technology awed him like a boy drooling over his first *Penthouse* magazine. Using his laptop housed in a ruggedized protective case, the signal would beam up to a constellation of satellites and would find its way to within a few miles of the conference, where Greta Thunberg and her merry band of incompetent do-gooders talked their nonsense. The signal would be downloaded and received by a microprocessor that Meridian had hidden in the utility pole, triggering a small explosion that would cause the unstable nitroglycerine acids to release enough force to kill all unsuspecting souls within 1,000 meters.

And best of all is that Mahdi would be sitting innocently on the other side of the Mediterranean Sea when it all happened. He would learn of the terrible news from Zurich on his phone at the same time as the rest of the world, and nobody would be the wiser.

Chapter 55

The less adventuresome Western travelers usually lodge in the newer section of Marrakesh. Contemporary museums, restaurants, and hotels located there had reddish stone exteriors to blend into the city's ancient roots. Smartly dressed tourists shopped for handbags, art, and clothes before eating tagine cooked in clay pots.

None of that mattered to Nasir, his security detail, George, and Chetan. They were not there for the luxury.

Nasir had worked inside the medina for many years as a Saudi spook and had developed a working knowledge of the area. The group stayed at a riad located inside the medina just past the western gate.

George and Chetan awoke in their separate rooms on the upper floors of the riad before sunrise, as planned, to the call to the *salat al-fajr* prayer blasting from a nearby mosque. They dressed and hurried downstairs, careful to be on time.

Nasir greeted them as they arrived at the ground floor.

"Good morning. Thank you for coming on time. We have a long day ahead of us. Eat up. It may be a while before we can feast again." He put his right hand out, gesturing for them to sit at the table in front of the marble fountain.

A Moroccan selection of breads, cheese, sausage, and eggs with salted lamb lay on the table. The trio began washing down the food with orange juice and coffee.

"We'll speak softly about a few pertinent details while we eat. I have some bad news, I'm afraid. My agents had surreptitiously searched the building in Zurich, posing as maintenance men. They were not able to discover any bomb."

"Could it have been planted outside?" asked George.

"They looked on the grounds and outside walls but couldn't find anything."

"What about a truck or car?"

"They'll be watching for that. We've done this before."

Interpol?" asked George.

"We talked to them. They talked to the conference organizers who *claim* that the building is secure enough. They are not willing to shut it down, without tangible proof."

"It's up to us, then. Terrific," Chetan said dryly.

"Yes, *inshallah*. Let me introduce you to my two assistants." Nasir motioned for them to sit at their table.

The assistants sat down.

Nasir said, "This here is Amir. Amir is carrying a Sig Sauer 226 handgun in his waistband. He's handy with a gun and other weaponry, all hidden of course. He and I will take point."

The tall man sported a thick black beard and mustache and wore jeans, sneakers, and a long-sleeve FC Barcelona soccer shirt and hat. He tipped his cap to George and Chetan.

After George and Chetan formally introduced themselves, Amir offered both 9mm Mossberg MC1's and belly band holsters. George accepted his with a frown.

"A starter gun? I'm a pretty good shot," George said.

Amir shrugged his shoulders while George emptied the gun, cocked the action, and checked the sight. Satisfied that it would work, he put on the belly band and made sure he could easily reach it if needed.

Chetan held her hand up, signaling that she didn't want to hold a gun.

"You should take it just in case, Chetan," George said before proceeding to give her a crash course on the basics in case of an emergency and demonstrating to her how to tuck the gun in her belly band.

When they were finished, Nasir introduced the second person.

"And over here is Habiba," he said with a broad smile.

George looked up at the woman and smiled. Like Amir, she also had a holstered pistol and wore black pants, but she had on a red shirt and white hat emblazoned with the words "Disneyworld" stitched in navy lettering. Her shiny black hair poked through the hole in the back above the adjuster.

"She's further proof of King Ali Salman's modernization efforts. She is also carrying a Sig Sauer. In addition to being proficient with her gun, she is an expert at computer programming, hacking, cyber warfare, you name it. She may be the most important member of our team since she has skills that will come in handy if we need to shut down a program instituted by Mahdi. She will be in the middle.

"The two of you will be bringing up the rear. We will be communicating through our earpieces. If we split up, Habiba will go with George, and Chetan will go with myself and Amir. George, you said before you knew this place. Is that true? You can direct your way around with Amir if we split up?"

"*Know* is relative, Nasir. I said I'm familiar. I've been here a few times, but nothing like you. If I need to, I can fall back upon the maps you provided. I studied them last night and before I came down for breakfast."

"Remember what I said before though. No matter how much you may have studied them, it gets all mixed up in there. Everybody should take careful note of their surroundings and what they may have passed. Buildings, people, shops all blend inside. It is very easy to get lost. Look for distinctions, something that catches your eye, like the person working the front of a store, steering shoppers, a display, or the type of wares being sold."

"And Mahdi? Any idea of where he is in this maze?" Chetan asked the obvious.

"Our trackers are still searching, although we believe he is in the far side of the medina. We will be stopping to talk to a friend of mine first," Nasir replied.

"Friend? So, no chance he's been compromised, right?" George asked.

"That's correct. I know him well. His name is Mohammed. We will use his shop to stage the approach. The only other people aware of it are in this room," Nasir noted. "Any other questions?"

"The meeting starts at 11:00 a.m. Zurich time?" George asked before glancing at his watch.

"Correct. It's 7:30 a.m. local time now and we're two hours behind. That gives us one and a half hours to find and disable him."

"Sounds doable," George said glumly, knowing that nothing goes according to plan *especially* in the medina.

"Any other questions?"

Nobody spoke, leading Nasir to wrap up the breakfast with a final instruction: "I suggest that everybody wash up, use the bathroom, and we'll regroup down here in ten minutes. Habiba and Amir, the two of you should double check your weapons. That's about it. The sun will be out in the next few minutes, and we should get going soon. Remember, it will be colder in the morning than the afternoon."

Chapter 56

Meridian waited patiently in Mohammed's shop of wares, past the food stalls. Mahdi had broken protocol, contacting Meridian directly on his cell phone and without obscuring his voice. He seemed excited passing on the lead that he had just received.

But he also seemed nervous and vulnerable. Meridian sensed he wasn't in absolute control – too confident and lost in the enormity of what was about to happen.

At least his boss had the foresight to set the trap, taking advantage of the intelligence he just received. Meridian felt like a spider. The only people able to stop the plot were heading into his web. Once the prey was snared, the real fun would begin.

Chapter 57

The group left the riad, beginning their walk up an alley. The sun had risen, but the sandstone buildings made it difficult for the light to shine through, and the narrow alleys remained obscured. The group was a target for the locals, some demanding they shop in their stores, others welcoming them as tourists.

Chetan noticed Habiba, Amir, and Nasir had their hands ready to react, eyes darting from one side to the other. She touched her holstered gun, getting used to the feeling, but hoping to not have to use it.

They walked through the carpet, leather, and fabric vendors, smells of raw leather dominating over the others. People were busy, darting into stores, talking, shouting, pointing, arguing even in the early morning in the densely packed area.

Next came an extensive network of food vendors. Nasir and then Amir and Habiba began saying "No thank you" or "La Shukran" to just about everybody that approached, shoving food samples into their faces. Chetan and George joined in, dodging eager salesmen.

Smells of tandoori, bread, and spices competed with the sludge on the ground and rising sulfur from the sewers. A mixture of sweet and putrid trailed after them as they passed the food stalls.

Fifteen minutes later, they reached their planned reprieve. Nasir had made arrangements with the owner of the store, Mohammed Bennani. He had known Mohammed for a long time, having befriended him while head of the Marrakesh station for Saudi Arabia.

The shop had been used by the Bennani clan since the Alawi dynasty days of the 17th century. Mohammed – a tall, muscular man sporting a thin black beard that came to a point under his bottom lip – told his friend, Nasir, that his grandfather expanded the business into clothing after the movie *Casablanca* blazed through the West, brightening Morocco's stature on the map.

Before the movie, the business sold only colorful lamps, hanging lights, and wooden and marble wares. After the movie, Grandpa began selling inexpensive replicas of Humphrey Bogart's charcoal fedora hat with the trademark black ribbon and high dome.

Years later, when Mohammed met Nasir, he explained his family's secret to success: "Tourists don't know what they want. Something catches their eye, and they walk in on a whim. That's our secret, to provide magnets for the eye."

The two developed a special bond, culminating in Nasir realizing that his shop, one of the bigger ones in the medina, could be used by his spies. And Mohammed's infectious personality made him the perfect liaison.

***

Nasir smiled as he entered the shop, an area filled with hanging light fixtures, each made of different shades of colored glass. The smell of lavender candles filled the air, another touch employed by Mohammed to make visitors feel welcome.

Nasir looked up to see the bottom of a metal door that Mohammed would slide down at closing time. It would provide a modicum of security when Mohammed closed the store, but Nasir also realized that security is a relative term in the wide-open souks.

Mohammed greeted Nasir with a broad smile and a hug, followed by a kiss on each cheek – old habits that survived the pandemic. Chetan, following close behind Nasir, entered, and looked around for a place to sit, eager to rest her weary legs.

Mohammed roped off the entrance as Nasir announced to the group, "We can relax here for about fifteen minutes. Mohammed here is a dear friend. There's a bathroom in Mohammed's office in the back, probably the only one without a pit toilet outside of the riads. You can use the toilet after Amir and I talk to Mohammed." Nasir addressed his group in English before turning to Habiba. "Habiba, you stay with our guests and watch out for our enemies."

Mohammed greeted them, setting out mint tea, sweets, and nuts on a table. He waved for them to enjoy themselves and then pivoted towards his office.

***

A wooden door with faded varnish and various scratches separated the office from the area where Mohammed sold his wares. Mohammed's musty office desk and couch, where he sometimes napped, and the bathroom were inside.

Today, someone else inhabited the space.

Meridian, tipped off by Mahdi, looked through a crack in the door. There, he watched Nasir address his foot soldiers, who looked more like they were going to a Halloween party than embarking on a pathetic attempt to stop the Benefactor. It was a bush-league plan that would have been smothered a long time ago, if not for the luck of George fucking Harper and his Indian compatriot. Their luck would end soon.

First, he would take care of the inept leaders of the apparent coup against the future king. And with them out of the way, he would move onto the weaklings, now fattening up on sweets and nuts for the kill.

Noticing that Mohammed, Nasir, and Amir were approaching the office, Meridian quickly repositioned himself next to the inner door, obscuring the toilet. There, he would wait for the right opportunity.

***

Mohammed entered the room office first, sitting on an old couch with Amir plopping down next to him. A small plume of dust rose from the cushions as they sat on the dirty surface. Nasir sat in a scratched wooden chair that he had moved from behind the desk to face the couch, ready to orchestrate the meeting.

Mohammed looked at his watch before saying, "It's now 8:30. You don't have a lot of time. Marrakesh is two hours behind Zurich, and the meeting starts in thirty minutes. Thunberg will be there, yes?"

"She's supposed to be the keynote speaker. Poor kid doesn't realize what's about to happen," Nasir said before looking at his watch. "We need to find Mahdi in the next thirty minutes for our plan to work."

"I understand. You need to time this right," Mohammed said. "Finding Mahdi too early could make it worse. You need to catch him in the act."

"That's right. After Khashoggi, we need to be even more careful. Arresting the nephew of our current king without catching him in the act or discovering proof would be a nightmare."

"Agreed, and, as you suspected, I've confirmed that he stayed last night at a riad near the tanneries. It looks like that's the place," Mohammed beamed.

"Ah! Makes sense. That is a great place for him to operate with impunity," Nasir said.

"What about cutting off his ability to upload the instructions to the satellite so he can't transmit anything?" Mohammed asked.

"That's possible to do, but we need to get closer to the source." Nasir said. "Any update on his location?" he asked.

"I received word before you arrived that he's in the tanneries," Mohammed trumpeted.

"That's a big area. He would be able to hide in there," Amir said.

Nasir remembered a large pit, the size of a small pool, that went deeper into the ground. It had a false top, making it look like brown dye. The inside served as a secret space where a person had privacy.

"I think I know where he is though. It's a –"

***

As Meridian listened to the exchange unfolding, he knew he had to attack before Nasir could reveal the exact location of his boss, Mahdi. Fortunately, Nasir's back was to the bathroom door. He was an easy target.

Meridian's movements were fast and efficient, executed with the silence of a professional killer. Wearing surgical gloves and a white doctor's gown, he popped out from the bathroom, grabbing Nasir. He sliced horizontally through the front of Nasir's neck with a scalpel, cutting the jugular vein. Blood spurted across the front of his doctor's gown.

Nasir slumped off the chair like a discarded doll, collapsing to the floor. His last thought was about the missed opportunity to reveal Mahdi's location in the tannery.

***

As Meridian attacked Nasir, Amir jumped up from the couch, unsheathed a knife hidden in an ankle holster, and attacked Mohammed. He could have used his gun, but he didn't want to alert Habiba, George, and Chetan about the attack, preferring to instead eliminate Nasir and Mohammed quietly. Cut off the snake's head before striking the others after.

Only Mohammed didn't cooperate with the plan. Calmly fighting back, he used a cushion from the couch to block the knife from gutting his stomach. As he warded off the attack, he screamed for reinforcements.

***

Habiba couldn't believe Mohammed's screams at first. She knew George and Chetan couldn't understand the words, although they would be able to figure out what was happening. Indeed, they followed closely behind her, approaching the door gingerly, guns at the ready, even Chetan.

The door flew open. The three of them moved back a step to avoid being hit while Amir approached Habiba, holding his stomach, pretending to be a victim.

Habiba fell for the ruse at first, but quickly reassessed the situation when Amir began to draw his gun. She was faster. Her instincts kicked in as she shot him in the stomach from a few feet away and lodged into the wall of the shop.

Meridian, outgunned with only his scalpel, sprinted past the trio, jumping over the rope that Mohammed used to signal that his store had been temporarily closed, and ran out of sight.

Habiba aimed her gun, but Meridian was just a few feet from a gaggle of shoppers. She wouldn't be able to get a clear shot. Turning back to her compatriots, she quietly took stock of what had happened. She was in disbelief at how one of their own, Amir, had been a double agent, a traitor working as one of Mahdi's spies.

Chetan hesitated before approaching Nasir. How could she continue? Weeks before, she had been the chief investigator for the Oakland Fire Department. And now? She was trapped in a deadly maze in a strange country playing the part of a spy.

Still, she had made the choice to help, and she wasn't a quitter. She had her own reasons and had already persevered through the tallest of obstacles.

After checking Nasir's pulse, she trembled, declaring him dead.

Mohammed closed Nasir's eyelids and said goodbye to his friend before taking his gun.

"Now, what do we do?" George asked as he and Mohammed moved Nasir's body deeper into the office, allowing the door to close. "Our window is closing. The medina is huge. And we don't know where to look."

Habiba looked at George.

"I need to find a phone to call our embassy," George said.

"You don't have time," Mohammed interjected. "The tanneries are deeper into the medina, almost at the other end. I'm going to call a contact at Moroccan Intelligence for backup."

"How long will that take?" George asked.

"Twenty minutes, but we're in Morocco. Twenty minutes sometimes means thirty minutes on a good day."

"Great, Mohammed, just great," George said before adding, "I've been to the tanneries before with Suzanne as a tourist. It's a big place, but I have an idea for finding Mahdi and that crazy doctor," George said.

Everybody turned toward him.

Chapter 58

Mahdi looked at his watch, waiting for the meeting in Zurich to start. Ten, nine, eight, seven… As the minutes ticked off, he sat at a makeshift desk in his private lair in a place where nobody could find him.

His human weapon, the faux doctor, had by now taken care of the dolts who thought that they would take him down. Lying in wait at Mohammed's shop, Meridian and the double agent, Amir, would team up to kill them all. Meridian would then join Mahdi for the final act.

And if Meridian failed, well…every good plan had a backup, and Mahdi had his.

Chapter 59

The tanneries are best described as organized chaos. Tall, red sandstone buildings overlook a gorge where workers toil in pits.

Tours are given to astounded tourists, who are shown the pits where hundreds of scantily clad workers sweat long hours in the hot sun. The action takes place in dozens of pools having different sizes, shapes, and colors. Fermented pigeon scat and other waste is used for soaking hides, lime and argan-kernel oil is used to remove any flesh remaining after the hides are deskinned, and dyes are used for coloring.

Tourists are kept safe on outer balconies that tower over the pits. The brave ones venture down to see the action and a few walk on the outer edge, watched over by nervous parents waiting at the top. And when it is all over, eager merchants begin the dance, shake, and shaming to pry as many Moroccan dirhams as possible before the next group cycles through.

***

George and Habiba walked up the stairs to the terrace of a shop located on the eastern side of the tannery pit. Ignoring the pleas of the merchants, they walked out onto the terrace and scanned the horizon, knowing that Chetan and Mohammed were doing the same on the western side. Mohammed had told them that it was still early in the day and there would be fewer people around.

George looked down upon a large squarish area where the workers labored, giving him a momentary reprieve from the impending fireworks. Hides dried on a larger, taller structure with a dirt roof. He scanned the area, looking for any sign of Mahdi, Meridian, or anybody else suspicious. Nobody stood out.

***

Like George and Habiba, Chetan and Mohammed perused the area from their store terrace. George and Chetan made eye contact from their elevated positions across the pits below.

A shopkeeper with an unkempt beard that barely hid the scar running down the length of his face approached Chetan. "You want tour? I take you. Only 100 Dirham for you."

Chetan replied calmly, "La Shukran. La Shukran," words she heard Nasir utter earlier in the day. Continuing to scan the area, she shrugged her shoulders at Mohammed, who looked at her with a frown.

But Scarface didn't back down. He began pointing more emphatically at Mohammed.

"One hundred fifty Dirham for you and your friend. Two hundred for the one over there."

Chetan repeated, "La Shukran. La Shukran."

The man pressed, "You buy then? Leather? Genuine leather? Come this way. You and your friends."

Chetan and Mohammed didn't move, continuing to look down at the pits, turning away from the man with the scar.

Mohammed whispered to her, "He will leave. He wants us to buy something or take a tour but will give up and approach the next group. Happens all the time."

Chetan and Mohammed continued to survey the pits, looking for any unusual activity.

The man grunted loudly. Ignoring the man turned out to be a serious miscalculation, as he signaled to somebody inside. Before Chetan and Mohammed could react, two locals from inside the store had already drawn their guns, putting them against their lower backs in a position that would be hard for somebody on another terrace to see. The locals motioned for Chetan and Mohammed to go inside the store.

Having little choice, they followed the instructions of their captors. Chetan said something in English, earning her a whack on the head with the barrel of a gun from behind, that made her ears ring.

Mohammed eyed the guns warily. He spoke apologetically to them in Arabic, but the words didn't calm the situation.

The men forced both of them to leave. Chetan realized that they now had their lead on Mahdi, only one with a pickle.

***

George watched the scene unfold from the other side, looking on as an agitated man threw up his hands in disgust at Chetan and Mohammed. *He's probably upset that they were not interested in buying anything*, he thought.

But he couldn't believe it and would never forget what happened next. The man who had harassed their compatriots didn't walk away. Two other people approached them from inside the store, ganging up on them.

He next witnessed the beginnings of a struggle.

"Habiba, come here," George whispered, beginning to point until she swatted his hand away, obviously not wanting to signal the perpetrators.

"We get out of here. Help them. Come! Now!" Habiba said in stilted English.

303

Chapter 60

George and Habiba raced down the stairs of the store onto the streets of the medina, making their way to the side of the pit where Chetan and Mohammed were last seen.

Habiba abruptly stopped, turned, and began passionately kissing George, a maneuver that drew looks of disgust, even in the more modern Marrakesh. A good cover is sometimes an awkward one.

George understood and reciprocated as three men escorted Chetan and Mohammed towards the south side of the pits, two of them holding guns to their backs. The third held two photos that George couldn't decipher from a distance. The gun was difficult to see. It was hidden by the shirt worn by the thug, but the bulge revealed the gun underneath.

He and Habiba followed, holding hands. Both were experienced field agents. They knew not to draw any unwanted attention and pretended to observe the different structures, or turned to embrace, leaving at least one with a full view of what they were watching. Their cover, lovers touring the medina, seemed to be holding.

Their task was to follow and wait for the right moment to rescue their friends. Following would lead them to Mahdi, who would be launching his program soon.

The cat-and-mouse game continued until Chetan and Mohammed made an abrupt left, turning back towards the pits with Scarface and his two gunmen directing the route. George peered around the corner, making sure the path was clear before moving forward, hand near his gun, ready to draw. Habiba followed cautiously.

A few more turns dead-ended into a gate. They couldn't see any structure on the other side of the gate.

"The pits must be on the other side," George said. "We're running out of time. We can't wait for the calvary. They must need them for something – maybe as human shields until they release the program."

Habiba nodded affirmatively.

George eased the gate open with his hand, allowing them both to slip through. Careful not to be seen, they walked down a narrow path. *This path must be used by the workers*, George thought to himself. *I hope nobody comes.*

He looked at his watch. It was close to 11:00 a.m. Time was running out.

George looked up at the pits on the left. Most were brown. But then he noticed a larger structure. While the others were made of uneven stone, the larger one looked as though it contained reinforced concrete. One section that had been partially damaged had exposed rebar. Unlike the other pits, the structure had no workers or activity that he could see.

He remembered that earlier, while standing on the balcony, he had seen a taller, wider area with dirt on the roof. Hides were hanging, drying out from the sun. At the time, he didn't give it a second thought, but now he began to wonder.

Without a noise, he tapped Habiba on the shoulder and pointed towards the structure. A small alley lay in between two of the pits, and George noticed what could be a gap.

They took a few steps towards the door and then dropped back. Noises filtered outside the holes from within. One person appeared to be shouting orders.

The voices grew louder. George thought he heard Mohammed's distressed voice. *They're beating him. Trying to get him to talk or do something.* Then George heard Mohammed cry out in pain, until his voice abruptly went silent…

George looked at Habiba. They had to move now with or without the reinforcements Mohammed had called in.

I hope they're tracking his watch or phone, George thought.

Habiba kicked the door open, firing at an emerging target. George, on the opposite side of the door, couldn't see inside, the door blocking his view. He tried to wiggle into the opening, but bullets whizzed past him, and he ducked away.

Habiba yelped, holding her right leg. Wounded, she fought back, firing her gun. George heard two men scream.

George leaned in further, but he didn't have a good angle. He could barely see. A shot whistled past his ear.

Chetan and Mohammed had both obviously been silenced, knocked out, or killed, otherwise they would be shouting for help. He thought about Suzanne and Chetan. His wife was in purgatory, and his friend was risking it all to help.

Habiba continued to fight. George, thinking again of both Suzanne and Chetan, took his chance, going further into the frame, gaining a view from which to fire. Two of Mahdi's henchmen appeared to be knocked out, but Habiba had been shot again, this time in her arm, and she fell to the ground close to the last remaining attacker.

She threw her gun in a desperate attempt to hit him. She was obviously out of bullets and energy. The gun deflected off the man, diverting his attention. George took the opportunity to fire three times.

His first two shots missed, but the third shot connected, catching the man in the neck. He gurgled and dropped to the floor.

George breathed easier, knowing he could now enter the structure. He couldn't see Mahdi or Meridian, and he assumed they were elsewhere. He saw a staircase on the far wall.

Maybe they were on a different level?

George checked Habiba's pulse. It was weak.

She whispered, "Go! Find them!"

George moved towards the staircase and found Mohammed lying on the ground at the bottom of the stairs, blood pooling on the ground from a gaping wound in his chest.

Wounded but not dead, he whispered to George, "Up there! Go! Your...friend...up there. Mahdi...watch out...monster...the scalpel. Careful!"

"Reinforcements?"

"On the way...but...remember...on...Moroccan time." he chortled, spitting up blood in the process.

"OK. Relax, Mohammed. You've done great," George said. He gently squeezed his hand and added, "the backup you called should be here soon."

Mohammed tried to smile but spit up more blood. His eyes darted in the direction of the staircase.

George worried about Mohammed's reference to "the monster." He knew this probably meant Meridian. He needed to tread carefully.

George walked up the stairs slowly, listening, looking up. At the top, he saw a room with a low ceiling and what looked like a cold slab of concrete. Although the room was dimly lit by two lightbulbs, he saw Chetan on the far wall at the right-hand side of the room.

Slumped in a chair and positioned as a human shield, Chetan's body protected Mahdi, sitting at a folding table next to her. Chetan's head hung in front of her; she was unconscious. Through the gap between Chetan's splayed arms and slumped chest, George saw Mahdi's fingers working furiously on the keyboard sitting in a thick case.

George surveyed the rest of the room, not finding Meridian. On the left side of the room, a wooden ladder led to an opening in the ceiling. George guessed that it led to the top of the structure.

George guessed that Meridian had left to check the outside, maybe scouting for Mohammed's reinforcements. Meridian had obviously worked the Moroccan over.

George looked over at Chetan and thought he detected a slight movement. It was now or never.

He crept slowly towards Chetan and Mahdi, careful not to make a noise. Finger on the trigger of the gun, his confidence grew as he made it past the entrance. George picked up the pace. He had to move fast, or it would be too late.

Chapter 61

As George advanced, he felt a sudden pain in his right shoulder. The shock caused his right hand to open, and he dropped the gun. He cursed at his sloppiness; having been out of the game for too long, he would now pay the ultimate price. He and Chetan had come so far, but Meridian had checkmated him in the end.

"Surprise! Happy to see me?" Meridian beamed.

As he turned around to face Meridian, he knew his only chance would be to close the distance between them, denying the monster room to wield his infamous scalpel. George rushed into him, trying to tackle him to the ground. He absorbed another blow, this one being a slash to the left side of his torso.

The maneuver worked, at least temporarily, and they both fell to the ground, with George on top of Meridian. But the pain was unbearable, and George weakened. Meridian rolled him over, gaining the upper hand. George tried to fight back, but the diminished former military operative proved no match for the younger, more powerful Meridian. With the scalpel held in his hand, Meridian began to slash down towards George's neck.

As he closed his eyes, not wanting to see the coming strike, George knew he would never see his wife again. He had failed. *Checkmate.*

Bang! Bang! Two gunshots into Meridian's chest blasted him off George, and he fell against the floor, the back of his head hitting the concrete with a loud crack. His nemesis had been killed – but by whom?

"Are you ok?" Chetan asked George before sheepishly adding "Lucky shot with the gun. I almost fumbled it, though, fishing the weapon out of the belly band."

Stunned by the turn of events, George could only stammer, "How'd you get free?"

Chetan grinned, "I managed to untie my knots. I had been working on them."

"Well, you saved my life. Impressive, especially for somebody who hasn't shot in while! I'm glad you didn't stay back. Where's Mahdi?" George asked as an adrenaline rush made him forget the pain.

"I pretended to be passed out. He ran up to the roof."

"And the laptop?" asked George while looking for his gun.

"He took it with him," she said.

"Good, that means he didn't launch it yet," he said.

"We need to get up there."

Chetan, faster than the wounded George, labored up the stairs first, pained by her earlier beating. George followed behind, with barely enough strength to make it up the stairs.

As George had guessed, the roof was flat with a thin layer of concrete used to air dry hides, blending in with the rest of the pits. It was the perfect cover for what lay below.

George saw the smallish Mahdi walking towards the edge of the pit. Mahdi's features weren't apparent to George when he was sitting at the folding table on the lower level. But looking up close at the man who had caused so much harm – Suzanne, Cindy, David, and the Techno House victims – Mahdi looked more like an overgrown child than an adult.

"Stop! Stop!" George shouted as Chetan rushed at Mahdi, readying her gun, looking for a clear shot, with George a few steps behind.

Mahdi screamed at George and Chetan over the noise of an approaching helicopter, "You're too late!" He threw the laptop in its heavy ruggedized case into a nearby brown pit, making a splash.

George and Chetan both fired at him but missed. As they prepared to fire again, a bullet flew from the air, hitting Mahdi in the head. His body collapsed, brain material splattering on the concrete roof. The gunman from the helicopter had fired through an open bay. George and Chetan looked up to see one of Mohammed's cavalry pump his fists celebrating the hit.

***

The whirling helicopter and gunshots snapped Meridian awake. Instinctively, he touched the two spots at his chest where bullets had hit his Kevlar vest.

Meridian counted at least three bullets being fired and heard the helicopter's sounds getting louder as it seemed to be hovering close to the roof. Although he didn't know if Mahdi had a weapon, he knew that his boss barely knew how to shoot. Meridian surmised that his boss would lose any gunfight. No longer his fight, the hired hand stood, walked the flight of steps to the ground floor, and snuck out the door into the medina.

***

George looked at the pit, but he couldn't see the laptop. He jumped in, ignoring Chetan who shouted, "No! That could be acid. You'll die! You're already severely wounded!"

But George didn't seem to care, dunking his head into the liquid to locate the laptop. Ignoring the intense pain, George reached deeper into the liquid until he retrieved the computer, grasping the handle of the ruggedized case.

Chetan reached down towards the pit and took the laptop from George. Splashes of the brown sludge hit her face and upper torso, seeping through her clothing.

311

Chetan saw the case was closed and sealed. Quickly, she handed the laptop to an agent, who had used a rope to drop down from the helicopter. She then returned to help George, who began screaming, struggling to get out, even with Chetan reaching into the acid pool to help hoist him up.

Chetan's skin began to sting, but nowhere near as much as what George must be feeling, she thought.

Medics approached from the ground and immediately began attending to George, whose body was limp, and Chetan, whose arms, face, and upper torso were searing. They applied a substance to the wounds, immediately calming but not eliminating the burning sensation.

George tried to ignore the pain, shooing the medics away. He was more interested in watching an agent dressed in green and beige camouflage, wearing a helmet with a face mic. Camo man was examining the laptop.

"Still on. In the system," the camo man shouted in stilted English.

He continued to work on the computer while others rushed toward them. "Hadawa. Quiet!" he shouted.

A few minutes later, he relaxed, a smile forming. "Order to, how to you say…activate program. Program no go through."

Mohammed, walking gingerly up the stairs, helped by agents on each side of him, made it to the roof. He announced haltingly, out of breath, "Received call. They couldn't jam upload to the satellite. But a Saudi agent jammed the download in Zurich. Bomb is intact."

Everybody relaxed. Thoughts about Meridian were lost in the chaos.

Chapter 62

As is the custom in many kingdoms, successful public work projects are named after the ruler or nobody. Failed projects might be swiftly renamed after a political enemy.

The best hospital in Morocco is named after King Mohammed VI. The ruler received high marks for modernizing the country. One of his more successful ventures is the Centre Hospitalier Universitaire Mohammed VI.

Chetan looked at the hospital as she and Mohammed pulled into the emergency lane. George and Habiba had been rushed there earlier by helicopter. The pink, three-story sandstone structure looked like a modern hotel from the outside. Finely honed palm trees and shrubs lined the pink stone driveway, which they entered after a private gate opened, letting them pass. It looked nicer than any building back at Rosebud, although that's a low bar, she realized.

The interior of the first floor to the hospital had wide open hallways, tall ceilings, and a reception and waiting room area on par with what she had experienced in the United States. A can't-miss portrait of King Mohammed VI – wearing a dark suit and sitting on a chair next to Morocco's red flag – hung on a wall in the far corner of the entrance. Mohammed took control once they entered, barking at the woman wearing a yellow headscarf at the circular reception desk.

Five minutes later, a rotund doctor wearing an untucked white shirt with red and yellow stains sauntered over to meet the group. Chetan started to doubt what she had been told about the hospital being Morocco's finest.

Maybe the king had put his money into dressing up the outside and interior while ignoring the staff, she thought with growing alarm.

Her worries were not alleviated after hearing what the slovenly doctor had to say in surprisingly good English, addressing both her and Mohammed.

"I'm the director," he said to Chetan's dismay.

"I have some bad news, I'm afraid. Mr. Harper is in surgery right now; his condition having taken a turn for the worse. One of the stab wounds may have penetrated his colon or his liver. We're checking on that now. Jumping into the acid pool allowed the acid to seep deeper into his body than we usually see. Then there's his skin, which was severely damaged, and his eyes, which were burned."

Chetan sighed and asked, "Prognosis?"

The doctor shrugged his shoulders. "Too early to tell. We'll keep you informed, though," the bedraggled doctor said before walking away.

Chetan grunted a mangled "Shukran" to the doctor's backside as he disappeared.

"Any sign of Meridian?" Chetan asked Mohammed.

"No sign. The operating room is being guarded just in case, but my guess is that he's long gone."

"Are the airports, bus terminals, and trains being monitored?"

"Yes, of course. His picture has been circulated, but he's good with disguises, right?" he asked.

"Yes."

"We'll do what we can, and hopefully, he'll turn up."

Chetan wasn't optimistic, but she was powerless.

"Is there somewhere I can make a call?" Chetan asked, thinking about George. Even though they had only known each other for four months, it felt like an eternity. *Overbearing and arrogant at times, but a real hero.*

"His wife?" Mohammed asked.

"Yes," she responded, thinking about the logistics of calling a jail from halfway across the world.

"I understand. I read his file. Need any help with the call?"

"No," she said before turning to walk to a quiet area in the lobby.

It took about thirty minutes to get connected with Suzanne's prison and another fifteen minutes to convince a guard to fetch Suzanne. Introductions were not needed, as George had apparently already told Suzanne about Chetan.

"There have been some developments," Chetan said in a somber tone before updating George's wife about the bomb. They had stopped Mahdi, and she hoped that she would be released soon.

"But...I can tell something's wrong. What happened? Where's George? Why isn't he telling me? Is he...?"

"No...he's fine. Well...I believe he'll be fine. He's hurt, but I'm with him now. The doctors here are excellent."

"Oh, my God. I can't believe it!" Suzanne said, choking up. "What happened? Walk me through everything. I'm a big girl."

"Yes, of course," Chetan responded before explaining all that had happened.

Suzanne took a minute to compose herself before responding. "Well, thank God he's got you there. George explained what he could to me. Can you give him a kiss for me and tell him I love him?"

"Yes, of course," Chetan responded. *He better make it.*

They talked for another five minutes before a guard cut the discussion short.

***

With the death of Nasir and the treachery of Amir, Habiba assumed the role as liaison to King Ali Salman. Habiba had been shot twice, both times in areas not covered by her protective vest. The shot to her right thigh had passed through her leg, hitting muscle and tissue, but missing bone. She

315

was not as fortunate with the second shot which shattered her arm, but doctors projected a full recovery.

It was fortuitous that she had survived and remained conscious. If she had been eliminated, nobody would been left to brief King Ali Salman – a rare feat for a woman in the Kingdom.

The furious king got straight to the point when his sole surviving agent called him from the hospital, where she had arrived by ambulance. Spare no expense, get everybody stabilized, including the Americans. They must be stabilized in time to board the King's plane being sent from Riyad. The surviving heroes and the bodies of the traitors Mahdi and Amir would also be flown back to Saudi Arabia.

After talking to the King, Habiba received a call of her own from Nasir's deputy, Ibrahim Khalil. King Salman had already instructed his government to begin working on compiling the information needed to convince the Americans of Suzanne's innocence.

"We need to leave and go to my embassy," Habiba told Chetan after she had returned from talking to Suzanne.

"No, you go. I'm staying."

"But I need you there. You know more than I do about the background. We want to dismantle the network."

"And get Suzanne released too?"

"Yes, of course. That's why I need you there," Habiba said.

"I understand. But I'm not leaving, now. I'll join you later."

Habiba nodded before leaving.

Three hours later, half of the time spent sleeping against the shiny granite square support pole, the disheveled doctor approached with good news.

"The procedure went well. George is resting. The wound wasn't as deep as it looked initially. It looks like the perpetrator used some sort of shallow knife like a scalpel. Strange."

Chetan suppressed a grin and said, "Yeah, the perp likes that instrument. Lucky for George, I guess."

"Yes, he is. He's resting, but he is expected to make a full recovery."

"Thank you!" Chetan responded with relief before calling Suzanne with the good news.

***

Two days later, George had recovered enough to travel. His arms and torso were bandaged, but he could walk on his own accord, except for a cane needed to relieve pressure on his left ankle and foot that had been severely burned. He could see fully out of his right eye but wore a protective patch over his left eye while it continued to heal.

He also spoke to Suzanne. While he wanted to return to Virginia to be with her, they both knew that he needed to go to Riyad first.

George slept for most of the trip to Riyad. Khalil met them at the airport and shuffled Chetan, George, and Habiba to meet the king.

***

King Salman greeted George and Chetan, wearing a headscarf and a wide smile. George had made sure to sit to the left of the king so he could see him with his good eye.

Ibrahim Khalil joined them for tea and an array of fine foods. Eat and drink before business. They knew the drill.

After a gut busting, hour-long meal, servants cleared the food. "Let's get down to business, shall we?" King Salman said. He looked at George. "Habiba tells me that you jumped into a pit of acid in order to retrieve a laptop?"

George shook his head affirmatively, but he wondered where Habiba was. She had been instrumental, but why wasn't she present? Even a more modern king has his limits in the still socially conservative Kingdom, he guessed.

The king interrupted George's thoughts, asking, "Not even knowing if the laptop would still work?"

"Yes, that's right. But I knew it was in a ruggedized waterproof container and would contain invaluable evidence."

"And you, Chetan, you stuck your arms in there despite the pain to hoist him out?"

"Yep. Sorry, King. Uh, I mean, yes."

"That was a brave thing to do. The two of you are real heroes."

Ibrahim looked at his phone before approaching King Salman to whisper in his ear.

King Salman said, "I have good news. We've filled in some of the gaps about the group."

"The Oilmen?"

"Yes, George," he said without any details.

"And my wife?"

"Of course. We have already talked to our embassy in Washington. We have arranged for a call with the agents."

"Agent Proctano?"

"Yes, I believe he will be on the call."

George stroked his chin as he thought about the guarded king's simple replies. He didn't trust Proctano. *Who knows what he'll say to defend his decision.*

Still, George didn't have any proof that the FBI had been guilty of anything beyond haste. He also knew that the Kingdom had deep ties to the American government, which had recently overlooked Khashoggi's brutal murder. Pointing fingers now wouldn't accomplish anything.

"Do you mind if I listen?" George settled, although he knew what the answer would be before he completed his question.

King Salman looked at Ibrahim, who shook his head no. Salman gestured to him to explain.

"Mr. Harper," Ibrahim began, "you should understand, given your background. Until your wife is released, it wouldn't be proper. I can assure you that we will explain the situation. I don't see how they could continue to hold her."

He didn't have any choice, George conceded. "Let me know what happens."

"Of course," Ibrahim said. "We will use our full influence to see that she is released by the time you land in D.C. You have my word."

"Before we leave, I want to ask again about the Oilmen," George said.

"About?"

"What happens to them?"

"My people are going to take care of it," Ibrahim stated confidently.

"Take care? How?" George asked.

"We have our methods."

"Even on American soil?" George asked, raising his eyebrows. "But..."

"Everything will be coordinated," the king said before pausing. "You look surprised. I understand. Fred Turner. Yes, I understand. Hmm. You need...how do you say it...closure? Is that it?"

George smiled.

King Salman returned the smile, saying, "I'll send you a souvenir."

George's smile turned into a frown as Ibrahim escorted him and Chetan out.

"That'll be all," King Salman said.

Chapter 63

The next day, George and Chetan left on separate flights from Riyad to their respective cities. The heroes were treated by the kingdom to first-class tickets.

George lay down flat in his seat, tucking his legs in the space under his high-definition television. He wanted to sleep, but he knew to wait until after service of the first meal, otherwise he might be awakened by attendants. Besides, he wanted to brag to Suzanne that he had been served lobster Newberg 40,000 feet in the air by Saudia, the nickname of the Kingdom's official airline.

He tried to sleep after dinner but couldn't. Taking 10 milligrams of Ambien, twice his normal dose, did little to calm his aches and thoughts about Suzanne.

After giving up on rest, he watched two movies and then tried to sleep. Finally, in the tenth hour after tossing and turning, he began to doze. Only it was too late. A mere three hours later, the cabin lights brightened in preparation for landing.

Clearing immigration and customs took 45 minutes. After being granted permission to step back onto U.S. soil, he texted his wife and began weaving through the baggage claim area as fast as his cane would allow. Nerves on fire, he waited for her to respond to his text.

"Running five minutes late," said her text response to George's prompt.

True to her word, she arrived five minutes later, after abandoning her car in the pickup line to the chagrin of shouting traffic cops on segways.

They limped towards each other as fast as they could, then held each other for a long minute while tears flowed down their cheeks. An elderly woman smiled at them as they separated.

***

A month later, all seemed back to normal – with one exception. Earthcare had received a large infusion of cash from the Kingdom, wired into its corporate checking account. The amount of $50,000,000 astounded Suzanne.

What should I do with it all? Her mind flashed to David. He had beamed when he told her at his job interview how he had developed a way to track methane gas emitted by cows.

A shiver ran through her. She would honor David's memory by using part of the money to expand Earthcare's program distributing improved bovine feed throughout the third world.

George liked the idea when she told him over dinner.

"What about you, honey? What are your plans now? Back to semi-retirement?"

"I could never do that."

"Not interested in golf or the newest rage, pickleball?"

"Ha! No. I have another idea but want to talk to somebody first."

Suzanne cocked her head at him but then understood what he meant.

***

Like George, Chetan was also treated to a first-class experience on her flight back to Oakland. She had replied to a text message from George bragging about his flight, "Wouldn't be surprised if I got stuck in coach!"

Celina greeted her at baggage claim with balloons emblazoned with the words, "Welcome Home, Hero." Fellow passengers smiled at her as they waited for their luggage, which in Chetan's case consisted of one lucky suitcase that had been to Barcelona, England, Rio, Riyad, Marrakesh, and now back to San Francisco. Best of all, Celina had brought a special friend with her: Zonta.

At first, the feline tried to ignore her owner who had disappeared for the past month. But then emotions got the best of her when they were in Celina's car driving home. Zonta couldn't resist climbing onto her lap and purring until Chetan gladly rubbed the fur underneath her chin.

Celina, worried about her friend. She wanted the juicy details of Chetan's experience and suggested that they take a walk.

"Any ideas about what you'd like to do now?" Celina asked.

"Trios?"

"Ha! You want to meet up with that singer. *Stairway to Heaven* – I noticed you choked up. I couldn't tell if it was the singer or just the song."

"Little bit of both!"

"True, but I was referring to your plans, honey. What now?" Celina asked.

"I don't know. I think I may have outgrown my job as chief investigator. It may be time to try something else."

"Like?"

"I kind of liked investigating something *other than* fire."

Celina smiled at her. "International woman of mystery! Sounds exciting!"

"Yep! And I can even get *you* involved."

"Oh! So, I'll be your Patty from *Goliath*," Celina said.

"Right! And I'll be Billy Bob Thornton," Chetan said, smiling.

***

George had approached Habiba before leaving Riyad. The last conversation he had with King Salman had left him unsettled. He and Suzanne had too much invested to walk away and trust somebody else to take care of it. Habiba had referred him to Ibrahim, shrugging her shoulders in frustration at having to defer the matter.

The king, through Ibrahim, struck a deal with George. Ibrahim would provide George with the kill list that he could watch from afar. The list would be his collateral, like taking out a loan with a bank.

It had only been four months, and George hadn't expected much progress. He was pleasantly surprised.

Everybody on the list had been eliminated, except for one. The speed in which the Saudis operated was even more impressive than the Israelis in their operation, *Wrath of God*. In that mission, the Mossad systematically eliminated Palestinians who had massacred Israeli athletes participating in the 1972 summer Olympic games in Munich.

The Saudi operation was quicker, which, to George, meant that they must have already known and gathered intelligence about several of the Oilmen before George and Chetan arrived in Riyad.

Some of the Oilmen had heart attacks. Others had freak accidents. Nobody reported a connection. The only one who knew of one was George and select members of Saudi and American intelligence.

Fred Turner was the one surviving member of the Oilmen. And George thought he knew why: let him suffer, knowing he would be next. But what if King Salman struck a special deal with him, enlisting his help on another project?

***

A few days later, Matthew, George's local Federal Express delivery driver, hand-delivered a small square box. George wasn't expecting anything, but when he opened it up, he knew instantly that King Salman had kept his word. A severed finger stared up at him.

George gasped when he saw the dried blood around the detached finger. It looked fake until he saw Turner's Texas A&M college ring still attached, still being worn. A true Aggie to his last breath.

***

A few weeks later, George and Suzanne met Chetan and Zonta, who ventured for another road trip, this time to the Indian Mission Cemetery located at the Rosebud Indian Reservation. A wire fence held up by fading, splintered wood enclosed the burial sites and monuments haphazardly placed amongst tall grass. A few evergreens offered scant privacy.

The visitors used umbrellas to protect themselves from the light cold rain. Chetan gently placed a bouquet of colorful flowers at the base of Hotah's marker. Everybody touched a hand to their lips and planted it on the marker.

The ride to a local hotel began quietly but then turned boisterous as Led Zeppelin's *Stairway to Heaven* began to play from SiriusXM's '70s channel. The first two verses caused a mixture of tears and laughter at the same time.

> *There's a lady who's sure*
> *All that glitters is gold*
> *And she's buying a stairway to Heaven*
> *When she gets there she knows*
> *If the stores are all closed*
> *With a word she can get what she came for*
> *Oh oh oh oh and she's buying a stairway to Heaven*
> *There's a sign on the wall*
> *But she wants to be sure*
> *'Cause you know sometimes words have two meanings*
> *In a tree by the brook*
> *There's a songbird who sings*
> *Sometimes all of our thoughts are misgiving*

Made in the USA
Las Vegas, NV
17 January 2024

84511403R00184